P9-DEC-611

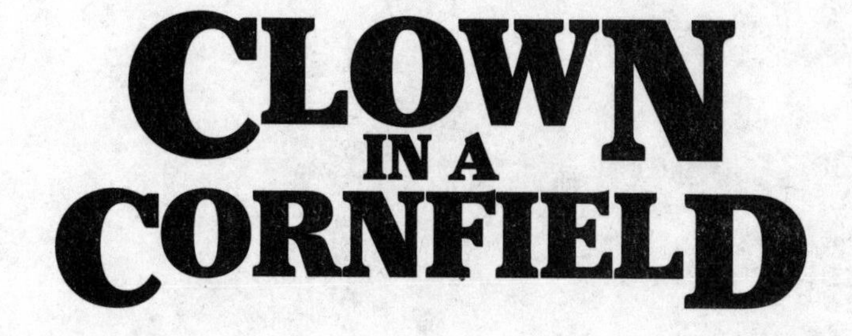
CLOWN
IN A
CORNFIELD

ADAM CESARE

CLOWN IN A CORNFIELD

An Imprint of HarperCollins*Publishers*

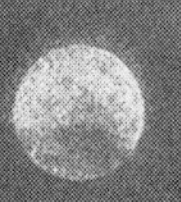

Clown in a Cornfield

 For information address HarperCollins Children's Books, a division of HarperCollins Publishers, 195 Broadway, New York, NY 10007.
www.epicreads.com
ISBN 978-0-06-285459-9
Library of Congress Control Number: 2020935558
Typography Jenna Stempel-Lobell
20 21 22 23 24 PC/LSCH 10 9 8 7 6 5 4 3 2
❖
First Edition

For Jen

PROLOGUE

"Can you see me?" Cole yelled over to them. He was standing on the south shore of the reservoir, barefoot and facing the water. He looked like he was thinking, but Janet knew better. The scrunch in Cole's expression came from trying to keep his belly in a six-pack.

"I've got you," Victoria yelled back as she framed her brother. She was using his phone and struggling with the device. "How do you zoom on this thing?" she asked as she shuffled to the edge, not looking at her feet and focusing on Cole. Janet could see a pink stamp of tongue at the corner of Victoria's mouth as she tried her best to get the shot her brother wanted.

"You've got to be in portrait mode when you go live."

Janet meant it as a polite pointer, but as the words came

out of her mouth, they sounded like a jab. She didn't mean it to be a dig, but she couldn't help it, either. Her tone was why people thought she was such a bitch. Her tone and that she kind of was. Whatever—it was fun to watch the sheep quiver.

"I, uh," Victoria stammered, propping the phone upright, then looking over to Janet for confirmation that she was holding it correctly.

"Never mind," Cole yelled, exhaling, letting his six-pack deflate to a four-pack. Cole was effortlessly hot. Really. And Janet thought he looked better when he didn't try. "Maybe just let Janet do it, okay?" Cole hollered, frustrated. "Please?"

Janet crept over to the edge to join Cole's sister, careful not to slip. As soon as Janet had the phone away from Victoria, she was adjusting focus and framing. It wasn't Victoria's fault she was inept. She was young, inexperienced. What was she? Twelve, thirteen? How old were eighth graders? It didn't matter. Victoria Hill was naive. Janet had mastered the stomach-in-ass-out art of the selfie before Victoria had been old enough to remember her own passcode.

Janet gave the signal and Cole performed a backflip—well, a half flip—with a splash into the water that was probably bigger than he meant it to be.

Behind her, there was a cascade of can tabs being pulled, twist-off bottles popped. Matt must have given a signal that the party was safe. It was Matt Trent's job to figure out when his fellow security guards would next patrol the reservoir. He must have seen them head back to their cabin at the mouth of the driveway. That meant they had about an hour until they'd need to think about leaving. Plenty of time for the lightweights to get wasted.

From over Janet's shoulder there was a deep rumble and then a familiar voice.

"Outta my way!" Ginger Wagner shouted. Ginger wasn't her real name; it was Annabeth. But she'd tried lightening her hair in seventh grade, the process had gone all sorts of wrong, and her hair had ended up this clown-red color. She'd kept it, claiming she liked it that way, and had been "Ginger" ever since. Janet turned, forgetting Cole's phone in her hand, and watched Ginger skateboard past.

"Watch it, slag!" Janet yelled as Ginger rolled by. She got a playful finger in response.

Janet smiled, eyes moving with Ginger. The wheels of the girl's skateboard were loud on the old, pitted concrete.

Janet tracked her with the camera. "You're live, Ginger! Do something," she shouted, and Ginger complied, popping her board over the knee-high lip of concrete that passed for a safety barrier. Ginger cannonballed into the reservoir, her board following her on the thirty-foot drop. Live content gold. Janet made a note to Boomerang the first few seconds of airtime and tweet it out when she got home.

Kids pushed to the lip of the reservoir, watched the water.

The party seemed to hit the pause button as they waited for Ginger to surface. Nobody opened drinks, nobody talked or laughed.

On the shore below, Matt had climbed down to join Cole at the edge of the water. Looking out of place in his security guard shirt and swim trunks, Matt had his phone out. It was a big Samsung Galaxy that used to be his mom's. Mom hand-me-downs, yuck. Janet shivered. Not that she was rich like Cole, but at least she didn't have to live in constant fear of her battery overheating and exploding.

"Uhhhh, dudes."

They were still waiting for Ginger. She had been holding her breath for a long time . . .

Matt yelled up, "If she drowns, I get to keep the body." Janet wasn't even sure what he meant, but assumed he was being disgusting. Even though he was the guy who let them into the reservoir to party, Matt was a fucking dick—and Janet knew she wasn't the only person who thought that.

They waited. Janet could feel her own lungs begin to strain—she didn't even realize she'd been holding her breath—but then Ginger's head broke the surface of the water. She was waving her bikini top. "Impact knocked it right off! Come on in!" she said. "Water's warm."

Kids didn't need any more of an invitation. The dam of propriety broke and everyone rushed for the water. Some climbed down to the shore, while some took the more direct route of a high-dive. *Fuck, who are all these people?* Janet recognized most of the kids from their year, knew all the juniors. A few more of the faces she knew, but not the names. Some she recognized as seniors of little note. A handful were older kids who'd graduated but hadn't gone off to college for one reason or another. The older kids made Janet a little uneasy, but then they were probably where most of the beer came from.

No, the older creeps weren't what was really troubling her. *There are underclassmen here.* Janet felt the back of her neck prickle with indignation. She looked at the young faces. Singling them out by the way they sipped their beers. They'd be taught a lesson later. Maybe she'd encourage Tucker to get them drunk and then abandon them out by Tillerson's field. Every year some drunk frosh wound up knocking on the Tillersons' front door to use their phone because no one could get a cell signal out there and the little punks needed to call Mom for a ride home. So why not a whole bunch of them, dropped directly from the reservoir?

No, it wasn't just the trespassing freshmen pissing her off, either. It wasn't like she'd remember tomorrow to launch a full investigation, but Janet was annoyed that someone in their group had open-invited everyone. Tonight should have been *their* night, just the six of them—seven if you counted Victoria (Janet didn't).

This trip to the reservoir was meant to be for *just* them.

"Give me that," Janet said, swiping a beer from a terrified-looking first-year. "We can't be drinking on camera, dick-head." She drained the half beer and tossed the empty can over her shoulder. The boy watched, something like admiration—infatuation?—creeping onto his face. Janet shoved him and told him to "Fuck off." It made her feel better.

"Yo, Janet," Cole called up. He was halfway up the stairs. "Ready to try the backflip again?" He made a "start rolling" motion with one finger.

Oh yeah, she still had his phone.

She didn't even remember ending the feed. That wasn't good. She hit the button to reconnect. There was a hazy moment of the phone fighting for a connection, then the five-second countdown.

"Look out below!" Tucker Lee yelled as he ran into frame with a lit M-80 in hand.

"What the fuck—" Janet heard herself starting, but then Cole lifted a hand. She cut the stream before it could go live again.

"What are you doing?" Cole yelled up, taking the stairs two at a time to join them on the overlook above the reservoir.

"I wasn't going to *actually* throw it," Tucker said. The fuse was still burning, but he didn't seem worried. It was a long and slow fizz. Those things were hard to put out. She'd once seen Tucker toss one into a bucket of water, and it still exploded. An M-80 wasn't a firecracker; they were quarter sticks of fucking dynamite.

"Put it out," Cole told him.

"Ah, seriously, man," Tucker whined, the fuse still a slow *phffffffzzzz*.

"Now," Cole said, stepping up right in his face. Or as close as Cole could get, being a full foot shorter than Tucker.

Tucker groaned, wrapped the fuse between two fingers, and pulled off the cherry without flinching, even though it had to have burned him.

"Pack of six costs me ten bucks," Tucker said.

"Here," Cole said, pulling a beer out of a cooler that'd appeared at their feet while they'd been talking. "Even?"

"Cream ale? Seriously?"

"Fuck you." Cole laughed. "Just drink it."

Order restored, Cole gave Janet a nod and she started the process to go live again.

"Hey, guys and gals," Cole said. He had his YouTube voice on and Janet couldn't help but smile. Such a doofus. Cole wasn't tall and broad-shouldered. He was compact and angular. Perfectly proportioned. He could throw a ball, but that was as blue-collar as he got. He'd never be working the fields or the production line at Baypen, but it didn't matter. The rich boy was not destined for *real* work. "We're coming to you live from an undisclosed location," he continued.

Janet couldn't figure out the need for secrecy. Everyone would know they were at the Kettle Springs Reservoir.

"Worldstar!" someone on the far end of the reservoir yelled, then did a sloppy somersault from one of the two concrete stacks across from them. The stacks flanked either side of the pool's overflow waterfall, and it usually took a few more drinks before boys were scrambling up their algae-slick sides. But tonight people were eager to party, apparently.

Janet caught the kid's flip in the background of the stream but didn't zoom in or pull focus away from her main subject. This was Cole's moment and she knew not to cut away.

"As you can see," Cole said, pivoting and indicating for Janet to do the same so she could catch more of the walkway behind him, "summer weather has overstayed its welcome, and the crew and I are celebrating the only way we know how." He came to a stop beside Ronnie. The girl leaned in and put her hand on his bare stomach, just above his bathing suit line. Ronnie Queen was shameless. And where did she get that bikini? Whether it was online or at the mall on Route 70, Janet and Ronnie usually did their shopping together. Janet kinda couldn't believe Ronnie would wear something so stringy without, at least, sending a snap to Janet for comment. Janet's approval. Whatever, that was probably why Ronnie had done it. The bathing suit and wearing it was a deliberate snub.

Janet could see in Ronnie's eyes that she'd gotten what

she wanted: Cole was noticing. Not in a pervy way—he was too cool for that—but a slight blush in his cheeks, a glint in his eyes that he knew what would keep people in their stream engaged.

"You're looking good, Ronnie," Cole said.

"Well, uh, thank you, Cole," Ronnie said, her delivery not nearly as smooth as his, a hand on his forearm, not to steady her but to flirt.

Dream on, Ronnie. He's out of your league. I *can't even get with him.*

Ronnie looked nervous, and she should have been. They were only a minute and thirty seconds into the feed, but Janet knew without having to check that the bikini wasn't enough . . . their audience was already starting to click away.

This shit was getting boring.

"You *are* looking good, Ronnie. But I will also say . . ." Cole smiled into the camera. He was a pro, seemed to have a natural sense that something needed to happen in their video and quick. "You're looking a little dry." He whistled through his teeth. Tucker appeared, scooped Ronnie onto one big shoulder, and flung her over the edge. There was very little theatricality to it, no buildup, but the toss played well because, even on the small screen, you could tell from her expression that Ronnie wasn't in on the joke. If she'd conspired with the boys beforehand, she definitely wouldn't have worn *that* bathing suit.

"Thanks, Tuck," Cole said, patting his friend on the shoulder as Tucker walked back to his circle of drinking buddies.

Cole looked beyond the camera: "So, Janet, out of a possible ten, what do we give Ronnie's dive?"

There. She was given permission to be catty, to do what she did best, and after that desperate bid on Ronnie's part to try to grab Cole's attention, the girl knowing that Janet herself had been chipping away at that mountain for years, Janet let loose.

"Her legs were all over the place. Never mind the thigh jiggle. I'm going with a four-point-oh-no," Janet said, happy, finally vibing with the party atmosphere.

"Nah, my girl's a ten. Even when she's a rag doll," Matt said, interrupting, his own phone out in selfie mode. He had his uniform top off now, not that it would take much of a detective to figure out who let them in. Was he serious? Splitting their audience like that? And who would be watching his stream when they had the choice of Cole's? Janet scowled at him.

"We're getting live comments," Janet said, bringing things back, reading the screen. "Dee says that you're starting to look mighty dry yourself, Cole."

Cole smiled, gave a bashful laugh, and started to make flirtatious conversation with the camera. But Janet couldn't focus on what he was saying.

Victoria Hill hadn't worn a bathing suit to the reservoir. And why would she? Cole's sister never went in. But now Janet could see that Victoria had stripped off her clothes. In just her underwear she was balance-beaming her way around the lip of the reservoir's pitched east side, headed for the stacks. Nobody walked the sides of the reservoir. If you wanted to get to the other side, you took the long way around on the dirt, not on the narrow concrete lip. Victoria had a half-empty bottle of strawberry vodka in hand and was wobbling like she'd drunk it all herself. Janet watched, her breath held for the second time tonight. But Cole's sister made it across safely. She was on the other side without slipping, without skinning her knees and elbows, before splashing into the water.

Janet continued watching Cole's sister because this—whatever *this* was—wasn't over. After taking a swig and tossing the bottle down, Victoria tiptoed to the ladder that led up to the first concrete stack.

This wasn't a public swimming pool and the stack wasn't meant to be a diving board, but as Victoria climbed, Janet found new respect for Cole's chronically basic little sister. Whatever she was doing, it wasn't easy.

Victoria Hill was quietly making a scene without making a scene.

Ignoring Cole's continuing monologue to the camera, Janet zoomed in on his sister's ascent.

"You with me?" Cole said, finally realizing the focus wasn't on him.

"Check it out." Janet pointed. Victoria had made it to the top of the concrete stack and had both her arms out.

Victoria's waving arms were either for balance or to hype up the crowd, it was hard to tell.

"Do it! We're bored of your brother," Tucker yelled, his arm around a freshman boy he'd been forcing to fetch his drinks. Tucker Lee clenched the boy tight to him, big hands and big arms like a vise.

"Jump!" Ronnie yelled from somewhere below them, down in the water.

"Yeah, jump!" Matt echoed, seemingly forgetting that he was being paid to guard everyone's security.

"Do it! Do it!" The rest of the party picked up the chant.

Janet had Victoria perfectly framed. The shot was grainy enough, far enough, to seem real, candid and improvised—and it *seemed* that way because it *was* all of those things.

What was Victoria waiting for? This was her moment. Victoria could make a statement here. Make the years ahead of her bearable. Be popular. Janet was in awe, impressed. Janet had pulled herself up the social ladder gradually, but Victoria was fixing to do it all in one night, in one stunt.

And then, finally, after two gymnast's pumps on the balls of her feet, Victoria jumped.

Later, Janet would swear she had no idea anything was

wrong, that the bump against the back of Victoria's head barely looked like anything. But she did notice. She saw it when it happened. The little jitter, the bounce of Victoria's face moving suddenly a half inch to the left as the back of her hair moved past the edge of the concrete stack.

Janet might have been the only person out at the reservoir to pinpoint the exact moment the descent changed from a dive to a fall.

Louder than the smack-splash of Victoria's back connecting with the water was the echoing "oooooo" from everyone gathered, watching. They all must've sensed something bad, but no one moved. No one thought to do anything. Why should they? A hundred million billion kids had made that dive before Victoria Hill. There'd been a couple of bent-back toenails and bloody noses, but outside of that, nothing *bad* had ever happened. So why now?

They waited, just as they'd waited for Ginger's dye job to reappear, but it didn't take nearly as long for Victoria to surface.

With her face down. Arms out.

Janet dropped Cole's phone. It would film the sky until the battery died two hours later. On the live feed, you could hear voices. Screaming. But you couldn't see Cole dive in. You couldn't see him pull his sister to shore. You couldn't see that she *looked* fine. Like she was sleeping, until you lifted her up and saw the gentle gush of blood at the back of her scalp, parting her wet hair. You couldn't see what the coroner would report, that the back of her skull had been caved inward on the edge of the stack.

Being there, you couldn't know what the kids watching the livestream had picked up immediately, down in the comments:

OH SHIT, that girl is dead.

ONE

ONE YEAR LATER

"Wait! Stop!"

The moving truck backfired and then groaned. Asphalt crunched as the vehicle began to roll forward.

"You can't leave like this!"

Quinn Maybrook watched, helpless, as her dad flung himself against the side of the truck. He steadied himself on the running board. His stringy forearms tensed, gripping the side mirror, climbing up to plead with the driver through clenched teeth.

It would have been a harrowing action-movie scene . . . except the truck was barely moving.

The driver applied the brakes, the truck shuddering and groaning again, and cracked the window:

"Look, Dr. Maybrook, you paid for delivery and load-out,

not load-*in*. We drove overnight to get here and it's going to be a whole day to drive back to Philly. We have another gig first thing tomorrow—"

"But I—"

"I'm sorry, but we gotta go," the man said, moving to roll the window back up. Dad slipped his fingers into the gap, putting his weight on the window.

The guy gave him a look that said *I will roll up this window and chop off your fingertips but please don't make me do that because it'll be a major headache for everyone.*

Her dad let go.

"Don't review us on Yelp!" the driver yelled, hitting the gas. The sudden start shook her dad loose. He stumble-stepped back to where Quinn stood, and they watched the truck pull down the street. All they could do was sigh.

Glenn Maybrook dusted himself off. He adjusted his glasses.

"Well," he said, clapping his hands as if he hadn't been trying to wrestle a truck, "I guess we're here." Quinn could see that his composure was about to crack. He muttered, began repeating: "We're here, we're here . . ."

"Come on, Dad. It's not a big deal. This isn't that much stuff," Quinn said. The move had been harder than expected, though, and now they needed to get everything inside.

Mom would have thought it was hilarious if she were here. But, of course, if Mom were still around, there's no way that they'd ever have left Philadelphia to move to Kettle Springs, Missouri.

But Mom wasn't here, and so they were.

Standing in the middle of the street, Quinn looked to the horizon, as if she could go on tiptoes and see the Comcast building back home. When her father told her where they were moving, Quinn had done some quick googling and concluded that the town would be, like, one big cornfield. That it would be quiet, sleepy, and boring. But that wasn't fair, because already there was more here than she thought there'd be. Which was good—she might be trying to view the town as a yearlong pit stop between her present and her future, but it'd be nice if the year was halfway enjoyable.

Their new house was a five-minute ride from downtown, which they'd driven through on their way in. Main Street seemed to be not just the main road, but the only way out of Kettle Springs, giving the impression that the Missouri town was more a glorified cul-de-sac. Passing through downtown, Quinn noticed a fifties-style diner and a bookstore that was probably all secondhand paperback romances and mysteries where the detectives owned cats. Or the detectives *were* cats. Not her scene.

But on the brighter side, there was also a second-run movie theater and not one but two thrift stores, one shuttered. The theater and thrift shops would have been full of hipsters back in Philly, but here they were probably what passed for premium, cutting-edge entertainment. She looked forward to checking them out.

Their new street, Marshall Lane, was lined with four houses on each side, and there were indications of life in each. Two houses had big green John Deere tractors parked out front. Or were they riding lawnmowers? Quinn wasn't sure what the difference was. But she'd learn. She'd learn that and more. Moving to Kettle Springs would be . . . a *learning* experience.

She looked back to the curb and their earthly belongings. In the early-morning light, what struck her most was how little of the front yard their stuff covered.

Outside of the boxes, most of which were supplies for Dad's new practice, there was a leather roll-chair with one plastic wheel chipped; two mattresses, different sizes but the same brand; a doll from when she was little that she hadn't picked up in years and couldn't believe had made the trip with them; two milk crates of her dad's old records but no record player; their TV that they'd wrapped in a frayed old comforter; a twine-tied stack of outdated medical journals that would likely wind up in the basement, never to be untied; an old couch that looked older and uglier on the lawn than it ever had in their old trinity apartment; a fading CRT computer monitor; and a poster tube that'd been bent in half during the move—Audrey Hepburn's face was almost certainly creased forever.

And looming above this assemblage was *the house.*

The siding was cracked, the windows shimmery, the front door in desperate need of firm sanding and a fresh paint job, and from what Quinn could see, the roof looked like her teeth felt—mossy. (She'd brushed before they'd left, but it had been a long trip with a lot of gas station food.) The bones of a nice house were there—the front porch and its deck swing were charming—but what was on those bones . . . damn.

No time to worry about what she couldn't change. There was work to do. Getting everything inside would take the better part of the day, and she was determined to get it all done. And quickly. It was still early and she hadn't spotted any neighbors, but the road to minimal embarrassment was getting everything inside before she and her dad could be seen having a reverse yard sale.

God. Quinn was exhausted. After they got this junk unpacked, she needed sleep. Tomorrow was her first day of school—her *second* first day of school this year, as it turned out—and she needed to be fresh.

Her dad caught her eye, saw that she'd been taking it all in, and threw up his hands. He gestured to their stuff and looked ready to cry.

"Don't worry. It won't take that long," she said, bending to pull one leg of the couch from where it'd sunken into the dew-damp grass. "But come on. I can't do it alone."

On the count of three they each hefted an end of the couch. Dust puffed into the air and Quinn muscled down a sneeze. They should have left it back in Philly. They could have bought another couch, a new couch, one of those sectionals that have cup holders, USB ports, and heated seats. Replacing the furniture had been *another* opportunity to start fresh that her dad had ignored. Yes, maybe new stuff would have been an extravagance, but her dad was a doctor and the cost of living out here was—he insisted—unbelievably cheap. But even if it weren't, she'd rather eat rice and beans for a month than live with musty relics of their past life.

The couch smelled like Mom. Fuck, now *she* was about to cry.

She looked up from the cushions and caught her father staring at her.

"You're amazing, you know that, kiddo?"

He might have been clueless sometimes, but Glenn Maybrook was often sweet enough he could convince her to push away the hurt.

"Yeah, yeah, yeah, I'm a rock, the wind beneath your wings. Swing your end around, okay? I'll go up the front stairs first," she said.

"No, no, I'll go backward." It was a chivalrous gesture, volunteering to walk in the difficult direction. But he was kidding himself. Dr. Glenn Maybrook was all knobby elbows and floppy feet and Costco four-to-a-pack reading glasses.

Her mother was the athlete; she was the one who'd pushed Quinn into sports. Like it was for her mother before her, volleyball was Quinn's game. She was long-limbed and quick, not the tallest girl on her team but with a jump that could get her shoulders up even with the top of the net. Her coaches had been crushed when she told them that the varsity squad would be without her this year, that she was moving to Kettle Springs. They tried to talk her out of it—as if it were her choice. They even volunteered to talk to her father on her behalf.

But the whole move happened so quickly she didn't even have a chance to tell them no. Dad had received the offer on a Monday and accepted by the following Friday. Within a week they were packing to go. He didn't ask her what she wanted. He just told her one day after school, framed it like a move halfway across the country was just something he had to do. Like he was telling her he'd already ordered takeout without asking what she wanted.

It was a package deal, a great opportunity: take the business *and* get the deed to the house. They could start over with just the turn of a key. "Please, Quinn," he'd asked when he'd finally thought to *ask*. "We really need a fresh start."

And maybe he was right.

For Quinn that was the sole appeal to leaving Philadelphia:

a new beginning. Or, if not a new beginning, a place she could detox for a year, recuperate before applying to Penn or Temple or any of the Philly-area colleges.

In Kettle Springs she could keep her head down, avoid the drama. No one here knew Quinn as the girl whose mother slumped low in the bleachers during last year's regionals, then puked down her chin.

Nobody in Kettle Springs knew how Samantha Maybrook had died.

Quinn could start over.

She hefted the couch through the threshold and set down her side in the living room, where the smell of stale sweat and cat piss sent her dashing to throw open the windows.

"Oh, what the hell, Dad?" she said.

"The last owner must have been a cat person . . . ," her dad said, rubbing his neck.

"And a fu— a freaking shut-in."

Dad dropped his end of the couch—probably leaving two more half-moon dings in the already ruined hardwood—and crossed to the opposite side of the room, throwing open the rest of the windows in the hope of welcoming in a cross-breeze.

It doesn't matter. Give him a break on the little stuff.

With the air fresher, but by no means *fresh*, Quinn took in her surroundings. They were coming from a three-story apartment in Fairmount. A trinity, three small rooms stacked on top of each other, where it wasn't Sunday if she couldn't hear their neighbors arguing. They had a postage stamp of grass that Mom liked to joke was her "garden." Quinn had never lived in a real house in her life, and yet it felt like she knew the layout of the house on Marshall Lane by instinct. Turn here and there is your den. Up there you'll find the bedrooms. Bathroom is the second door on the right.

There was a level of comfort in that familiarity.

Quinn pulled the couch over against the far wall. They were going to need more furniture, newer furniture, to distract from both the size of the room and the general sense of misery and neglect you got from standing in it.

While they were out furniture shopping, maybe they'd pick up a blowtorch and some accelerant, too.

"Going to grab another box and check out my new room," Quinn said. "Always wanted to live in an attic."

Her dad frowned, and she put a hand up before he could start to apologize for things he didn't need to apologize for.

"No, really. I mean it. There's a bedroom upstairs with pitched ceilings, right?" she said, remembering the pictures her dad had shared. Then she squeezed out more forced optimism: "This place is actually kind of cool. It's got . . . personality."

"I'm glad you like it," he said, struggling to open the last window and seeming not to hear the snark in her tone. Dad whacked the frame with the heel of his hand and loosened the crumbling paint enough to open the window an inch. "Needs a little work, but it does have promise, doesn't it?"

Quinn smiled and nodded. With enough work and love, you could save anything.

Well, almost anything.

The screen door slammed behind her, sounding loose, and Quinn leaped down the front stairs in a single bound, grabbing the first box she came to labeled "Quinn's stuff."

The house was not as intuitive as she'd first tricked herself into thinking, but after two closets and the hall bathroom, she found the stairs. The stairwell was narrow and the steps were rickety, cracked, and unfinished. No sneaking out of the house, she figured. Or at least more difficult sneaking out.

She climbed the steps. With no banister, she'd have to be careful at night. She set the box down in the middle of the unfinished wood floor and began to take stock.

Bzzt.

It was a message from Tessa. The text read: **Gone but not forgotten. Quinn in our hearts 4eva.** Under the message, there was an attachment, but her phone was taking forever trying to download it, the blue progress circle only a quarter filled.

The cat-piss smell in the living room was one thing, but Dad better hurry and get the Wi-Fi sorted.

There was a *BANG* downstairs, and Quinn rushed to listen at the top stair.

"Dad! You okay?"

"Yeah, yeah, yeah . . . ," he yelled back, sound carrying disconcertingly well through the empty house. "But we're going to need a new screen for the door."

Quinn forced a sigh, then a deep breath, pulse still quick. Glenn Maybrook was wrecking the house already, but at least he hadn't killed himself. She wasn't a complete orphan, not yet.

Outside, the sun was rising higher. Quinn pulled open the blinds on the window overlooking Marshall Lane. The effect was immediate, the room warmed with the sunlight.

She turned to get the box she'd brought up and whacked her head on the sloped ceiling as she did.

Fucking pitched ceilings.

Quinn muttered something awful, rubbing her skull and realizing she would need to crawl on her knees if she wanted to touch the north or south walls of her new bedroom.

Below the angle of the ceiling to one side was a vintage metal bedframe and a mattress that looked like it belonged in a movie about the Civil War. There was also a simple desk pushed against the wall under the window that faced Marshall Lane. The red luster of the wood was enough to let Quinn know the desk was real furniture, not cheap particleboard.

The house's former owner was also the town's former doctor. Glenn Maybrook had taken over his practice on

Main Street. Quinn didn't realize that Dad had bought the house partially furnished, if that's what you could call the furniture in the attic, and she suspected neither did he. But whatever. She wasn't going to touch that mattress with her bare skin, but having a few things already here would make life easier. No trips to IKEA, if there even *were* IKEAs in the Midwest. No late nights trying to put together bed-frames with just an Allen wrench and twenty-seven-step Swedish-language instructions. But no veggie meatballs or lingonberry sauce, either, so it was a give and take.

Quinn checked her phone. The attachment had finally downloaded. Tessa had sent a short loop of her and Jace each emptying a carton of apple juice into the cafeteria's garbage can. They were pouring one out for Quinn. The text on-screen paraphrased Boyz II Men, something about the end of the road. Quinn smiled, remembering the three of them driving around Philly, singing at the top of their lungs.

She watched the video a few more times, then felt her vision blur. It wasn't the memory of cruising South Street that made Quinn's heart hurt, but the fact that she'd be receiving fewer and fewer texts like this over the coming weeks.

It sucked, but the friends were bound to drift apart. She loved Tessa and Jace, but their joke felt too true; soon enough, Quinn would be dead to them.

Quinn sent back a quick lol and allowed her phone to autocorrect to the leaning-sideways-crying-laughing emoji. No. She couldn't spend the day texting with her old friends. There was work to be done. She needed to get busy starting over.

She put down her phone on the desk and glanced out the window.

Dad was on the front lawn, talking to a kid who looked about her age. He had short dirty-blond hair and was wearing jeans and a plaid button-down shirt that made him look like a lumberjack. Hanging off his shoulder was a camo-colored backpack that appeared mostly held together by safety pins.

Backpack. He's going to school.

Oh shit! Dad's meeting him first.

The boy extended a hand, her father shaking it, and laughing at . . . Well, whatever Glenn Maybrook was laughing at, Quinn couldn't quite tell.

Dad pointed at a box and Quinn could see the boy's lips ask: "You need some help?"

But her dad waved away the boy's offer, then said something that—in hindsight—must have been "Don't worry, my daughter and I can handle it." Glenn Maybrook half turned and pointed up to the window, and Quinn locked eyes with her new classmate.

Glenn Maybrook waved, goofy as ever, as the boy nodded

a restrained hello up to her. Quinn didn't return the greetings; she just took a big step back into the attic and wished that she could disappear entirely into the gloom. She stood, not breathing, out of their line of sight and counted to thirty. When she dared return to the window, the boy had stopped looking up. He was walking away down their street, backpack hitched to both shoulders.

A moment later, there was the sound of her dad fighting with the broken screen door. "That was the neighbor!" he yelled up. "Don't worry, I didn't embarrass you!"

"Not your call to make," Quinn yelled back from the corner of her empty room.

The floorboards creaked as she crossed the attic room. Everything in this house seemed to creak. And all the creaks meant there would be no hiding from her dad. No staying up late and pacing, picking at her homework until dawn. Which sucked, because that was her process.

Moving to the window at the opposite end of her bedroom, the one facing the backyard, she despaired. There were no blinds, no drapes. But then again: there were also no neighbors facing the back of the house.

The back lawn was uneven and overgrown, with spots of dead grass and a birdbath tilted at such an angle that it probably wasn't bathing many birds.

The lawn wasn't the totality of the view, though.

Their property abutted a cornfield. Miles and acres of

the crop. Which shouldn't have surprised Quinn. She'd seen the house on Google Maps. The whole town was encircled by corn.

Quinn looked to the horizon as the cornstalks swayed with the breeze. The corn itself could have been waving hello, or it could have been breathing. Missouri itself a sleeping giant under their new home. Enormous, indifferent. The thought could have been comforting or she could let the idea freak her out, that she was living on the back of a monster named Missouri. It was all a matter of how she chose to look at it. Perspective.

Quinn peered out into the distance. The corn wasn't all she could see. Out in the fields, breaking the horizon, looming above all like a warning, was a large, dilapidated warehouse and factory. Even small on the horizon, she guessed the structure was five stories tall, not including the chimney stack tilting out the back. The factory's roof was sagging like an animal with a broken back.

On the side of the building was what looked like a mural. There were plenty of murals in Philadelphia, a whole municipal department dedicated to them, and maybe this would be a nice reminder of home. The mural needed a wash, though; it had been blackened and sooted-over by whatever calamity had ruined the building in the first place.

She took out her phone, unlocked to the camera, and used the digital zoom to get a closer look.

There, painted on the side of the factory, was a clown.

An old-timey clown with a porkpie hat and red, bulbous nose. The clown had faded greasepaint stubble on his chin, and his once ruby-red nose was pocked with blisters from where the paint had bubbled. His painted white face had long gone gray. But his eyes had been more or less untouched by the flames, and something in the way they'd been painted made it seem like the clown was staring straight into her window, straight at Quinn.

Across the top of the factory building was the word "Baypen." It must have been the name of the company, but Quinn felt no strong desire to research it.

And under the clown was a slogan that was illegible but for the word "EVERYTHING" written in all caps and a looping, fake-fancy scrawl. Quinn snapped a picture of the clown. Maybe she'd send it to Tessa later. Her friend liked creepy stuff, would get a kick out of it. She'd make Quinn feel better about having a pervert clown watching over her. And then she'd tell Quinn what Quinn already knew: that her next task was to find some damn curtains for that window.

TWO

Quinn woke to a phone alarm she didn't remember setting.

She flopped onto her back and blinked for a second at the unfamiliar ceiling, then looked over to the poster that'd come loose overnight and was hanging limply by three corners; the new desk; the boxes still to unpack . . .

Nope. She hadn't imagined Kettle Springs.

There was a knock on her door, the sudden noise shoring up Quinn's consciousness.

"I made breakfast," her dad said. A pause. "It's downstairs. I'm going to head into the office to see what I'm dealing with, okay?"

There was another pause and Quinn stretched. Her dad was waiting for confirmation she'd heard him.

"Okay. Good luck on your first day." Yeah, why not? It didn't cost her anything to be nice. "Love you."

"Love you, too," he said as he descended back down her attic stairwell. "And good luck, yourself." But Quinn didn't need luck. Only one of them was nervous about the fresh start.

With the house to herself, Quinn showered. The hot and cold knobs were a finicky puzzle that she only halfway understood, but it felt good to be clean again after all the moving and dust. She then dressed and dried her hair. She looked at the flat iron, deciding if she was going to start out the school year with her kinks or without.

It took fifteen minutes, and while some days she hated the iron, today the warm, smooth pull of the device put her at ease. She got the curls from her mom and with her mom they would stay, at least for a little while.

Quinn came downstairs to find that the "breakfast" her dad had mentioned was a chip-clipped bag of Lucky Charms. Dad had unpacked a single bowl and spoon and placed them on the kitchen counter. No milk. It was hard to tell if he was joking or if he thought this actually qualified as "making breakfast." Before what happened with Mom, Glenn Maybrook had been a funny guy, but now that humor was . . . subtle.

Class started in forty-five minutes. Judging from what she could see of the town out her bedroom window, she estimated a ten-minute walk to school. She could take her time and still be early.

Quinn sat on the floor with her cereal bowl and scrolled on her phone. It didn't take long to find herself frustrated at both the sluggish speed and that there seemed to be no morning messages from Tessa or Jace. And thanks to time zones, it was an hour later in Philly.

They've already forgotten about you. And you haven't even been gone a full forty-eight hours yet.

She grabbed her empty book bag and set out for school early, just to be moving.

There were two cross streets that would've led her toward the school building, and Quinn opted for the one that looked less depressing. The houses were larger, farther apart, all carrying that "cat lady" vibe in both decoration and upkeep. And it wasn't just the faded porcelain frogs holding signs that read "Bless This Home," or the strings of Christmas lights drowning in overflowing gutters, or the pots of flowers dying either from neglect or because it was their season to die. No. There was plenty of shabbiness back home, but there was also new life creeping around the edges. Philly ate its rot, was constantly demolishing the old to make way for the new. Looking at these houses, Quinn was struck with the feeling that Kettle Springs had left its best days behind. The town had given up.

Quinn was so lost in her thoughts, she hadn't noticed her

neighbor following her. The boy was two houses behind, on the opposite side of the street. When she looked over her shoulder at him, he caught her eye and started to double-time it to catch up.

Quinn had asked her father about him last night, over dinner, but Glenn Maybrook couldn't remember the boy's name. Years of medical schooling, memorizing every major bone, vein, artery in the human body and still he couldn't hold on to the neighbor's name for a few hours.

"I want to say it was . . . Rodney?"

"Dad. If *that* kid's name was Rodney, then *two* people in this family are set to have a nervous breakdown."

They'd both laughed at that. It was a nice moment, even if her father's iffy memory now felt like one more thing that she ought to be worried about.

"Hey. Hey there."

Quinn looked across the street. Not-Rodney's pace slowed to stay parallel with her. Still flannel-clad, the boy waved two fingers to get her attention.

"Hi," she said. She didn't feel like talking, but there was no escape now. He crossed the street between parked cars, not bothering to look both ways. Nobody was going anywhere in Kettle Springs anyway.

"I'm Rust. Ruston Vance," he said, voice friendly but laced with—what?—Midwest dirt and grit? "I live next door. I met your dad yesterday."

The boy stuck out his hand. Not how she usually greeted classmates, but she took the hand and gave it a firm, if awkward, shake. His hand was callused, something Quinn was unsure she'd ever felt. That and his general demeanor gave the impression he was an adult; maybe that was just the calluses and the crooked—broken and reset?—nose. Or his dirty-blond stubble, now tawnier that she was seeing it up close, but still impressive and fuller than she was used to seeing on guys her age. But then again there was also something goofy about Rust that kept him from being intimidating. Maybe it was the wide smile or the ancient stains on his flannel shirt. Or the shirt itself, its pairing with the camo backpack. Which was it, did he want to blend in or stand out?

"I'm Quinn." She nodded at the school, the tallest building on the horizon, and added: "It's my first day."

"Dr. Maybrook mentioned that."

Ha. Dr. Maybrook. She snorted back a laugh. Rust scrunched up his face like he'd misspoken.

"Oh, it just sounded very formal. I think of him as Dad."

"Yeah, well, he seems nice. Seems . . . cool. My dad's never worn sneakers in his life."

Quinn remembered the white Reeboks, how happy her dad had been to buy them before the move. More evidence of a new start. For the last fifteen years as an emergency room doc, he avoided white shoes. Blood spatter was a work hazard.

"He has his moments," she agreed.

"He also mentioned Philadelphia? Is that where you're from?"

Maybe it was Rust's downhome presence, or maybe it was that the sky had brightened, but talking to him made Quinn feel better, more relaxed. For a moment, she forgot that she was in Kettle Springs, that she knew no one, that her life was a wreck. Life, Quinn had decided on the long ride out here, was a matter of perspective and attitude. There was a way to look at anything and make it seem okay. She felt sure of it, because . . . well, what other choice did she have?

"It's a nice little city," Quinn said about Philly. It was the same attitude she would have taken if she were talking to a tourist, some opposing volleyball player in from New York who just said her hometown was "better than expected." But putting it that way to Rust made Quinn feel like Philly was somewhere she'd visited once, not the place she'd lived for seventeen years.

"Going to be a big adjustment here . . . ," Rust said. He was right—the intersection they were passing had white picket fences on either side. The houses closer to the school were nicer, looked less neglected.

"Yeah, well, I've decided a change will do me good," Quinn said, not realizing that was the attitude she wanted to take until she'd said it.

Rust nodded in agreement and they lapsed into silence for a block until they crossed the street in front of the school.

Up ahead, kids were milling, taking a last moment outside before they'd be inside all day. Quinn watched one car, then another, turn into what must've been the school's parking lot, a cracked expanse of blacktop ringed in chain-link fencing.

One of the boys near the handrail was spitting into a water bottle of . . . Quinn felt her gorge rise. Gross, chewing tobacco.

"It will take some getting used to, I'm guessing," Rust said, picking up where they'd left off, probably seeing her turning green. "But I think you'll learn to like it. Don't judge it from how it looks." He smiled, seeming to indicate himself, then added: "Not totally."

"What's there to do around here?" Quinn asked. "I mean, for fun?"

He considered. "I'm probably not the best guy to ask. There's great fishing and hunting, if you like that sort of thing."

She blinked at him. She'd fished once on a family trip to Florida, but hunting? Never. Not in a million—

"Ducks're in season . . . ," he fumbled.

Quinn blinked again and tried not to wince, but something in her expression must've given her away.

"Oh. Right. I'm probably not helping any stereotypes with

that answer," Rust said. "Yeah. Well, there's also a movie theater on Main Street. The Eureka. Mostly old stuff, but sometimes they get newer flicks. Color even." He widened his eyes to show he was joking. "There was a frozen yogurt place, too, before Baypen closed down, but that's gone. You can drive to Jamestown if you want to go to the mall. It's only about twenty miles, once you get to the highway. It's a good place for a hang—or so I've heard."

Quinn remembered the window, the dilapidated factory, and the clown. "Baypen, what *is* that? I saw the factory from my window. What'd they make there . . . clowns?"

"Ha! No, that's just Frendo, the mascot. Baypen made corn syrup, but, uh, the refinery burned down . . ." Rust trailed off as he looked up ahead at the school building, where crowds of kids had all gathered to wait for the bell but where no one seemed to be waiting for him.

"It's a long story—"

"Oh yeah?"

"They shipped their product out all across the country. You probably had our syrup and didn't even know." He said that last part with a weird amount of pride, like it was *his* corn syrup. "My father used to work security there. Started when he was my age, actually."

"Until the fire?"

"No, it closed before that," Rust said, climbing the stairs two at a time. She moved to catch up, then realized Rust was cutting ahead not to outrun her, but to hold the door.

"The fire happened recently, actually," Rust said.

"Well, I'll have to get the long version of that story out of you later," Quinn said. She pointed a thumb at the front office. "I have to go get set up."

"For sure," Rust said, smiling before offering his hand to shake again. Somehow, shaking hands with Rust felt less like she'd made a new friend and more like her first job interview. "Maybe I'll see ya in class. But probably not unless you signed up for metal shop?"

She gave him a shrug, tried for her best irrepressible smile: "Who knows? Maybe I did."

Turning, she nodded goodbye and pushed into the front office.

The woman behind the desk was squinting at an old computer screen, the colors warped and faded. Quinn cleared her throat and the woman looked up, haggard and unhappy.

"How can I help you, young lady?" the woman asked. A friendly statement rendered somehow . . . not friendly.

"Hi. Quinn Maybrook. My dad called. I'm new."

The woman didn't speak; instead she plucked a manila envelope from her desk. "Here's your schedule. Good luck," she said. Looking Quinn up and down, she gave a scoff that said *You're going to need it* and turned back to her emails.

Oooookay. Quinn picked up the envelope and hurried out of the office to open it.

Her locker wasn't hard to locate, but the combination inside the envelope didn't seem to work.

29 . . . 6 . . . and . . .

"Did you hear?" someone said as they walked her way.

Oh no. She was already being gossiped about as the new kid. The new kid from the city. Which—and she didn't want to sound conceited here—was probably big news.

"Of course, I heard!" someone yelled in response. "Everybody's heard."

"I can't believe they let him back!"

Wait. *Him?*

"I can't believe he *came* back, but I'm glad he did." The first voice returned, settling at a locker across from hers. "I mean, it's not like anyone can prove he did anything."

"I'm sure there's evidence. But my dad says who's going to press charges? I mean, *his* dad owned the place. More than anythin', I'm pissed that he only got a three-day suspension."

"Yeah. I got two days once for a shoving match."

Quinn was so engrossed in eavesdropping she didn't realize she was staring into her locker door, motionless like a lunatic, until a voice beside her said:

"You have to start at zero."

"Huh?" Quinn turned to the speaker.

A girl with close-cropped hair, dark at the roots and light at the top, and a hoop nose ring—the septum, not the nostril—was suddenly in Quinn's personal space. The girl snatched the combination from Quinn's hand and began to read.

"They all start at zero for some reason, but they don't put instructions on the printout," the girl said. She was wearing a *Thrasher Magazine* sweatshirt and cargo shorts, the kind built for function rather than fashion, but on her, they seemed somehow fashionable.

"There you go," the girl said, pulling down with a sharp *CLACK* and letting gravity swing Quinn's locker open.

"Oh. Thanks," Quinn said, realizing that she didn't have anything to put into the locker, not yet. She'd been opening it to make sure she *could*, to give her something to do before the bell. But now she felt too self-conscious to just close it up again.

"I'm Quinn," Quinn offered lamely. The punk girl seemed content to let the interaction be over, but Quinn wasn't sure she wanted it to be.

"People call me Ginger." And before Quinn could ask why, she added: "My hair used to be lighter."

"Oh."

"You new?"

"Is it that obvious?" Quinn asked, smiling.

Unlike the woman in the front office, Ginger gave no up-and-down, didn't seem interested in Quinn at all, merely looked Quinn in the eyes and offered: "It's a small town."

Okay. A little rude, Quinn thought. But Ginger had

helped Quinn open her locker, which had been a nice gesture. In a hallway where the kids were dressed well enough to look like an ad for American Eagle, Ginger presented an intriguing alternative. At the very least she looked like she came from an ad for a *different* store at the mall.

But before Quinn could think of something else to say, the doors down the hall slammed open.

All heads turned as two boys entered the hallway.

The boy in front, while on the short and stringier side, held himself with confidence that made him seem somehow bigger than the meathead marching in lockstep behind him.

Everyone in the hallway was watching the two boys—even the students who'd turned to face their lockers and friends, the kids trying to look like they *weren't* looking.

No. Not the pair. They were just watching the boy out front. The other guy, big as he was, a neck so thick that it wasn't a neck at all, just an extension of the guy's head, that guy was simply set dressing.

"Cole . . . ," someone whispered. That must have been his name. No last name yet, just Cole. Or maybe that *was* a last name.

Halfway down the hall, Cole looked to Quinn, effortlessly finding her in the crowd, his glare lingering. He had a button nose, a puckish grin, and perfectly tousled dark hair. There were circles under his eyes that could have been from partying or lack of sleep or both, but he wore the fatigue like makeup. His shirt was unbuttoned enough for Quinn to glimpse the edge of his undershirt, a white V-neck. As he passed, she took note of his jeans, distressed around the knees, near the pockets, and fitting like jeans should.

Standing in Cole's wake, Quinn heard someone whisper: "My mom says she can't believe he's not dead."

And someone else added, "My uncle says he ought to be."

The Neanderthal trailing behind Cole seemed to overhear that last comment. The big guy sneered in that direction, his job to squash all Cole criticism. He wore a rumpled football jersey with a picture of a mean-looking, steroidal goat on it. It must've been the Kettle Springs High logo, blue and gold the KSH colors.

Quinn watched the pair of them go. Cole bounded up the stairs at the far end of the hallway. His bodyguard-friend was slower, using the handrail like he was too big to win the fight against gravity without it.

"Wow. Who was that?" Quinn asked, trying to get Ginger to look up from working on her own lock.

"Cole Hill. We used to be friends. Back when my hair was lighter," Ginger said, then tossed an eye to the side and smirked. "And, yeah, he's pretty cute," she said, pausing before adding: "for an arsonist."

THREE

Quinn was late to her first class. Not a good start, but how the hell was room 207 located on the *first* floor?

Her schedule listed the class as "Science." Quinn had no idea what kind of science she was about to walk into. She took a deep breath outside the closed door for room 207, grabbed the knob, and . . .

Inside, the lights were off and a diagram of a plant cell was being projected onto a pull-down screen at the front of the room. She'd taken bio twice now, both in middle school and high school. The transparency looked like it dated to before she was born, so she doubted Kettle Springs High was offering some kind of super-duper AP upgrade.

In the darkness, faces turned to Quinn. Her plan for today had been to keep a low profile, and then repeat that for around two hundred more school days, until she was packing for college. It was only day one, and she was already doing a shitty job.

"Close the door," someone yelled, light from the hallway streaming in behind her.

"As I was saying," her new science teacher said, glowering at her. He didn't ask for a late pass, didn't ask for her name, so Quinn stumbled her way to the only open seat: the front row, next to the dusty hot vent of the projector bulb.

"Just because it's Founder's Day Weekend doesn't mean there won't be a test on Monday," the teacher said, crossing thin arms across his chest.

The classroom around Quinn groaned as one. "But Mr. Vern . . . ," someone muttered.

"Stop it. Stop that," Mr. Vern said, stepping into the spotlight of the projector, his mustached upper lip quivering. Mr. Vern wasn't wearing a sweater vest, but Quinn felt sure that the man owned more than a few. He uncrossed his arms. "We're *a month* into the school year. Exams happen. Time for all you juniors and seniors to grow up and deal with it." Juniors *and* seniors? Wait, was this a mixed class? Were some of the kids around Quinn in the darkness juniors?

The class groaned again. Someone in the back, hidden in the dark, let slip more loudly than he probably meant to, "What a dick . . ."

"Okay," Mr. Vern was quick to snap, leaning forward. "If

that's going to be your attitude, clear your desks and we'll have the test today instead."

Sighs and scoffs surrounded her.

"Mr. Vern?" a voice asked above the murmurs. Quinn turned to see a hand raised, phosphorescent pink nail polish glinting as Quinn's eyes adjusted to the dim room.

"Yes, Janet," Mr. Vern said, exasperated. Quinn couldn't see much, but from the outline of her profile Janet had smooth skin and glistening lips. A valley girl who'd found herself in the wrong valley?

"Well, I've been looking over the syllabus," Janet began, pausing dramatically to flip open the large, organized three-ring binder in front of her. The binder was as well put together as its owner, a reflection of exactitude. "And it says that the first exam will cover nutrition and, uh, we haven't even touched on that yet. Nutrition is *chapter 12* in the textbook. Were we expected to be reading out of order?"

"That, that—" Mr. Vern started, his hands flailing as if trying to grab the answer out of the air just in front of him. "That must be a misprint. Must be from an old syllabus."

"Oh, I figured that. Just wanted to double-check," Janet said, a smile in her voice like she'd just won the argument. No further questions, Your Honor. Quinn suspected the point wasn't to be right so much as it was to fluster the teacher.

"So, wait," another voice cut in, this one behind Quinn's

left shoulder. She turned in her seat and saw the meathead guy who was walking behind Cole earlier. He somehow looked even bigger in the harsh shadows cast by the projector lamp. It was like he and his desk had fused together in the dark and become one big inky blot. "Mr. Vern. You mean to say that we aren't going to be tested on nutrition?"

"No," the teacher said with a sigh. "No, Tucker, you aren't."

"That's not fair! I've been studying the wrong thing, then."

"You haven't been studying anything!" Mr. Vern shot back. With a few stomps, the teacher crossed the room and flicked on the overhead lights. There was a smile on his lips as the class grumbled against the sudden burst of the fluorescent bulbs. Quinn thought he meant the lights to seem defiant, but really, to her, it felt like an admission of defeat, the house lights brightening when the show was over.

"Mr. Vern!" Janet said, gasping. With the lights on, Quinn was surprised to see that Janet didn't look at all like what she'd pictured from her voice. She was Asian, for one thing—the first hint of difference among what to this point had seemed like a pretty buttermilk school. Janet's makeup was there not to conceal, but to accentuate natural beauty. She had shoulder-length black hair, a lightness around the edges that was either highlights or sun-kiss, and a cute, round face that probably helped her get away with gaslighting her teachers like this. “You can’t say he hasn’t been studying! You know that I tutor Tucker after school.”

“It’s true,” the girl behind Janet said. Quinn bounced from Janet to the girl. She had blond ringlets and a side ponytail. Chewing gum snapping. White jeans and a T-shirt so tight it might’ve been body paint. She looked how Quinn had expected the popular girls in Kettle Springs to look, how she had imagined Janet looking, from her voice and lipstick.

“Ronnie. Please stop helping,” Mr. Vern said, sighing, before swiveling around back to Janet and Tucker. “I . . . I’m sure you do tutor him, Janet, but the test has been on the syllabus since the start of the year . . .” Dark spots had grown under the teacher’s arms as he stood in the heat of the projector’s spotlight and struggled to control the class. Quinn didn’t usually have much sympathy for teachers, but she could see her dad reflected in this man’s anxiety.

“It’s true,” Tucker said. “Mr. Vern. I’ve been studying all about nutrition.” The boy seemed to strain for some further proof, scratching one side of his weeks-old buzz cut. “Learning about what’s, uh, good to eat.” Mr. Vern looked away from the speaking boy and the lamp of the overhead projector, trying to gather himself.

“Oh come on,” a final voice yelled from the back of the room. “Just move the test already, Mr. V, and let’s get on with class.”

There, in the back corner behind her, a seat chosen to be out of the way or so the student could keep an eye on everyone in the room: Cole Hill.

Quinn hadn't noticed him on the way in.

He had a pen in his hand and a notebook open in front of him. He seemed ready to work if the world would let him.

"Oh, is that what you think I should do, Mr. Hill?"

"I'm just saying . . . ," Cole began, trailing off as soon as he realized that he had the whole class's attention. "I'm just saying," he repeated, continuing more quietly, "we're wasting time. We should just push forward with the lesson."

"Well, now that I have your *permission*, maybe I will," Mr. Vern said, then pointed both hands out, overlapping accusatory fingers. "But you and your friends won't be around to see it."

"What?" Janet blurted, a record skip in her steely, lip-glossed composure.

"You're out, Ms. Murray." Mr. Vern pointed to Janet. "You are disrupting this class on purpose by arguing about the test. You and Ronnie. Out. Tucker, too. Gather your books. Cole, you too. Go to the in-school room. Now. Have fun wasting your own time. Not your classmates' time."

"I was trying to help! This is bullshit," Cole said, standing.

"You know what's—" Mr. Vern stopped himself. He was upset, shaking. In the slapped silence of the classroom,

Quinn swore she could hear his teeth grinding. "You will *not* talk to me that way. What's upsetting is that you're all"—he took a beat to point at each student who'd interrupted him—"you're all out of control. *You* think the world was built for your amusement. And for years we've—the town has just taken it. But people are waking up. That you're a b-b-blight on this community." He took a deep breath, tried to slow his stutter. "And you're not ruining my lessons for a moment longer."

Cole was standing now, closing his notebook, clicking his pen. "Okay, sure, fine. We're going."

The fifteen or so kids who *weren't* being sent out of the classroom all stared at Cole as he hitched up his bag and exited without further protest, followed close behind by Tucker.

The tension in the room was so thick, so palpable, as the rest of the group made their way out that Quinn couldn't help it: she laughed.

It just came out. A small giggle. A perverse, nervous, involuntary response.

"Oh, this is funny!?" Mr. Vern whirled, pointing to Quinn.

It wasn't funny. The tension, the absurdity of the teacher's tantrum, the very fact that she was so far, so surreally distant, from her home: the sound slipped out before she could cover her mouth.

The teacher moved to his desk to consult what must have

been a roll sheet. "Maybrook? You find this funny?" Quinn felt the blood drain from her face. She didn't know how to answer—or if she was even supposed to. "No, this isn't funny. This isn't one bit funny. This is insane! Your new friends are an impediment to learning at this school and that's just in class. In the real world, on the internet, they are a . . . a . . ." *Blight.* She filled in, when he couldn't find the word. Mr. Vern swallowed hard.

Okay. Maybe Quinn had misjudged the situation. This was about something bigger than senioritis, fucking with a nerdy teacher, and not wanting to take a test. "I, for one, am fed up with their antics, with their videos and their . . . their . . . their *bullshit.*" There it was, it was out, the word he'd so clearly wanted to say earlier. He held three fingers to his lips, then hissed: "They're probably filming this right now. Isn't that right, Janet?"

If they were, this guy was done. A filmed tantrum like this was the kind of thing that parents brought to school boards.

"Isn't it, Janet?" Mr. Vern repeated.

Janet and Ronnie had been hovering at the doorway, Cole and Tucker already out in the hall.

"Go! Detention! Now!!"

"All Tucker did was ask a question," Janet complained.

"A question! A question—right. Well, you've got *in-school* suspension. Do you want to make it *out of school*?"

Janet threw her hands up, resigned, started back out the door.

"Wait. Come back here. Give me your phone. Now! You can pick it up at the end of the day."

"You can't do that!" Janet snapped. "That's private property!"

"We weren't even filming!" Ronnie seconded.

"Yours too," Mr. Vern said, beckoning Ronnie to return back down the center aisle.

The two girls fumed, but both handed over their phones to Mr. Vern.

"And take your new friend with you." Mr. Vern tapped the edge of Quinn's desk. "Make sure she gets down to the ISS room without getting lost. I'll be calling the office to let them know you're coming."

"Me?" Quinn asked, still astonished at the sudden turn her morning had taken.

"Yes, you, Maybrook. Go giggle with the *cool* kids outside of my classroom. In fact . . ." Mr. Vern seemed to have an epiphany, his mood manic. "Janet, Ronnie?" he asked.

The two girls stood at the doorway, arms crossed.

"Tell the boys, who are no doubt standing right outside, snickering at me. Tell them you're all banned from Founder's Day," Mr. Vern said, turning to the rest of the class with an *Ain't I a stinker?* look on his face.

There was silence in the room, nobody else wanting to

react and earn themselves a ban from . . . whatever Founder's Day was.

"Like you have the power to do that. It's a public event," Janet said. Not a whine, just a statement of facts. Her phone was private property, this was a public event: Quinn had met girls like Janet before. Amateur lawyers.

Quinn didn't know what Founder's Day was and didn't care, not at this moment. She was being tossed out of class. She repeated that fact to herself in numb disbelief. Quinn grabbed her bag and stood to leave, her hands and arms not feeling like her own. She'd never gotten in real trouble—nothing worse than a few skipped gym classes marred her record at her old school, and with those there had been no punishment: she was a volleyball star.

"Yes, tell yourself that I can't," Mr. Vern said, his voice more even than it had been. "I'll let the sheriff know to be on the lookout for you and your friends. That you're banned. That you're unwelcome at the 'public event.'"

"Whatever," Janet said, shrugging off the proclamation. She exited the room, Ronnie in tow.

Still in a daze, Quinn followed them.

"Come on, new girl," Cole said, waiting for them all outside the class. Mr. Vern was right—he'd been listening and smiling. He didn't seem at all troubled by what had transpired.

Cole's smile put Quinn at ease. Or, at least, it calmed her enough that she no longer felt like she might cry.

"Follow me," he said, closing the distance between them, leaving his crew behind.

His hand touched the small of her back, guiding, gentle:

"We'll show you the way."

"Fuck me!" Tucker said. "I mean, who cares about Founder's Day, but if they call home, my mom's never going to give me the car on Saturday."

Quinn suspected that the in-school suspension room hadn't been built to *be* the in-school suspension room. Instead of anything official-looking, it was a bare, unused classroom. They took chairs down from stacks in the back of the room to have a place to sit. Despite Mr. Vern's threat of "alerting the office," there was no adult supervision and seemingly none forthcoming.

Security at KSH seemed lax, but maybe that was because back home at Quinn's school, there were metal detectors at every entrance, security guards with zip ties poking from their back pockets.

Even without disciplinary infrastructure and climate officers, Cole, Janet, Tucker, and Ronnie all acted like they knew the drill for in-school suspension.

They took their seats to the front of the room, arranging the desks there in a half circle.

"You can't miss the party," Janet told Tucker. "You're my ride."

"Mine too," Ronnie said. She had taken down her side ponytail and was now in the process of putting it back up on the other side, swapping out the neon band with one of the others she wore at her wrists. "I mean. It's our party—"

"Well, you helped. It was Janet's idea," Tucker interrupted.

"I know," Ronnie continued, pivoting. "Man up. Tell your mom, you're taking the car. What's she going to do?"

"She'll kill me," Tucker said. "And anyway, what do you care, Miss Queen?" He said "Miss" like "Mizzz" and Quinn was unsure if it was a last name or a pet name. "Matt'll drive you. Probably. If he didn't just redo the seats."

Ronnie pouted. "Sucks. I had a cute outfit ready for Founder's Day."

Quinn wondered if the ban extended to herself. Or if her punishment was just this detention. She could ask Mr. Vern later, if she stopped by his classroom, ready to apologize. But it was probably better to let it be for today, have a fresh start next class.

"We're still going. What about the phones?" Janet asked.

"Oh," Ronnie said, flipping an iPhone out of the waistband of her white jeans.

"Yes, girl!" Janet smiled.

"I hope Mr. Vern has fun with old 6s."

"Holy shit," Quinn said. Again, she'd wanted to remain an observer, hadn't presumed to angle her own desk into the group, didn't know if she wanted to, but she couldn't hide her amazement. "Did you really give the teacher decoy phones?"

Ronnie smiled for a moment, taking pride, but then her grin disappeared, a look of realization that Quinn was the new girl. "I'm sorry, was I talking to *you*?"

"Be nice," Cole said. It was the first time he'd spoken since they'd arrived.

Ronnie snarled, a *Don't tell me what to do* look, but then turned to Quinn and apologized. "Sorry. That was childish."

"Maybrook, was it?" Cole asked. "Kicked out of class on your first day. That's a hell of a statement."

"We got a badass over here . . . ," Janet muttered. It didn't sound like a compliment, but it didn't quite sound like an insult, either.

Quinn ignored her.

"It's Quinn. And it's not usually how I like to start off. But the guy went crazy. He should be fired . . ."

"Yeah, Mr. Vern's a bit high-strung," Cole explained. The others nodded. "But he's old-school Kettle Springs."

"KSOG," Tucker offered.

"He grew up here. Never left. He thinks everything was better before kids started wearing ripped jeans in like 1983."

"And that satanic music they all love," Janet said. Ronnie rolled her eyes in response. What was their deal? Not lock-step agreement like most mean girls, that was for sure. Competition with each other? Over Cole himself, maybe?

"Dude kicked me out of class once for wearing a Vikings cap," Tucker cut in to add. "On game day."

Well. That didn't seem weird to Quinn. Dress codes were dress codes. Or was that a city thing? There didn't seem to be a strong gang presence in Kettle Springs.

"Did you catch any of his rant on there?" Janet asked Ronnie, motioning to the phone.

"No! I wasn't even filming! He really did throw us out for nothing!"

"You really missed it?" Cole said. "And look where it got us." He motioned around the room.

"Not to mention the fact that if we're banned from Founder's Day, I'm now missing out on a churro," Tucker said.

Ronnie looked ready to apologize like before, but instead Janet interrupted and doubled down.

"Oh, like we're not going anyway. And how were we supposed to know Mr. Vern was going to flip out over something so small?" Janet said. "That would have played well on the channel, too. Did you see how red he was? I thought he was going to pass out . . ."

"You have a YouTube channel?" Quinn asked, finally admitting to herself that simply dipping her toes into the social scene wasn't going to be possible. She was in it now. The deep end. The five of them were doing time together . . .

"Yeah, *we* have a YouTube channel," Ronnie corrected.

"They *used to have* a YouTube channel," Cole said, a further tweak. Distancing himself.

"They," Janet scoffed. "*We* still do. Even if some people don't like to be on camera as much as they used to." Janet nodded at Cole, both of them looking different flavors of exasperated.

"What kind of channel?" Quinn asked Janet, breaking the moment of awkwardness.

"Stunts, pranks, we have—had, whatever—almost six thousand subscribers. A few videos have gotten, like, fifty thousand views. We're growing. Or at least were until a little over a week ago." Another withering look to Cole. "Seems like we might *really* be done now."

While Ronnie and Tucker seemed to be under the boy's thumb, Janet didn't seem to give a shit. Quinn liked that.

"Check it out," Tucker said, handing over his phone. "There's no Wi-Fi here, but I've got the page cached."

Quinn scrolled through videos with names like: "Roof Jump on a Moped—Must Watch!!"; "Old Lady Freak-Out—Waitress goes H.A.M."; and "KILLER CLOWN—HAUNTED BARN STUNT TrY Not to LauGH :-D"

The last video's thumbnail showed a familiar-looking clown in a porkpie hat, grasping an oversize plastic sickle and sliding out from behind a barn door.

"That clown," Quinn said, recognizing the hat more than anything else.

"You've seen him before?" Cole said, surprised, happy.

"Yeah, I meant to ask someone what was up with him"—she thought of Rust, but didn't say his name, as it didn't seem like her neighbor fit with this crowd—"I've seen his face around town. On buildings and stuff."

"Oh," Cole said, seemingly disappointed that she didn't know the clown from their videos. "The town loves Frendo. He's, like, our mascot. But he's lame, so we've been trying to give him a makeover. Rehabilitate his image. Make him a little more . . . homicidal."

"That reminds me," Janet said, a sidebar with Tucker that was only a little distracting and rude. "You should get in touch with Dave Sellers, see if he'll trade shifts with you tomorrow."

"Shifts?" Tucker looked confused for a moment. "Ah. Gotcha," he said, figuring out whatever she was asking. "I don't think the guy has a phone, but I can try to find him around town. Five bucks and he'll hand over the suit."

"Whatever you two are planning," Cole said, pointing between Janet and Tucker, "leave me out of it."

"So what happened? Why aren't you making videos anymore?" Quinn asked, trying to get the conversation back on track.

When he spoke about the channel, it was obvious that Cole was proud of their work.

Nobody answered.

Tucker, Ronnie, and Janet squirmed, looked to Cole as he thought about it.

"We had an incident last week." Cole paused. "I got drunker than I should have."

Tucker coughed, put a hand on Cole's desktop. "That's one way to put it, man. But you didn't mean it. We all know that."

The hand moved to Cole's shoulder and he shrugged Tucker away. "I'm good," Cole said to the bigger boy. Tucker looked ready to stand, give Cole a full shoulder rub, if it was requested. It was extreme, even for sports bro fraternity, and Quinn had to wonder if Tucker knew how sad his hero worship looked.

"He burned down the factory," Janet said, cutting through the fog of Tucker's coddling.

The pieces of town gossip she'd gotten from Rust and then Ginger began to knit together, giving Quinn a better picture of what was going on.

"It was *my* family's factory," Cole corrected, as if that made it less of a crime. "My dad's at least. And it had been empty for over a year. At the time of the fire."

He's pretty cute, for an arsonist. Ginger's words came back to Quinn.

"No one got hurt or anything," Tucker said, coming to his friend's defense. "It just got out of control, but the way everyone is reacting, you'd think no one in this town ever threw a rager before." Tucker was clearly used to standing up for Cole, no matter what.

Cole looked over and up to make eye contact with the big kid. He smiled. Even beaten and sad—and with that unattractive air of *I'm the boss*—Quinn could tell that Cole had the capacity for kindness. Or at least she hoped he did, that she wasn't just developing a crush, ready to give more slack to someone who . . . maybe just admitted to a major felony?

"I made a mistake," Cole said, voice soft. "I fucked up. But in my defense, the factory's been boarded up too long and all it was doing was sitting around and slowly rotting. It was a stupid reminder of the way things used to be. I'm not sad it's gone."

"Mostly gone," Janet corrected him. That was right, the inside might have been burned out, but the structure was still standing. Quinn almost told them that she could see Baypen from her bedroom window.

"Say what you will about Kettle Springs . . . ," Ronnie seconded. "The volunteer firefighters are on point."

"Fine, *mostly* gone," Cole said, glaring at Janet.

"Cool," Quinn said, then, reaching for a change of subject, a way *in*to this group she wasn't sure getting involved with was a good idea: "So, where'd you shoot the creepy clown video?"

"At Tillerson's barn—" Cole stopped mid-thought, mid-word, and snapped his fingers, pointed to Janet.

"Don't look at me, it's open invite."

"That's very neighborly of you, Janet," Tucker said.

"What she means to say is she's spent most of this week putting together a party," Cole explained, some life coming back into his sad-dog eyes. "And you're definitely coming."

She looked at the room around her, everyone seeming to be ready for what came next, for her answer, different levels of involvement on their faces. Everyone except Ronnie, who was taking great pains to look like she didn't care.

"I am?" Quinn asked, buying time for him to elaborate.

Cole's invitation was phrased like a command, but somehow it felt like a challenge.

"You bet you are. Day after Founder's Day."

Founder's Day. She wanted to ask what it even was. Whether they thought Mr. Vern had formally banned her from the "public event" like he had them, but there was no time.

Cole looked to Janet, tenderness in the expression. He nodded.

Go on.

"You saw a little bit of it, in class. What it's like around here," Janet started. "There's so many people—and Mr.

Vern's the least of them—trying to shut us up, trying to make us who *they* want us to be. Trying to tape our mouths shut and tie us in bubble wrap."

"But for one night we're going to say fuck 'em," Cole said, picking up the energy. "We're going to do it where nobody's around to stop us. Out in the corn, drink and smoke and do—"

"All the things that make Kettle Springs great," Ronnie added.

"Kettle Springs is great?" Tucker sneered.

"It could be," Janet said, suddenly wistful. "It will be for one night."

"And you," Cole said, winking at Quinn, "cannot miss it. Not if it's the last thing you do."

FOUR

"Everything's so cheap, it's like living in the fifties," Quinn's dad said, turning the menu over to begin again from page one. "Salisbury steak for five bucks! And it comes with a side."

"A side of diabetes?" Quinn asked. Tentative.

She was relieved to see him smile. It'd been a rough afternoon since getting home. The school had called Dad, letting him know she'd gotten detention for "disciplinary issues." He didn't take it well, began pressing her with questions about acting out. But by the time she'd recounted her story, explaining about YouTube channels, celebrity boys, a factory fire, a science teacher's Mr. Hyde moment, and a mysterious party invitation, Glenn Maybrook could only chuckle and say:

"Well, I guess don't make it a regular thing."

Whoever he'd spoken to from the school hadn't mentioned Founder's Day, and neither had Quinn.

Quinn looked around them at the Main Street Eatery. Yes, that was the actual name of the restaurant. The establishment was a cross between the greasy spoons that peppered South Philadelphia and the proper diners on the other side of the Delaware River in Jersey. They were seated in one of the booths next to the windows and watched the sleepy late-afternoon rush of Kettle Springs.

Quinn picked at a splotch of crusted ketchup in front of her. It came off easily against her fingernail. Otherwise, the place was clean enough but not antiseptic. This was not a chain restaurant, hadn't been plopped down whole cloth in a weekend. The knickknacks dotting the walls had earned their spots. A "Missouri's Best Chili, 1998" runner-up plaque hung with pride alongside pictures of the decades of Little League teams the restaurant had sponsored.

As Quinn scrutinized the decorations, she noticed that, oddly enough, nothing seemed to date beyond the early 2000s. It was like time had stopped for the Eatery just after the turn of the century. The effect made the Eatery seem less like the walls were celebrating the restaurant's place in the community and more like they were preserving the artifacts of a time long past.

Quinn's dad was looking down with a private and doofy smile, still perusing the menu. "They have chicken-fried steak. I haven't had chicken-fried steak since—" And he stopped mid-sentence. Quinn knew where the thought was going to end up, more or less. Glenn Maybrook had last had chicken-fried steak with Mom. Somewhere. On a road trip, maybe. Probably before Quinn was born or before she could remember. If he were able to without crying, he'd tell her that it tasted great but that it kept them both up all night with indigestion. "Anyway," he soldiered on, shaking his head, "that dish sounds like it will be good for business. A real artery clogger."

He kept at it: "Do you think it's okay to order something from the breakfast side *and* something from the lunch?" Poring over the menu was the happiest he'd looked in weeks.

"I think here in the fifties they let time travelers get away with anything they want," Quinn joked.

He deserved this. Samantha Maybrook might have robbed them both of any enduring optimism toward the future, but snatches of occasional fried food–inspired happiness really shouldn't be too much to ask.

Their waitress came over, looking harried. The woman wore her hair up, in a style that Quinn had only ever glimpsed in pictures and old movies: the beehive. Despite the worry lines on her face and smudges in her makeup, the hairdo was perfect. The waitress wore large, mermaid-scale earrings that gave her face an unpleasant reptile quality when paired with her blue eye shadow.

Warmly and professionally, the woman fielded Dad's questions about the menu. Quinn glanced to the window to keep from staring at the mole that'd poked through the waitress's thick foundation.

Across the street, she saw a group of men on the corner, one with a banner draped at his feet, the other two pointing up. They were hanging a sign welcoming everyone to Founder's Day. They seemed to have things under control, so Quinn let her eyes drift down the street. There'd been plenty of interesting bumper stickers around town, but she couldn't help but pick out the truck with the gun rack, the "Don't Tread on Me" magnet, and an American flag sticker with a dark blue stripe. Back home, the truck wouldn't have belonged to a Philadelphian, the sticker representing a Pennsyltucky bingo, but in Kettle Springs it was starting to look normal.

A kid Quinn didn't recognize walked by the window and she turned away to avoid meeting his gaze.

With fresh eyes, Quinn realized that the Eatery's clientele skewed much older than at the diners she knew back home, which mostly served as after-school hangouts this early in the night. She remembered how much the waitresses hated the groups of teenagers. Sometimes nursing hangovers, kids would take over three or four tables for hours, order milkshakes and fries and demand free refills on Cokes. All that while not historically being *great* tippers.

In fact, Quinn noticed, there wasn't a single other teenager in the Eatery. Unlike the town itself, which seemed sleepy for so early in the evening, the Eatery was bustling. A veritable sea of liver spots, soup noises, and mothball stink.

After settling on an order, Quinn's dad leaned over the table and said, "I'm going to hit the head before the food comes."

"Thanks for sharing."

Quinn pulled out her phone. Usually picking up her phone was muscle memory, but right now she had a purpose. She was going to try looking up her new classmates—fellow detentioneers—on Instagram.

Unlocking her phone, she overheard her dad say: "Heya, I'm Dr. Maybrook. Pardon me, but it looks like you've got a cane there. Why don't you stop by and I'll be happy to take a look. I'm at Doc Weller's old practice."

Glenn Maybrook conducted a version of this conversation with three separate customers, trying to sell his new practice, but none of his potential patients seemed eager to talk with her dad. Which wasn't surprising—a strange man was approaching them and asking how long they'd had that scaly patch of skin below their elbow. It may have been that Quinn was a conspicuous eavesdropper, but every time she raised her eyes above the back of the booth, she saw old, dull eyes staring back at her.

Her dad's awkward glad-handing wasn't the problem.

No. It wasn't her imagination, wasn't paranoia. The old folks in the diner weren't talking to her dad because of her. The patrons were responding to her dad's pleasantries by giving Quinn a stare-down.

Instead of creeping her out, like those old, rheumy eyes staring at Quinn probably should've, all they did was make her angry. Quinn almost thought to bare her teeth and growl to really give them something to be afraid of, but caught herself and toyed with the beads of condensation that had formed on her glass of water instead.

"Tough crowd," her dad said as he slid back into the booth. Their food arrived a moment later. Quinn's dad cleared his throat to ask the waitress a question and for one horrible second Quinn was terrified he was going to ask if she'd ever had that mole biopsied. But, instead, he asked for syrup. "I like it on my bacon," he said as if the request needed explanation, and then, inexplicably, he winked. The waitress smiled and winked back, if only by gratuity-based reflex.

Quinn had to admit the food was good. Putting the fifties prices aside, chipped beef on toast had its charms.

"This can't be every night," she said between mouthfuls. "We need to do less eating out, less takeout. There's got to be a decent supermarket around here. We're in farmland, right? Where's the farmers' markets and cute roadside stands?"

"I don't know sweetie, but . . ." Her father trailed off. She heard the sleigh bells affixed to the restaurant's door jingle.

Please don't be Cole. That was her first thought and it surprised her.

But she turned in her seat to see it wasn't Cole at the door. It was a grown man clad in what Quinn had always thought of as "highway patrolman tan." There was a star on his chest. Not the silver badge that Philly cops wore on their belts, but an honest-to-goodness sheriff's star with more points than seemed necessary. This was a massive man, with the reddened, visible pores of someone who was both old *and* prematurely aged. His thick, rectangular gray mustache was as standard-issue as his belt, handcuffs, and sidearm. Quinn tried to imagine him ten or twenty years younger and just couldn't. She suspected he might have always looked this way.

The lawman tipped his hat to her father, then removed it. He winked at Quinn and then sat in the booth behind theirs without "waiting to be seated" as the sign instructed. Quinn felt the vinyl of the booth's upholstery pull tighter as the man sat back-to-back with her. She could hear the sound of his spurs settle as he sat, despite the fact that he probably wasn't wearing literal spurs.

"Sheriff Dunne, what can I get you?" their waitress said, patting the side of her beehive, searching for the pencil nub that might've disappeared in the early eighties.

"The usual. Thanks, Trudy," he said.

"Black coffee and a baked potato with cheese, coming

right up. Yer a creature of habit, George," she said, a girlish giggle in her voice.

This exchange revealed two things: that Sheriff George Dunne didn't understand how meals worked, and that their waitress was—of course—named Trudy.

After the sheriff ordered, the Main Street Eatery released a collective sigh. It didn't seem like fear exactly, but the same kind of star power Cole had exhibited at school, playing to a different audience. With the normal din of arthritic hands on silverware resumed, Quinn felt comfortable enough to ask the question she'd been holding in since she'd gotten back from school.

"Are you nervous?"

"About my little girl going out to a party?"

"No, Dad," she said, suddenly not wanting to joke about the party, especially with the sheriff right behind them. "About seeing your first patients?"

Her father paused, considering the question. "I'm not nervous. A bit of first-day jitters. Never easy being the new kid—even when you're not a kid anymore. Why? Do I seem nervous?"

"On your way to the bathroom, you offered to give that lady a pelvic exam." Quinn pointed across from them using her pinkie.

Her father managed both a laugh and a disapproving look at the same time. It was a look he'd been working on since she'd begun testing adult conversational waters. After Mom died, Quinn had to do a lot of growing up, quickly, and while Dad might have needed her to be his friend and confidant and sometime shoulder-to-cry-on, she knew he also missed having her be his—in his words—little girl.

"So, are you asking if I'm going to have a breakdown?"

"Yeah. I guess I kinda am."

"I love you, Quinn. You know that, right?"

"I know."

"I'm good. I'm in a good place. Kettle Springs is . . ." He searched for the word, then settled for something different. "This is what I needed," he said, putting a hand on hers and then correcting himself, "what *we* needed. And you say this like I wasn't at the office all day today."

"Yeah, but you didn't see any patients."

"Dr. Weller's departure was really sudden. It's weird. He literally didn't advance the paper on his exam table, just left it there with someone's butt imprint still on it. I'd canceled today's appointments, but I probably didn't need to." Her dad fiddled with the salt and pepper shakers, mismatched, the salt in simple clear glass and the pepper a ceramic clown face. "The good news is that the office has all his equipment. Was expecting to have to do some orders, run at half capacity. I'm amazed he didn't sell the house furnished, too, if that was how quickly he needed to get out."

"I guess it's not that weird. Wherever he's moving, he

probably needs chairs," Quinn said. For the first time since unpacking, it seemed to sink in that their house had been someone else's house earlier this month.

It didn't feel right to her, the brevity of it on both ends. It was like Dr. Weller could turn his car around, use his spare keys to walk in when they were at home tonight, and be like, "Sorry, changed my mind. GTFO."

"Anyway"—her dad kept talking, bringing her attention back—"it's exciting taking over a practice, but the office also feels . . ." He paused.

"Don't worry. You'll make it your own soon enough. How many you seeing tomorrow?"

"There are three patients on the schedule. Was supposed to be four, but one called this morning to cancel. I have no idea if the rest have even been told there's a new sheriff in town."

At this turn of phrase, Quinn felt the *actual* sheriff behind her shift in his seat.

"So to speak," her dad added, flicking his eyebrows up and looking over Quinn's shoulder as Trudy came over to ask how their dinner was.

Dad gushed about the food itself, then went on to rave about how the prices were so much more reasonable than back home in Philadelphia. It was more of an answer than Trudy expected. Dad was trying too hard to be neighborly. And he wasn't great at it. He wasn't the kind of doctor who excelled at small talk or bedside manner. It wasn't really his nature. He was a quiet guy, big-hearted, soft. He cared too much but didn't give voice to the care. Which was a big part of why they moved to Kettle Springs. Working at a big hospital owned by one of the nation's largest corporate healthcare conglomerates had gotten to Glenn Maybrook. He'd had to tell too many families that this procedure or that medication wasn't going to be covered by insurance. He'd seen too many kids come in with gunshot wounds and sent them home with bills they couldn't afford to pay. The stress wore on him, but after Mom overdosed, he was done. He was just hollowed out. He went through the motions for a year after, afraid to upset the routine, unsure that the ground beneath him wasn't about to open up again. But his mind was somewhere else. He couldn't keep his head in the game. He wasn't sleeping. This diner food was the most she'd seen him eat. More than once, Quinn had woken in the middle of the night to find him sitting in the dark, arguing with a ghost, with Mom. So when the opportunity in Kettle Springs came, Quinn didn't fight it. A fresh start was exactly what they needed; even if it was not what she wanted.

"Since you bring it up. I think I've decided. I think I'm going to the party," Quinn said after Trudy was finally able to pry herself away from her dad's compliments.

"Good, you should," Dad said. "Is the neighbor kid

going? I like him. Doesn't strike me as the kind of guy that gets kicked out of many classes."

"No idea," Quinn admitted. "And *Rust*. His name is Rust, Dad," she said, hoping repetition would help the information set, congeal, in Glenn Maybrook's brain.

Her dad took a toast shovel of chipped beef and nodded absently: "Weird name."

Across Main Street, a few doors down, Quinn spotted Janet and a few other kids preparing to cross the street. Janet had her phone out, laughing to Ronnie, who mugged for the camera, side ponytail in yet another new configuration. Next to Ronnie was a guy Quinn hadn't seen before. He was shorter than both girls, but no one would ever call him small. He was built like a fire hydrant, squat and solid. He held his arms out at his sides like he'd recently finished working out and was still enjoying the burn. Janet led the way as the three of them shot between parked cars.

Was brazen jaywalking another indicator that Janet and company didn't give a fuck, or was there just not much traffic to pay attention to in Kettle Springs?

Quinn realized she'd been staring too long and that her dad had been trying to talk to her the whole time. Then came the fear that her classmates could very well be crossing to the restaurant so they could grab a bite to eat.

She stared intently at her mostly eaten toast and tried to think invisible thoughts.

"The girls are in my bio class," she said into the table, interrupting her dad's idle chatter.

"*The* bio class?" he asked.

Behind her, Quinn felt Sheriff Dunne once again shift in his seat. Her father's attention pivoted away from the window as the lawman behind her stood from his booth. Quinn didn't turn, but she could hear the sheriff's boots on the tile. Isolating that tiny sound caused her to realize another hush had fallen over the restaurant.

Quinn raised her eyes. She could see the sheriff in the reflection of a hazy wall-length mirror at the back of the room, leading to the bathrooms.

The sheriff left his hat on the table to save his spot as if to say, *This won't take long.*

Walking over, the sheriff stopped inside the door to the Eatery and waited. Janet and her group paused on the sidewalk outside and looked up, wordlessly communicating with the man through the glass.

And in that moment of stillness, Quinn saw it: the glass of the door was like a magic mirror out of a movie. On one side there were yellowed newspaper clippings about giant pumpkin pies made from giant blue-ribbon-winning pumpkins, little old ladies wearing kitty sweaters they'd knit themselves, and over that delicate small town, the huge, aged sheriff protecting law and order. On the other side—in what seemed like a different dimension—there were the kids with their iPhones, taking in the world through electric eyes a gigabyte at a time, there were boys in V-necks and girls in boy shorts, and that world was led by Janet, a vision Norman Rockwell never painted, black hair perfect, dressed in pink to match her nails, looking like a new stick of bubble gum.

Was it Quinn's imagination, or did the sheriff's right hand subtly drift toward his gun as he peered out at the teenagers? No, couldn't be; the big man was simply adjusting his belt.

Whatever he'd done with his hand, it was enough to defuse the situation. Janet smiled a "just kidding" smile to the sheriff, and the teens continued, zipping right past the door.

The sheriff made a show of stretching, so tall, his arms so long that his knuckles nearly grazed the stucco ceiling, and then he turned and headed to the back of the restaurant toward the men's room. The murmurs, the sounds of rattling knives and forks against china, resumed.

"Oh wait," the sheriff said, doubling back. He clapped one large hand on her dad's shoulder. Glenn Maybrook looked immediately uncomfortable. The sheriff smiled, wide and warm as if he hadn't just had a Mexican standoff with a trio of high schoolers.

"You're the new doctor!" the sheriff boomed, almost announcing it for the diner, as if that hadn't already been told.

"Why yes, I am. Hi, Glenn Maybrook," her dad said, visibly nodding away his discomfort and attempting to slip back into professional mode.

The two of them shook, her dad's hand disappearing into the sheriff's like the big man was wearing a catcher's mitt. Glenn didn't get up, so the sheriff loomed over her dad, holding all the power.

"Sheriff Dunne. Welcome to town, Doc." Her dad held his dopey smile, nodding. "I'm not going to interrupt your supper, I just wanted to say hello. We're so glad you made it. And just in time."

"Yup, er," her dad faltered. "Happy to be here. It's a great little town you have."

"Sure is—" The sheriff looked up, remembering something, or making a show of remembering, at least. "Actually . . ." He reached into the top pocket of his shirt, behind his badge, and took out a small, folded paper. "You probably heard already, but tomorrow is Founder's Day." He looked down, acknowledging Quinn for the first time. "I bet you're excited to have your first Friday in town be without school, sweetheart. Looking forward to seeing you there."

"I . . ." *I'm not your sweetheart, motherfucker.* She didn't know where the rage had come from, a good feminist upbringing or maybe just the way the man said the word. But—as far as the sheriff was concerned—at least she wasn't banned. "I didn't even know I had school off tomorrow."

Quinn smiled, squeezing her own thigh under the tabletop to control herself.

"You sure do," Sheriff Dunne said, then turned back to her dad. Kid time was over, apparently.

"Explains why my patients are canceling, I guess," her dad said, but Sheriff Dunne seemed not to hear or care, just continued on with his prepared spiel.

"The town's undergoing a bit of a transition at the moment, and as our doctor, I'd love to get you involved in a positive way in the community. I know it's short notice, but we've got a town meeting tonight," the sheriff said, punctuating the words with a squeeze at Dad's shoulder. "Be nice if you could come. Refreshments will be served—if you've still got room." He chuckled, eyes down to Dad's empty plate.

Her dad stood, apparently tired of being talked down to. "That's mighty nice of you to ask."

Quinn winced at her dad's attempt to sound folksy. *Mighty nice*. God.

"I'll," her dad continued, "certainly try to be there."

"You can be there or not, right? There's no trying." The sheriff smiled wide. Nobody in Kettle Springs minced words, apparently.

"Uhhhh. With unpacking and all. I don't think . . ."

"Relax. I'm just making you squirm, Doc. But I understand. We'll get you at the next one," Sheriff Dunne said, and slapped Glenn Maybrook on the back hard enough to send her dad's side into the tabletop, spilling both their waters.

"Trudy," Sheriff Dunne said, then whistled between his teeth. "A slice of pie for the doctor and his little gal. Any flavor they want, but they want cherry."

"That's very kind," her dad said, Quinn still hung up on being called both a little gal and a sweetheart.

"And some napkins." The sheriff gave a firm nod and continued to the restroom.

Her dad turned back to Quinn.

"Where were we? Oh yeah, you said you were going to the party," her dad said.

But Quinn wasn't listening. She watched their waitress pass the sheriff and grab his arm: "Thank you. That girl and her friend, they . . ."

The sheriff held one massive gray-haired hand up and waved Trudy away: *Think nothing of it.*

Quinn's dad cleared his throat.

"Right. The party," Quinn said, snapping back to the present. "No worries—and, yes, I promise if there's drinking and driving, I'll just call a Lyft."

"A Lyft in Kettle Springs?" her father snorted.

"Yeah, I guess you're right. Lyft probably hasn't made it here yet." She shook her head.

Her dad looked down at his hand. He unfolded the paper the sheriff had handed him. He had a familiar curl at the sides of his mouth, one Quinn recognized from before Samantha Maybrook had died, leaving them alone. "But you know what *has* made it here?"

"What?" Quinn asked, almost afraid of whatever cornball response was coming from her dad next.

Glenn Maybrook kept his impish smile, turned the flyer around to her, and spread its headline wide.

The paper read:

"Make Kettle Springs Great Again"

FIVE

"And how exactly are we supposed to do that, Harlan?"

"Yeah, with what money?"

The questions hit Harlan Jaffers like waves. They were tossing him, drowning him. These people, his constituents, needed to give him one fucking second to *think*.

He should have had his assistant spring for a few extra cookies to toss onto the refreshment table. Maybe a sleeve or two of Chewy Chips Ahoy would have soothed the rabble.

There. That was it. There was a way Harlan could quiet them. At least buy some more time to think.

"Everyone quiet please!" Harlan said, feeling a droplet of sweat slither its way down his spine, ending in the waistband of his briefs. How was it this hot in here? With the windows open? In October?

Body heat. Angry bodies. That was how.

"Before y'all keep yellin' about canceling Founder's Day, I want you to know that this is an event that your neighbors have been putting their hearts and souls into for weeks. And with only a quarter of the regular budget! I know times are tight and we have to do more with less, but I can honestly say that this is the best these floats and costumes have looked in *years*. Downsizing the fair helped, too." He paused and dabbed his forehead with his handkerchief. For the moment, he had the room's attention and he was determined not to lose it. "Honestly, let's give a hand to Mrs. Murray, who hand-painted the banners for the Shriners and the 4-H Club. She's not just a pretty face, she's an artist." Harlan motioned to the Asian woman in the second row. Beside her, her husband uncrossed his arms and clapped, but looked annoyed while doing it. Murray. Harlan hated that shitbird. Pudgy cue ball didn't know how good he had it.

"Banners are all well and good, but what about the pump engine that was damaged while putting out the Hill boy's fire? It ain't gonna be ready for the parade!" Fred Vassar yelled, cupping his hands even though it wasn't needed in the cramped, hot lodge.

"Yeah, not to mention if there's *another* fire," Grady Lidle hollered, piling on.

"We should have taken out a billboard on I-44 like I suggested," shouted Helen Mars. "More out-of-towners would come, then. They'd visit downtown. It'd help local businesses."

"People. People. Listen to me. Flyers have been distributed at the St. James Mall. We'll have a crowd. And as far as the rest of the money problems go, I have it on good authority," he said, then paused. Well, here goes. He was beyond the point of no return: "Arthur Hill is considering attending the parade." They stopped yelling. That had shut them up, even temporarily. "I don't want to speak for the man, but if he likes what he sees on Main Street, he might reinvest. Reopen things."

A hush fell over the room. Hill hadn't been seen in town for almost a year. The only person going in and out of that big fancy house was the boy, who mostly just caused trouble and heartache when he did.

Townspeople looked at each other. There were smiles and whispers, no more barked commands on how to fix things, what to spend their nonexistent treasury money on.

Harlan was satisfied. It felt like he'd quelled the insurrection. That was until a voice from the back of the room had to speak and ruin things:

"Are you sure that's true, Harlan?"

It was Sheriff Dunne, barely raising his voice as he walked his boots down the center aisle. Harlan hadn't even seen him lurking back there. But, come to think of it, where else would the bastard be but lurking?

"Of course it's true," Harlan shot back. "Wouldn't have said it if it wasn't. I . . . I just got off the phone with him."

The sheriff seemed to consider this, fiddled with the hat in his hands, then looked back up. *Was that a smirk on his face?*

"Well, then that *is* good news," Dunne said, more to the gathered townspeople than to Harlan.

Huh. Harlan breathed a sigh of relief.

"Sheriff?" a voice asked from the crowd, tentative. Dunne turned to face the question and managed to eclipse Harlan, draw all the authority away from the mayor, by simply moving down to the front of the room.

"I don't mean to bother," Cybil Barton continued. She was a timid woman, so much respect for her sheriff that she didn't have any leftovers for her mayor. "But how is the Baypen investigation going? The charges against Cole Hill were dropped, but—"

Sheriff Dunne held up a hand to interrupt her. Not rude, but soothing. "Unfortunately, I can't comment on an ongoing investigation, Mrs. Barton," Dunne said. "We're doing everything we can to bring those responsible to justice."

There was a slight wave of disappointment from the crowd.

"But what I will add," Dunne continued, "off the record, of course . . ." He nodded to Janice Perry, busy scribbling out what would eventually become the official town meeting minutes. She put her pencil down.

Dunne hiked up his belt and everyone leaned forward, desperate for news, for gossip, for justice.

"What I personally think is that we are looking at a situation where what's *legal* and what's *right* are two separate things. And I've expressed this to some of you, but I think that there may soon come a time when the powers of law don't go far enough to keep Kettle Springs the town we know and love. But we're all coming together as a community to say a firm 'no' to this kind of behavior. Earlier today our dear science teacher, Mr. Vern, was telling me how he discouraged certain students from attending tomorrow's event."

Harlan took a half step toward the edge of the stage. He opened his mouth to interrupt, to bring the meeting back to the issues at hand, but with Sheriff Dunne standing in front of him, no one seemed to notice his call to order.

"Now, Arthur Hill is one of my oldest friends—even if we don't talk much on the phone these days," Dunne continued, not even bothering to shoot a glance over to Harlan to let him know he was wise to his bullshit. "I don't know if Arthur is going to pop in for Founder's Day, but I know that even if he does, the town has lost the love of one of its most important citizens. He's not invested in us anymore, emotionally or financially. And can you blame him? After what they've taken from him? From us?"

Dunne let these rhetorical questions sit for a beat, then continued.

"Last year, he lost a child. Last week, his factory burned down. Not an easy thing. A lot of grief. I know before the fire we were all waiting, holding our breath, for the refinery to reopen its doors. That's where we want Arthur to put his money. But I can say that he ain't going to do it with Kettle Springs what it is now. Population dropping and overrun with kids who don't give a—excuse my language—a rat's ass about our history or heritage."

The assembled members of the PTA, the City Council, and the Neighborhood Watch all nodded in response to this. Not a single churchgoer pretending to be outraged by the mild vulgarity. Not something Harlan had ever experienced.

George Dunne. Harlan hated him. And he loved him. But he envied him more than both of those things.

When the Hill girl died last year, there had been plenty of blame and anger to go around. The busybodies, dirt farmers, and small business owners of Kettle Springs couldn't agree on much, but they all seemed to agree that Harlan Jaffers had screwed up the situation with Arthur Hill's daughter.

"This new generation," Dunne went on, shaking his head and sucking his teeth, "they need to be brought in line. And the people in this room are not blameless!"

There was a theatrical gasp that Dunne pushed through, fire in his voice now: "We need to stop feeling sorry for ourselves, stop pining for a rescue that might never come. We need to take action."

"Yeah!" Fred Vassar yelled, but it wasn't time for that yet. Dunne held up a finger and continued.

"We need to pull this town back to life. We need to bring back what made this town . . ." He searched for his word: "What made this town *decent* in the first place. And all that begins . . ." And then Dunne looked up to Harlan and smiled, a look on his face that said *Continue with yer meeting.*

Oh. All this had been to set up Harlan for a win. He hadn't been expecting that.

"Tomorrow! It begins with the parade tomorrow," Harlan Jaffers shouted, and the audience exploded with applause. They were applauding Sheriff Dunne's words, not the parade itself, but Harlan didn't care. He'd take it.

Harlan Jaffers had been in politics long enough to know you take your wins where you can get them.

SIX

This morning Quinn had been reluctant to attend, and couldn't think of a good reason to give her dad as to why she *wanted* to skip the festival. But they'd been here for an hour and nobody had approached to ask her to leave or tell her she was banned.

Turns out, Founder's Day was a bigger deal than she'd expected.

Food, music, and a crowd that must have been bolstered by visitors from neighboring towns. There was even a small carnival, a few rides and midway games pulled into the school parking lot on trailers.

Honk! Honk!

A sound like an angry goose came loud and fast behind Quinn.

"Shit!"

She hopped out of the way, nearly run over by a massive clown riding a tiny bicycle. No, not a clown, *that* clown. The town's clown. The one who stared all night into her bedroom window, peering from the side of the burned-down Baypen factory. *Pervo? Mervo? Frendo? Yes, Frendo.* That was it.

Frendo swooshed past, faster than looked possible, a big man on little wheels. The clown wended between pedestrians, pom-poms dangling from his handlebars, squeeze-horn honking.

"Watch where you're going, dude!" Quinn yelled.

He stopped, wheels skidding, and turned around in his seat. In the process, nearly power-sliding into a family with little kids.

"You watch yourself, new girl," the clown shouted back, cackling with glee. "Enjoy the show."

Well. That was cryptic.

Quinn blinked, trying to place the voice. It took a moment, but she was pretty sure it was Cole's erstwhile bodyguard, Tucker. The big guy was more high-energy behind the clown mask than he had been in detention. And he certainly hadn't taken Mr. Vern's ban seriously.

Down Main Street, the Founder's Day festivities included a sidewalk sale with fried food stands interspersed to distract passersby from all the shuttered businesses.

"Oh, Tucker," someone said, sidling up to Quinn. "Such

enthusiasm when he wears the costume." The girl beside Quinn wore a thin cardboard half mask, but the paper clown nose and eyes weren't much of a disguise. Janet smiled, her chin and mouth not obscured by the masquerade mask in the shape of Frendo the Clown.

The girl slipped her hand into the crook of Quinn's arm. It seemed an overly familiar gesture, as if they were best friends, but Quinn didn't shake her off.

Tucker had stopped his bike and was staring at them both. He was wearing a plastic Frendo mask, yellowed at the edges with age and sweat. He not only had the complete jumpsuit, but his mask was much more elaborate and "official" than the one Janet was wearing.

Tucker nodded to Janet, giving her the okay sign and a horn honk, then disappeared into the crowd.

"That's, um . . . sanctioned?" Quinn asked.

"Totally sanctioned. Tucker even gets *paid* to play Frendo sometimes, when the town has the money. He wasn't scheduled to work today, but it didn't take much convincing to get him suited up. Tucker loves playing Frendo. And kids love him playing Frendo, which is even weirder. Because without the mask, I feel like he shouldn't be allowed *near* kids."

"So weird," another masked girl cut in. Because of the mask, Quinn hadn't seen Ronnie Queen approach. The girl's distinctive ponytail was hanging over the side of her cheap mask and she was squeezed into another too-small

T-shirt, this one possibly an actual child's size, advertising the "Kettle Spring Brownies Fun Run 2007." The design was a cartoon version of Frendo in running shorts, sweating into his porkpie hat.

This must be the "cute outfit" she'd mentioned.

"He's, like, the town's dumb-ass mascot," Janet said. "Frendo, I mean. But Tucker, too, I guess."

"It's nice to have one of our friends *not* be universally loathed," Ronnie said, an eye roll in her voice, even if the mask was obscuring her face.

Janet didn't take whatever bait Ronnie's remark was supposed to provide.

This close, Quinn could tell that it wasn't only Janet's *look* that was carefully cultivated. Janet smelled like a dessert. One of those fragrances you could get at Forever 21 or Claire's. Pineapple Upside-Down Cake or Butterscotch, something Quinn would have said was meant for younger girls, but on Janet the scent seemed to work.

Quinn noticed that there was a stamp at the corner of each of the cardboard masks that said "First Bank of Kettle Springs." They were being handed out as some kind of promotion. There were more of the masks scattered around them in the crowd. And Frendo wasn't relegated just to the masks, Tucker's costume, and Ronnie's shirt, either: the clown was everywhere today. Quinn noticed his painted face on signage, a mannequin propped in front of one of the thrift stores, and porkpie hats on random bystanders waiting for the parade.

"And Frendo ties into it being Founder's Day how?" Quinn asked, glancing over her shoulder to make sure her dad, who was somewhere in the crowd searching for "the perfect" food stand, wasn't on his way over, ready to embarrass her while holding a basket of fried Oreos.

"Because he *is* the Founder," a voice said. Quinn turned to see that Cole—mask barely obscuring his sharp features—and another boy were pushing through, ready to join them. People needed to stop popping out of the crowd; it was putting Quinn on edge. Especially people who Quinn knew had been banned from attending this event.

Cole and his friend were both holding large fountain drinks. There was no brand on the side of the cups, just a simple red-and-white checkerboard pattern. Which struck Quinn as weird, but then she remembered that she hadn't seen a Wawa or 7-Eleven, or any kind of chain store, in Kettle Springs.

The squat, unfamiliar boy who'd arrived with Cole wasn't wearing a mask. He lunged forward, wrapping an arm around Ronnie and kissing her neck. At this, Quinn was able to place him. He was the guy she'd seen out the window of the Eatery last night.

"Stop it, Matt. You reek—" Ronnie started, shoving him away, playfulness becoming actual might. Matt, that was correct, Tucker had mentioned something about a boyfriend who was precious about his car's leather seats.

Quinn sniffed and realized that she could no longer smell Janet's perfume. Because Matt stank of booze.

Quinn looked back to Cole.

If Cole Hill was also drunk, he was doing a better job holding it together, but she didn't think he was drunk. Better impulse control? A higher tolerance? Why was she going so far out of her way to see this guy in only a positive light?

"Yeah. He's the founder," Cole explained, eyes behind his mask a little glassy. Quinn noticed now that she was *looking* for signs of intoxication. "That's the story the town tells. That Frendo was a real guy, performed for the town's kids back during the Depression. When everyone was eating dirt or whatever. Frendo was around, helping to keep spirits up."

"That's nice," Quinn said, unsure what the proper response was, going back to scanning the crowd for her dad, worried he'd return and she'd need to introduce him to her new friends, the ones dressed like they were about to do a high-stakes bank job.

"Yeah, it would be nice. If it were true," Cole said, taking a sip of his drink. Quinn watched him as he spoke. Even with the mask obscuring some of his face, his body language told her he wasn't comfortable being in public, like at any moment he'd be recognized, swamped with requests for his autograph. Or run off Main Street because of a science teacher's ban. "Frendo's an invention," Cole said. "Property. My family holds the trademark. My grandfather liked to draw. He drew a clown in a hat. Put that clown in a hat on the first Baypen labels."

Matt laughed, was pushed away from Ronnie, and tried to lean on Cole for support. Cole ducked away. "That was the forties," he continued. "Clowns were fun then. I don't know if Granddad also came up with the story afterward, about the Depression and founding the town, but people believe what they want to believe. Because it's like Baypen and Kettle Springs are the same thing."

Cole's voice became harder to focus on as Quinn caught sight of Glenn Maybrook. Her dad was standing across the street. He had a chili dog in hand, his quest for fairground food a success. He met Quinn's eyes, bopped the end of his nose with one finger, and mouthed *Good luck*. For all of Dr. Maybrook's neurotic behavior, he was still capable of reading the situation well enough to know when to give her space.

She turned her attention back in time to let Cole have his grand finale: "Frendo is dead," he added, smiling wanly, his cheeks pushing up the thin cardboard. Clearly, Quinn had missed some parts of his speech. He held up the drink. "So long live Frendo!"

"Aaaaaaanyway," Matt said. "Speaking of Frendo. That

Tucker over there?" He nodded over to Tucker, who was standing beside his tiny bike, across the street and a few businesses down.

"I think so, why?" Ronnie asked.

In response, Matt produced four airplane-sized bottles of liquor, holding them by the necks between his fingers. In his palm he clenched a lighter. At Quinn's arm, Janet's fingers tightened for a moment. "Because he's got the good stuff and I'm going to trade. And he texted me that he forgot his lighter . . ." Matt looked to Janet and his eyebrows did a conspiratorial jiggle. Not subtle.

"Gimme that," Ronnie hissed. She ignored the lighter, tweezing away a miniature bottle of vanilla vodka and hurrying it into the back pocket of her shorts.

Quinn looked down the block. The parade had rounded the corner and was beginning to make its way up Main Street. Not that she'd been expecting Macy's Thanksgiving, but the Founder's Day Parade looked even shabbier than the lower end of her expectations. The high school must not have had a marching band, because prerecorded John Philip Sousa began playing over the loudspeakers that topped the streetlights.

"Hold that," Matt said to Ronnie, motioning down to his cup. "And don't drink it all."

Ronnie took a big sip in response, a bead of liquid wicking across the bottom of her cardboard mask as she pulled the straw away. Matt narrowed his eyes at her and she sipped again, a provocation between girlfriend and boyfriend that, Quinn had to admit, was kind of cute.

Matt started to go, but Janet reached out and grabbed him by the wrist. She let go of Quinn's arm for a moment, and Quinn weirdly felt the loss, suddenly alone in the crowd.

"Wait," Janet said, then turned back to Cole. "Is this all right?"

"Is *what* all right?" Cole shrugged, miming wiping invisible sleep out of one eye, not touching his mask. It was an exaggerated motion, but it drew attention to how tired the boy *actually* looked, how haunted and sleep-deprived the set of his jaw and the jaundiced sink of his cheeks. "I don't see anything, I don't hear anything. Whatever you guys are planning, I'm not a part of it. You don't need my permission."

"Just a little fun," Janet said, still keeping Matt tethered to them, the drunk boy looking impatient. "The tiniest of 'fuck you's' for trying to keep us away."

"God. We're pushing it," Ronnie muttered. The girl looked uneasy, busied her free hand with swapping out a hairband, mistakenly tugging at the elastic of her mask, revealing her face for a second before she could replace the disguise. Quinn didn't know why they were bothering—it wasn't like anyone familiar with the kids wasn't going to be able to place them, even with their eyes and noses covered.

"Just don't hurt anyone," Cole said, voice suddenly

serious, his eyes, dark beneath the mask, narrowing, moving from Janet to Matt.

"Wouldn't dream of it, boss. That's your thing," Matt said. There was a mean-drunk smile on his face, and that was the last Quinn saw of the boy before he darted into the street.

"Maybe you shouldn't," Cole started, reaching for his friend. But it was too late, Matt was already scurrying down the middle of Main Street, the first float of the parade bearing down on him.

Janet frowned at Cole. "Don't worry. I wouldn't let them do anything too crazy. Not while we're under the microscope." But now Janet sounded unconvinced, worry creeping into her voice.

Cole nodded. He tapped Quinn on the shoulder, then motioned to where Matt was running.

"Would you believe Trent's the best tight end the team's had in a decade?" Cole said, his anxiety wearing at the corners of his composure. Quinn was good at recognizing that. Like saw like.

The four of them watched the drunk boy weave through the crowd on the opposite side of the street.

Matt Trent, tight end. Tucker Lee, linebacker. Was Cole on the football team? Cole Hill, quarterback? It would complete the cliché if he was, the good-looking leader throwing touchdowns to his friends. But still, Quinn couldn't picture it. Even with the best defense in the world, Cole seemed too fragile to be tackled. Which was sexy, in an emo boy way.

On the opposite curb, Frendo-Tucker had moved positions. He was bent down in front of a group of kids, tying off a pink balloon sword—or at least Quinn hoped it was a sword—for a little girl who looked half-terrified, half-enthralled by the big clown.

With all the stealth he could muster, Matt Trent sidled up behind Tucker and whispered something in his ear. Tucker nodded without looking back, finished the final balloon twist, handed over a sword to a kid, and stood to take the mini liquor bottles and the lighter from Matt. He secreted them into one of the folds of his clown jumpsuit. Then Matt took something from Tucker in return.

Exchange finished, Matt slapped the bigger boy on the back and returned across the street. Matt narrowly avoided being crushed under the wheels of a pickup truck towing a giant ear of corn. The corn was constructed out of papier-mâché and fiberglass. Along the topmost row of kernels, in red lettering, were the words "Happy Founder's Day" and under that, freshly painted and in different handwriting, "Kettle Springs!" Quinn could see that the words "From Baypen" had been painted over, but neither the yellow of the corn nor the red of the new slogan was opaque enough to block out the company's name.

Matt slipped back into place next to his masked friends on the sidewalk.

Ronnie returned his cup, wiping the condensation on the back of his shirt with a pat that he didn't seem to notice.

"Feels a little light," he said, shaking the ice, but Ronnie ignored him.

"They like to do this," Janet whispered, not a stage whisper, but words just for Quinn, barely audible over the patriotic clash of recorded cymbals and tubas. "Kind of like hayseed foreplay." Janet took Quinn's arm again. They giggled together, Quinn given a little thrill that she was already somehow over Ronnie in the pecking order.

"Oh God," Ronnie said. "Check. It. Out." Quinn and Janet glanced back up to the parade.

"Just ignore them," Cole said, squeezing Janet's shoulder, taking up a position on the other side of the girl.

"Why?" Janet asked.

Quinn followed Cole's gaze to where Ronnie was now pointing.

The second float was beginning to roll by and Quinn could smell the diesel. In the bed of another pickup sat an oversize gold-and-crimson plush throne, tethered to the truck bed by bungee cords to keep it from sliding.

Sitting atop the throne were a king and a queen. The queen was a slight Asian woman in her forties, maybe fifties, who bore an uncanny resemblance to Janet. She wore a sash over one shoulder that proclaimed her "Miss Kettle Springs."

And the king sitting next to her was . . . Frendo.

Or, *another* Frendo, Quinn confirmed by glancing over to where Frendo-Tucker was finishing doing magic tricks in front of a new group of children. He handed a child a rose, started waving his goodbyes to the tots.

The Frendo sitting beside Miss Kettle Springs was also in the full, official mask and costume and had a Burger King crown resting over his porkpie hat.

"Good morning, everyone—" Ronnie started, her back turned to the parade and her phone held high in selfie mode, the other hand making sure her mask was symmetrically placed. She was angling to film something behind her, and Quinn's stomach dropped as she wondered what, and how embarrassing it was going to be for Janet.

"It's afternoon," Matt corrected his girlfriend, poking his head into the shot.

"Get. Out," Ronnie said, shoving him away. "Ignore the douche. Hello, everyone, I'm sexy Frendo the Clown and this is the Kettle Springs Founder's Day Parade. And we're in the presence of *royalty* right now."

"Would you guys knock it off?" Cole said from the other side of Janet. He lifted his mask toward Ronnie and Matt so the two of them could see the seriousness in his face. "Can we just have a normal day?"

"It's fine, Ronnie. Laugh it up," Janet growled. "Just keep the camera on the parade." Janet had her phone out. Quinn looked down and saw a single word typed on her screen:

Go.

"Janet's mom's looking so pretty, don't you think?" Ronnie said to her phone, narrating. Was she live right now? Seemed like it. "And who's in that Frendo costume beside her? Mr. Murray? Could be. Oh, next coming up, looks like the volunteer firefighters. My favorite. I do love a man in uniform. Matt used to have a uniform, if you remember our videos about—"

Suddenly, from farther down the parade route, there was a loud, shrill whistle-hiss.

To punctuate the end of the artillery sound, there was a loud pop.

The crowd around them gasped as one, a mass flinch that worked outward from the sound in a wave.

The familiar crackle of gunpowder sparks in the sky above them seemed to soothe the crowd, who hadn't been expecting fireworks. Not in the daytime.

Fireworks, yes. Quinn knew it was just fireworks. Had to be.

Around them, the crowd turned to one another, mothers to sons, fathers to grandfathers, smiling, laughing.

Janet turned to Cole. "See? Kids' stuff. A few light pyrotechnics."

Cole rubbed his neck. "How'd you—" He cut himself off, waved a hand. "Never mind, I don't want to know."

There was more hissing, turning the crowd's attention to the front of the parade. Like Cole, Quinn wanted to know *how*. How had Tucker lit fireworks all along the parade route without anyone noticing? Long fuses? Some midwestern magic?

A shower of sparks erupted from the four corners of the platform hauling the giant ear of corn.

"Ohhhh," Ronnie said into her stream, still smiling for the camera, catching the action in the background. "I smell popcorn."

More whistles and pops from down the block, the volunteer firefighters looking to one another, bewildered. They didn't know quite what to do.

The crowd was clapping and cheering now, thinking the sparks and snaps from along the parade were part of the show. And even though Quinn knew none of this was part of the official program, she smiled, too.

This might have been an act of defiance engineered by Janet Murray, but it was still giving joy to people.

It was still *fun*.

God. Her new friends were going to get in *big* trouble for this. And would she find herself lumped in with them? Quinn tried to wave the anxiety away and enjoy the moment. She was a good kid, but she'd never been *that* much of a narc.

Whoever was wearing the King Frendo costume wasn't amused, though. The clown in the truck bed stood, trying to surf along the motion with his arms out, his mask muffling his yells. "What the hell is going on?"

The driver of the throne-float pulled up short as the corncob in front of him ignited, a single spark catching the whole thing all at once. The sparklers were too close to the plaster. Suddenly the cob was a rolling fireball, cruising down Main Street.

"Uh-oh," Janet said, the small noise an understatement.

Janet's mom was sent sprawling from her seat. King Frendo tried to grab for her, but he moved too late and only succeeded in ripping free her sash.

"Oh shit, no," Ronnie said into her feed. Then pleaded into the camera: "I told them that messing with the parade was a bad idea! This is *not* my fault!"

With the firefighters scrambling out of the way, the third float rear-ended the truck and sent Janet's mom and Frendo, whiplashed, flying back the opposite direction. The third float was carrying the town's Cub Scouts on what seemed to be a large trout of some kind.

Extinguishers were already blasting the corncob, some of the men of the fire department working fast, but they seemed oblivious that a slow-motion wreck was still happening behind them!

Atop the fish, most of the Cub Scouts were crying, and a couple of them stumbled and fell off the edge of the platform as people in the crowd gasped, helpless to stop whatever was happening.

There were more pops and hisses as the last few fireworks shot off down the street, a delayed reaction in the *We're no longer having fun* chaos.

On the sidewalk the onlookers, Quinn included, collectively held their breath, watching, afraid for the kids caught in the middle of this accident.

But it was okay. The crash was beginning to settle. Everyone around her exhaled with the realization that the kids were safe. There were uneasy chuckles as everything on Main Street came to a complete stop. Nobody had been rolled over by an unlucky truck wheel or a giant largemouth bass.

But it *could* have been so much worse. Someone could have been killed.

Quinn saw her father run out into the chaos. Always the first responder, he stooped to help one of the kids. More parents charged out into the road to gather up their Cub Scouts.

"Is this you?" Quinn spun around. "Was that you?" the angry voice asked again.

Sheriff Dunne had Cole by the shirt. The sheriff was red-faced. He swept a big hand over Cole's head, swiping the cardboard mask away. He hadn't been fooled by the disguise, had probably been watching the boy from the crowd. Waiting for him to slip up.

The big man kept yelling over and over, "Was that you? Was *that* you?" He brought Cole off his feet, actually *lifting* him by his shirt, the fabric tearing. The sheriff was shaking the boy like he could jostle an answer loose.

"I didn't do anything," Cole was able to choke out.

"Sheriff, he didn't!" Janet screamed, suddenly not at Quinn's side, but instead batting at Dunne's huge arm, trying to get him to let go of Cole.

Beside them Ronnie Queen was still filming.

"I will *end* you," Sheriff Dunne hissed. "You and your friends were told to stay away from here!"

"I haven't done anything!" Cole yelled, wriggling.

"Let him go. He didn't do anything! We didn't mean—"

"Bullshit!" the sheriff shouted at her, specks of spit flying from his mouth as he flung Janet to the sidewalk, shaking her off violently, his attention still on Cole. In the struggle, Janet's mask had twisted into a blindfold and on her knees she pawed at it, dazed.

"You're done! Hear me? You're done here in Kettle Springs."

"What the fuck, man," Cole said, trying to turn in the big man's grip. "Janet, are you—"

There was a loud bang, different from the others. The

boom came from farther down the block, toward the Eureka Theater. There were gasps again, but only for a split second until the sound morphed into screams.

"No M-Eighties!" Janet screamed, trying to get up from the sidewalk and stumbling, still blind behind the mask. Panic spread.

"Look out!" someone yelled.

Metal groaned and Sheriff Dunne dropped Cole and ran against the tide of scrambling foot traffic. The sheriff might have been a jerk, but like her dad, he'd chosen to run *toward* the danger.

Whatever had exploded had shredded the front tire of the truck towing the float representing the Elks Lodge: an elaborate ten-foot-tall papier-mâché buck.

Kneeling on the sidewalk, a protective arm over Janet, Quinn watched.

The vehicle swerved, missing the displaced riders from the second and third floats. Headed straight for where her dad was seeing to the injured Cub Scout.

Quinn's dad launched back from his crouch, pulling the boy out of the path of the runaway float at the last moment.

The truck sailed past, fender colliding with a lamppost on the south side of the block. The impact stopped the truck, but forward motion sent the buck sculpture toppling from its platform.

From somewhere in the crowd there was one final horror-movie scream as the giant elk antler sliced down.

The smoldering ear of corn was carved in two, splitting the words "Kettle Springs" in half.

SEVEN

"It's an Elks Lodge, Francine!" Harlan Jaffers yelled. "I doubt they even know what Wi-Fi is."

He was wrong. Someone in the back of the room gave Francine Chambers a password that sounded to Harlan like alphabet soup.

"Ladies and gentlemen. Order," Harlan said politely once, then twice, before shouting "ORDER!" as loud as he could on pack-a-day lungs and still getting no response.

There were fewer people at this emergency town meeting than at last night's planned one, but the audience seemed twice as hostile.

Harlan wished he had a lectern—then he could take off his shoe and bang the heel like a gavel. Oh well. One of the many things on his mayoral bucket list he'd never get a chance to try. His term was up at the end of the calendar year. Elections were only two months away. He'd been in politics long enough to know that after what had happened with the parade today, he was done. He'd lose the election to a frozen Butterball turkey, if someone drew eyes on it and filled out the proper paperwork.

"Now you all listen. I'm still your mayor. Hey! I said *shut your mouths* and listen to me."

Faces turned, the necks creaking. Someone whispered loud enough for Harlan to hear, "*What* did he just say?"

Harlan sucked in his breath and clenched his fists in his pockets.

"Everyone quiet," Sheriff Dunne said, backing Harlan up before the crowd could pounce.

Dunne looked to Harlan, nodding. The sheriff sat front row, uniform clean of the day's action, freshly pressed. For a moment, Harlan wondered how many pairs of those tan pants George Dunne owned. He couldn't remember the last time he'd seen the man in a pair of jeans.

"Give him a moment of your time. Mayor Jaffers has something to say . . ."

The crowd quieted and those who'd been milling at the refreshment table took their seats. "Thank you, Sheriff," Harlan said, forcing a smile.

"My pleasure." George Dunne nodded, then leaned back, not finished. "But before you start, Harlan, I think everyone here has a right to know something. I have reason to believe the explosives from the parade to be the work of a minor. And while I won't say the boy's—or girl's—name until charges have been filed, I think that many of you can come to your own conclusions."

"Say it, Sheriff! We all know!" Bill Stevens, assistant principal at the high school, shouted from the back row.

Someone else, the voice female: "Thought you said they'd been *discouraged* from attending! That sure as heck didn't work."

Dunne stood, the floor officially his. Dissent ceasing as he raised his arms.

"First, and if you've been coming to the Kettle Springs Improvement Society meetings, this won't come as a surprise to you. But I want to ask everyone who's willing, able-bodied, and of age to be deputized. We need to unite as a town and we need to take action. And I'm going to have to ask everyone who's *not* willing to be deputized to leave."

There were murmurs of amazement and enthusiasm from the crowd.

Harlan cringed. "You've got to be kidding, George. Is this the Wild West?"

Swearing in deputies? Right now? Infuriating, and not only because the meeting had been so utterly swept out of his control for the second night in a row.

"Do you have a better idea, Harlan?" Dunne turned

back, eyebrows up, expectant, the mob behind him ready to pounce.

But maybe this was the time for Harlan to try a different tactic.

If you couldn't beat them . . .

"I'm in!" Harlan shouted. "Deputize me, Sheriff." He hadn't been to any of their stupid meetings, but if this was what it took to build back a little trust from his constituency: so be it.

Dunne frowned. "Wish I could."

"B-but you just said."

"A mayor can't be deputized, Harlan," Dunne said, conciliatory. "You know that."

"The hell I do. What do you mean I *can't* be deputized? That doesn't make any sense," Harlan replied, hating the whine he heard creep into his voice.

"That's the rules," Dunne said, looking up to the rest of the gathering. "If you'd like to head back to your office and check the bylaws, we'll wait."

Harlan paused, trying to think for a moment. He was sweating again. "But—"

"Oh, can you just get out, Harlan?" someone in the back rows said, voice barely raised. There was silent assent from the rest of the room. "We got work to do," someone else seconded.

Harlan looked at Dunne and wished, for a moment, he could knock that shit-eating grin off his face in front of everyone. But Dunne had six inches and fifty pounds on Harlan, not to mention a gun in his holster and the hearts and minds of the whole town in his pocket. Seeing no other option, Harlan Jaffers began to gather his briefcase from the side of the stage.

"Now, I have some inside information, straight from a trusted source—a source in the know—that there's going to be . . ." Dunne paused, looked over to Harlan. His expression said that this was privileged information. Deputies only.

"Fine. I get it. I'm going," Harlan said, feeling pathetic.

His footfalls sounding loud in his own ears, Harlan trudged toward the back door of the lodge.

He knew when he was licked. Three terms, ended by a few fireworks. Sparklers. A four-vehicle fender-bender where the only casualty was a lamppost and some construction paper. He'd have to go back to being a small-town attorney, dealing with property disputes and nuisance lawsuits. And probably make more money than he did as mayor, but that wasn't the point. He loved being mayor, thought he was a pretty good one, too. Sure, the town had gone through tough times on his watch, but that wasn't his fault. The townspeople would never know how much worse it would have been if he weren't around, watching out for them.

He pushed through the back door and stepped out into the cool night air. "Should have brought a hat," he said aloud to no one.

No one standing in the darkened parking lot. No one in the shadows.

Harlan Jaffers was overcome with emotion, kicked out of his own meeting. His vision shimmered and he choked back a sniffle. He worked his keys out of his pocket and fumbled for the fob, dropping it into an oil-glazed puddle.

Great.

He bent, barely hearing the quiet shuffle of footsteps of someone behind him. Maybe someone else leaving the meeting through the back door, tired of Sheriff Dunne's bullying tactics.

It was the reflection that alerted him, a rippling shadow in the wet asphalt.

A silver-and-red swoosh, familiar colors. Specks of white greasepaint with a smudge of cigar-ash beard.

He turned, more curious why someone dressed as Frendo would have followed him out into the parking lot. He didn't even have time to be afraid.

The ice pick missed Harlan Jaffers's temple, where the clown had been aiming, and entered halfway up the mayor's neck, its progress interrupted only when it nicked a vertebra.

Harlan Jaffers dropped to his knees, joining his keys in the puddle as the clown pushed forward, parting nerves and cartilage to bury the weapon up to the handle in the mayor's neck. The clown didn't even need to put a gloved hand over his victim's mouth to muffle the sound. Instantly weak from the ice pick, the mayor was unable to work up a scream.

Jaffers lay on the pavement, a puppet with its strings cut, staring into the nearest streetlight, gurgling for two minutes before losing enough blood that he was rendered unconscious.

Frendo transferred him to the back of a waiting van where—alone, in the darkness—Harlan's final thought was: "Still mayor."

EIGHT

Tucker didn't mean to do it. Not all of it.

He'd been drunk. Drunker than he thought—he'd admit that was his bad. But it was those little bottles. He read somewhere they were like a shot and a half each, and it was hard to keep count when you had to do decimals.

The M-80s were meant to be for later. Founder's Day was a celebration. Like Janet had said: What kind of celebration didn't have fireworks? It hadn't been hard to pull off, swapping days with Dave Sellers and then hiding the sparklers, but he didn't mean to turn the parade into a multi-float pile-up.

Now, in a post-nap haze, he wasn't even sure he *did* it. He knew he'd started out with the right stuff, used his bicycle to hit the fuses in record time. But did he stash the M-80s . . .

Whatever. No one would care about his side of the story. That much was obvious from the note his mom had slid under his bedroom door.

Confess now and I can help you.

God, Mom. Way to be melodramatic. He'd pay for Herman Lacey's new tire. Tucker had some money squirreled away from his Frendo appearances. And the little kid who'd fallen off the float wasn't hurt bad—just a twisted wrist and a few scrapes. He'd pay his doctor bill, too, if he had to.

He flipped the note around in his hands. On the back, Mom said he was grounded. Which was total bullshit. Hadn't the hangover and the chewing-out been punishment enough? She knew tonight was the party and that he wasn't going to miss it. She couldn't stop him from going, but she *could* stop him from taking the car.

He'd have to secure a ride.

Tucker looked down at his phone. Though the screen was cracked diagonally from the home button up to the middle of the right side, the top quarter of the glass spiderwebbed, it still worked. At least, it did when the town's shitty service would let it.

With his thumb over the screen, Tucker considered sending out a text. Cole's car was probably full up, but Matt would be able to squeeze him in. If Ronnie would share.

Holy shit, it was already after seven? Before he'd napped,

he'd intended to play a few rounds of *Fortnite* to clear his hangover. He hadn't realized the time had gotten away from him. He had to hurry. There'd be no getting Matt to turn around if he was already on the road.

Tucker leaned back in his chair and considered his options. The frame beneath him began to creak, and he caught himself, straightened up. Tucker had already broken three desk chairs this year. This chair had been part of their dining room set. Mom had whined when he'd brought it upstairs, but when was the last time they had anyone over for dinner anyway? Never. She and whatever dickhead boyfriend-of-the-month never wanted to eat at home. Whatever.

With a practiced gentleness, Tucker swiped to unlock the phone.

Nd ride. Cum pick me up?

He paused before sending.

Wait. Where is *Mom?*

He looked out his window. The driveway was empty. Was she at one of her boring town meetings or had she simply parked the car around the block in an attempt to hide it from him? She'd done it before. And she'd also threatened to call the sheriff if he took the car without asking.

He unlocked his bedroom door and yelled downstairs: "Mom!"

He waited. Nothing.

He looked back at his cracked screen: 7:29. This wasn't

like her, to leave him alone without saying where she was going or when she'd be home.

But, then again, Tucker was going out to a party, so why should he give a fuck if she gave even less of one? Tucker suspected that her douchebag boyfriend had surprised her and that they were probably boning at some roadside motel right now. Tucker shuddered just thinking about it and then hit Send on the message to Matt.

It was marked as delivered, then a few moments later marked as "Read at 7:31."

But no response came, so he texted again:

Fucking better come pick me up.

His text was again marked as delivered, again marked as read. But no response.

Matt can be such a shithead, Tucker thought. He should have texted Cole first. But now Cole would be pissed if he went out of his way or turned around to get Tucker, only to have Matt *also* show up. And Tucker couldn't jeopardize his thing with Cole. The rest of the gang could sometimes be dicks to Tucker Lee, but that didn't matter. Cole Hill was the coolest kid in Kettle Springs and Tucker's best friend. Some people used to joke that he was Cole's bodyguard, but Tucker knew he was more than that. Cole had his back as much as Tucker had Cole's. Now that he thought about it, it was Tucker's *duty* to get out to Tillerson's. Under his own power. Cole shouldn't have to fuck up his plans with the new girl, come halfway across town to give Tucker a ride. And besides, Tucker was a big guy, didn't feel like being the third wheel in the back seat of Cole's two-door car.

So if Matt was going to pull this bullshit and not respond, and ditch Tucker, that was fine. Fuck him and Ronnie. Tucker would give them another minute and then he'd start calling the JV squad. Part of him was tempted to text Ronnie directly. After all, it wasn't that long ago that she was sneaking in the back door once or twice a week. She always swore him to secrecy—he hated not being able to tell the guys that they were hooking up—but it seemed a small price to pay.

When was the last time they'd chilled? It'd been months; she was taking things more seriously with Matt now. Still, if Matt didn't write back soon, Tucker would try Ronnie next. And if she was with Matt? Wouldn't be the worst thing to break them up. It wasn't like they loved each other or anything. They just liked having that . . . "power couple energy" was how Ronnie explained it.

Tucker put down the phone and opened his laptop.

After Dad left, his mom had insisted that she needed to feel safe and had ordered two wireless security cameras. With Tucker's help, she'd installed one over the front door, next to the porch light, and the other looking out onto the backyard. The front camera's motion sensor triggered whenever raccoons came for the garbage. Tucker kept an air rifle by the front door.

He rubbed the sweat of his palm off on his pant leg and refreshed the camera. Tonight he was hoping for pests. Shooting something would make him feel better.

Finding signal. Please wait.

The image resolved itself into a view of his front porch and . . .

What the fuck!

Tucker nearly fell out of his chair.

On his laptop screen was a clown. The figure stood stock-still with its feet on the welcome rug.

In the desaturated, low-light vision of the camera, Frendo looked like a ghost. His pom-pom buttons were spots of infinite darkness running down his chest. There was a glossy glow at the corners of the mask's painted smile. The slight fisheye of the lens made the clown's features distort, made his nose even more bulbous than usual.

Goddamn it. Tucker's heart was racing. As much as Tucker loved pranking an unsuspecting dweeb, he hated to be scared himself.

His movement jerky on the camera, the clown at his front door reached out one gloved finger, placed it over the doorbell, then poked it forward.

Bing, bong.

Tucker had to admit, they got him good. If it weren't for him checking the camera, whatever this plan was probably would have succeeded. He squinted at the screen, trying to see if he could spot where Ronnie was hiding. She had to already be filming so she could catch his reaction. But he couldn't see her. Well, it didn't matter, time was wasting. They didn't know he'd seen them.

Tucker stood from his desk. Time to beat someone's ass. He padded downstairs, cracking his knuckles along the way. In a way, this was better than a raccoon, would release more stress.

Stepping wide around the windows, Tucker snuck up to the front door, turned the knob slowly, silently, and then quickly pushed open the screen door. He was hoping to crack the clown right in the face.

But as he jumped out on the front porch: nothing.

There was no clown. No friends laughing in the bushes. There was nothing but the faint sounds of crickets chirping on his cold, empty block. Even emptier than usual, and then he remembered why. Everyone was at Tillerson's already.

"Yo," Tucker said, his voice echoing down the street. "Good job, guys, you got me. Come out now and take your beatings. Make it easier on yourselves."

He waited for a response. Silence. He looked down at the doormat: *Enter and Be Blessed. Leave and Be Blessed.* His mom had a QVC problem.

"Fine," he said, exasperated. "Fuck it. Never mind. I won't kick your ass. Can we please just go to the fucking party?"

Still, no response.

He looked up.

Across the street, Ms. Olsen's house was dark, as were all the other neighboring houses down the block. Kettle Springs was a quiet, sleepy town, but something about the vibe outside felt too quiet, too sleepy, too dark.

He began to swing the door shut, intending to slam it, then stopped himself.

Whoever it was, they were probably creeping around the back of the house. What they wouldn't expect would be to be pursued.

He stepped out the front door, looked inside to the air rifle, then thought better of it and continued down onto the grass. At Tucker's size, stealth was difficult, but he tried to keep to the shadows.

The lawn was damp. Tucker Lee shivered against the chill. Reflexively, he touched a hand to his pocket to make sure he had the house keys and hadn't just locked himself out.

Shrubbery brushed against him, dotting his shirt with moisture, as he tried to stay as close to the cover of the house as possible.

He undid the latch to his backyard gate, then listened. Nothing.

Oh, was there going to be an ass-beating tonight. He smiled.

There was a concrete path that led to the back door. If he swung around the side of the house quickly enough, he'd scare whoever was there *and* they'd be close enough that he could grab them before they could escape.

But he'd only have one shot to do it right.

Flattening himself against the back corner of the house, Tucker Lee took a deep breath and leapt out.

But there was nothing and no one on the back steps. Only the soft amber glow of the backdoor light, the tiny red LED of the security camera, watching him.

What the fuck? If they had started to pull a prank and then called it off and ditched him . . .

He thought about how embarrassing that would be, how much it spoke to what his friends—besides Cole, never Cole—*really* thought of him.

Oh, he'd make these backstabbing fucks pay.

He unlocked the porch door and let himself back into the house.

As he was crossing through the kitchen, he opened his phone, going easy on the cracked screen.

Nice try assholes.

Tucker entered the living room as he finished texting, not bothering to turn on the lights. He was so focused on his phone and the thought of stealing a beer from the basement fridge that it took a moment to register that he wasn't alone.

"Shit!" Tucker said, jumping a little, then putting his phone over his heart to emphasize his surprise.

Frendo stood in the living room, his hands behind his back. The clown was between the coffee table and the media center. Even in the darkness, Tucker could see that Frendo had tracked mud onto the carpet. He must have come in through the front door while Tucker'd gone around back.

"Okay. Mask off, dickweed," Tucker said. "Let's see who's earned the beating."

As he spoke, he closed the distance and realized that whoever was in the costume was bigger than he was.

Huh. That was weird.

Had to be Ed. Matt was way too puny. Weird. Matt and Ed didn't usually hang out. Why would he be giving him a ride, too? Where the hell was he fitting him in his car? Tucker couldn't figure it, but it didn't really matter.

"Did Matt drive you here? I'm in a forgiving mood, so clean up your muddy fucking footprints and let's get out of here."

But instead of responding, Frendo tilted his head. It was a slight movement, like a bird eyeing a crumb, but still not committing to take flight.

And then Frendo revealed what he'd been holding behind his back.

The knife was impossibly long, the kind of exaggerated blade that only existed in video games.

"Cool," Tucker said. "You went to Party City."

The clown said nothing, but he extended his arm, the knife toward Tucker.

"Come on. Put that shit away. There's carpet cleaner and rags in the hall closet."

Tucker swatted at the knife with one hand, expecting the toy to go flying across the room, but it stuck firm. The clown's grip was strong.

And then Tucker looked down at his hand and saw that the webbing between his thumb and forefinger had been split. In the half-light, the wound across his hand looked like cut wax for a moment, and then dark blood began to well.

"Are you kidding m—"

Frendo lifted the tip of the blade and gently pressed it into the area beside Tucker's belly button.

A searing coolness spread across his stomach.

Tucker's phone tumbled out from between his fingers. It hit the ground, then took a bounce. The screen flashed, illuminating the room for a second as the device slid under the couch.

Not a fake knife!

It took a moment, but the sensation was unlike anything he'd ever felt.

It didn't hurt. Not really. It felt more just . . . wet.

But a second later, as the knife was pulled out, the wound hurt plenty.

Zzzzslllip.

Frendo nodded to hear the sound, and that nod snapped Tucker into action.

Tucker backhanded Frendo, catching part of the clown's jaw. The clown's porkpie hat stayed in place, the molded plastic of his mask shifting, hopefully enough to blind him. Whoever wore the clown suit was heavy, but hadn't been expecting the blow. Frendo stumbled back into the TV. The entire console rattled against the clown's weight. Mom's Hummel figurines and fine collectible crystal clattered in the cabinet.

Tucker placed a stabilizing hand on his stomach. All the shows said that you had to put pressure on the wound. Easier said than done; the puckered lips of the cut screamed. Tucker pressed, the cold of blood loss becoming the fire of a chemical burn.

He screamed. Blood ran down his fingers, soaked into his shirt.

The phone. Tucker needed an ambulance.

He squinted into the darkness, catching sight of the face-down phone under the couch just as Frendo did the same.

No, wait, he could try the house phone.

They were both going to go for the cell phone, not the corded handset on the end table beside it. Tucker had a chance.

Tucker roared, reaching his free hand out and grabbing hold of Frendo by the costume's coveralls. Pom-pom buttons shook and Tucker swung down hard, the clown's momentum from pushing back off the TV sending their weight down through the coffee table. It was an extreme wrestling move, something that would have been badass if it weren't so painful, the glass shards so sharp.

The way they landed, Tucker was much closer to his cell phone than the landline.

Glass crunched and bodies wriggled as Tucker moved for the phone, hoping that the fall through the tabletop would keep the clown dazed for a moment.

A strong hand gripped Tucker by the ankle. He reared back, horse-kicking with all his might and connecting with the clown's shoulder, missing his face, but still doing some damage.

No time to look back.

There was so much blood it was difficult to hold the phone. Tucker rubbed his free hand on the carpet, the other trying to keep pressure on his stomach.

With his thumb clean of jellied blood, Tucker swiped to unlock and quickly navigated to the call screen.

9.

The tinkle of glass behind him. Frendo was still moving. Was on his feet.

1.

The drip of blood, his own blood as it slipped through his fingers, the living room carpet drinking it up in thirsty *whick-whicks*.

1.

The fingers pulling on his scalp, fingers in bunchy white gloves, the kind that made it difficult to manipulate balloon animals. Tucker was only ever able to make fucking balloon swords because of those gloves.

With his thumb ready to touch the green dial button, Tucker felt his head jerked back, his skin drawn taut and painful.

The blade ran across his neck and, like that, Tucker Lee didn't feel much anymore.

NINE

"You okay?" Cole asked, looking over to Quinn while shifting gears with a steady hand.

She wasn't okay.

She was in a strange black muscle car with bucket seats. They were on a dark stretch of road, corn on either side, going too fast and . . .

"She's fine," Janet answered from the car's skinny back seat. The girl was ashing out a Newport into an Altoids tin. "Tough as nails, that one. You picked a winner, Cole. I can tell. Look at that laser focus."

Janet managed her smoke while keeping her hair in place, wind whipping into the car from the opened-a-crack front windows. Vaping and a little weed, sure, but Quinn couldn't think of a single kid back home who smoked *actual* cigarettes.

Cole made a throat-cut gesture. Janet flashed him a frown in the rearview mirror and quieted.

Quinn held the side handle to keep herself upright and to fight the motion sickness coming from the soft bounce of the car's suspension.

They took a tight curve without slowing and Quinn felt like she really might be sick. She quieted her stomach by focusing on Janet, who was mugging for Cole in the rearview. Was Janet her new frenemy—was that what they were destined to be? Or straight-up enemy? It was hard to tell; her behavior was erratic, her attitude sometimes sweet, sometimes aggressive. But Quinn had seen at the parade how close she'd been to melting down when Ronnie had started joking about her mother, and she couldn't bring herself to hate the girl.

Quinn couldn't help but notice that Janet was wearing the same pink lip gloss that she was. Why did she care? She just did. Outside the lips, Janet had a fresh dust of makeup under her eyes to hide . . . what? Exhaustion? Emotion? Quinn could only guess. Janet must have gotten in massive trouble after the parade. Quinn was amazed neither Janet nor Cole had been grounded. Or maybe they had, and maybe they were the kind of kids who ignored orders like that.

Cole reached over and adjusted the radio. No aux cable or phone hookup—it was one of those old-fashioned AM/FM jobs where you had to keep fine-tuning the knobs, searching for reception. In this case, Cole was dialing between an oldies station and a Billboard countdown. "Free Bird" was a really long song, so the two stations became a kind of impromptu mashup where Kendrick Lamar would occasionally lay a few bars over southern rock. Quinn looked over. In the harsh shadows of the dashboard light, Cole looked handsome. He was wiry and thin, pale but still attractive. Jared Leto–y, almost. He'd probably never look *bad*, but today he did look sadder, more serious than when they'd first met. The events of the parade and Sheriff Dunne's accusations had rattled him.

"It's not much farther," he said, pitching his voice lower, like it was just the two of them in the car. "And sorry we had to drive her." Cole motioned to the back seat. "I thought it was just going to be you and me. But with Matt driving Ronnie, and then Tucker . . ." He turned to the back seat. "Wait. Why couldn't you go with Tucker again?"

"I tried! I must have texted twenty times!" Janet said in a tone that made Quinn want to call BS. "I even tried calling. Went straight to voicemail."

"His mom took his phone, probably." Cole rolled his eyes and grinded the gearshift down as they entered a turn Quinn could hardly see in the dark. There were no landmarks on either side of the car, nothing but an unending wall of corn.

"When does the corn get, uh"—Quinn looked out the window and searched for the right word—"harvested?"

"Never," Janet said, smirking. "Not anymore."

"What she means is," Cole started, "not these fields. There's a subsidy for corn farmers. The government pays the rebate when you *plant*, not when you harvest."

"And without Baypen and your papa to sell to, clearing the B-fields is probably more trouble than it's worth, right, Cole?" Janet asked. The question had the air of an accusation. It made Quinn want to ask Janet what *her* family did, but she kept to herself. She wanted information but didn't want to be the nosy new girl.

They lapsed into silence when Cole didn't answer Janet.

With no streetlights, the greens, yellows, and browns of the cornfield seemed to swallow whole the glare of the moon and stars, leaving nothing but a void.

"You drive much back home?" Cole asked, trying his best.

"No," Quinn said. "I have my license. But nobody has a car in the city."

"What city was that again?" Janet asked.

"Philadel—"

"We know." Janet gave a soft kick to her seat. "Jeez, I was kidding."

Quinn caught herself staring daggers at Janet through the rearview reflection, but the other girl refused to play, return her glare. Why the switch? Why had Janet held Quinn's arm for most of the parade and now was acting like this? A bad mood from a botched prank? Close quarters?

Quinn didn't care. She was going to make the best of this: "So what do you guys like to do on—"

"Oh shit!" Janet yelled, the girl kneeing Quinn in the spine, *this* kick involuntary.

In the middle of their lane, illuminated in the cold stare of Cole's high beams, stood Frendo. The clown had appeared out of nowhere, it seemed. Dead-eyed. Staring down the speeding car without so much as flinching.

Quinn heard a scream. Not Janet's, not Cole's. It was her own voice, her own scream. They were going too fast. Frendo wasn't getting out of the way, probably couldn't. They were going to hit him.

They were going to—

Cole slammed on the brakes.

Quinn reached out to the dashboard, wedging herself in place as she gripped the door handle. The rear tires squealed. Cole jerked the wheel, the car spinning. The back end came around perpendicular to the road, putting Frendo directly into the path of the passenger's side window . . . and Quinn.

She had an unobstructed view as the car slammed straight into the clown, sideswiping him off his feet, sweeping his polka-dot body over the low roof with a padded thud.

The car shuddered to a stop.

"Oh shit oh shit oh shit," Cole said to himself, not loud but hopeless, broken, some kind of a final straw that Quinn hadn't witnessed the entire buildup to.

It was that sound of terrible realization that sent her spilling out of the door onto the asphalt, the back of her throat burning with stomach acid.

Hands on the cool ground, beginning to retch, that was when Quinn noticed what was fluttering down around her—

Hay?

She picked up her hand, stared at her palm in the moonlight, her lifeline cut by a sliver of golden hay. She straightened to her knees and plucked another blade out of the air.

Confused, she stood slowly, unsteady, to see Cole exit the driver's seat, kicking the clown in the head in his rage.

Frendo's skull exploded in a puff of hay.

"Scarecrow," Janet said, sliding the front seat forward and then slipping out the passenger's side door behind Quinn. "Frendo, the scarecrow."

"Who the fuck did this?" Cole yelled into the night, voice trembling.

Matt came out of the corn, laughing so hard he could barely catch his breath. He wore a chunky sweater and what in the dark looked like corduroy pants. He had the appearance of a clean-cut pro athlete, the kind you'd see clips of on the local news, apologizing about his behavior off the field, sorry to disappoint his fans.

"You should have seen you motherfuckers," Matt said. "Best prank yet."

The word *motherfucker* with a midwestern twang . . . it just didn't sound right to Quinn.

"W-where's Ronnie?" Janet asked. Quinn found the anger in Janet's voice comforting. She was glad that whatever this was, Janet hadn't been in on it. Janet had enough sense to put a twenty-four-hour hold on the pranks.

"Right here, bitch!" Ronnie Queen said, coming out of the cornrows on the opposite side of the road. The taillights cast the blonde in a demonic red glow.

Janet closed the distance to her friend, looking ready to throttle her. *Oh, please do it,* Quinn found herself thinking. But then, a half step away, Janet gave Ronnie the finger. "You both suck," Janet cursed. And then, surprisingly, with a sigh: "Did you at least catch it on camera?"

"Hell yeah we did!" Matt yelled, pulling a beer out from who knows where and popping the top. As he commenced chugging, he tossed another over to Cole, who caught it but didn't start drinking. Didn't toast Matt and Ronnie's "accomplishment." Instead, he threw the can as far as he could into the cornfields and got in Matt's face.

"You could have gotten us killed."

"But I didn't," Matt shot back.

"But you could have."

"But I didn't," Matt said again, more forcefully, now bumping chests with Cole. "So chill out. Look around.

You're alive. We're alive. And we're at fucking Tillerson's! Janet worked hard to plan this." Matt took a long swig, pushed his head back, sprayed beer into the night air, and let out some sort of wolf howl that would have freaked Quinn out if her nerves weren't already shot.

Quinn watched as the two boys stared each other down. The pain in Cole's eyes, the game-day ferocity in Matt's, she could only imagine all the shit that hung, unspoken, between them. Cole was the star. Matt was supporting cast, but he had ambitions, was making moves. Cole set the tone. Matt followed. Ronnie was clearly in love with Cole, even though she was *with* Matt. Janet, too. And for all the tension in the air, for all Quinn knew, Matt might have *also* been in love with Cole, just to even out the overlapping love triangles. Wouldn't surprise her one bit. She could see Cole clenching and unclenching his fists.

Was violence inevitable?

They all flinched as Cole made a sudden move.

He grabbed the beer away from Matt and chugged whatever was left.

"Fucking Frendo," Cole spat. "I hate that goddamn clown."

"How can you hate Frendo? Frendo *is* Kettle Springs," Ronnie said, and for the life of her, Quinn couldn't tell if Ronnie was joking.

And Cole didn't hesitate to add, with a steady finger shutting up Ronnie: "I know what he is, and I know what I said."

Janet moved next to Quinn. She took a drag on a fresh cigarette and then flicked it, half-smoked, into the cornfields. Definitely a fire hazard. "Well, while we're making shocking admissions: I hate all of you. Biggest party of the night and we're standing on the side of the road, arguing about who hates their life more . . . fuck you all."

"Yeah, fuck y'all," Ronnie agreed.

"Party!" Matt yelled, belching loudly. "Fuck everyone! Fuckin' orgy. I love you, man," he told Cole, enfolding him in a hug. Cole started tense, then patted the squat boy on the back.

Whatever had just happened, the screaming and the drinking and the hugging: it was a kind of exorcism.

Quinn felt the sudden urge to yell "Mazel tov!" in congratulations. But it didn't seem like her place. Or that this group of midwesterners from churchgoing families would know what the hell she was trying to say.

"Grab Frendo's head," Matt said to Cole, nodding toward the demolished clown. Cole had kicked the side of its head in. The plastic mask was bent out of shape, lips upturned in a smirk, one eye socket collapsed. It looked like Frendo, but a creepier, more warped version, if that was even possible.

"Why?" Quinn asked. "He's destroyed."

"Never leave a Frendo behind," Matt said. "That's rule number one, two, and three." He smiled as he staggered into the road, where he grabbed Frendo's head, the stuffed torso coming along with it. He tossed Ronnie the disemboweled, deflated Frendo, and the girl caught it, one hand gripping its neck.

Throttling Frendo like a mic stand, Ronnie smiled and sang, "A lit-tel drop of Baypen makes everything bet-ter."

It took Quinn a minute, but had that slogan been on the side of the factory?

Everything. She remembered the one legible word.

"Wait, Cole," Matt said, turning back, already in the ditch, presumably headed back to his own car. "Why don't you just pull your car in here? We're close enough to the meeting place, we can walk the rest of the way."

Janet answered for him. "No. You want to wander around in the dark, be my guest."

"Was I talking to you?" Matt asked.

"Forget them, baby," Ronnie said.

They rounded the car, Janet climbing into the back first, then Quinn sliding in.

"Does it really make everything better?" Quinn asked, still in the afterglow of the adrenaline, nausea, and fear. "A little drop of Baypen?"

Cole pulled shut the driver's side door, the three of them watching Ronnie and Matt disappear into the corn.

"Corn syrup's just sugar. So at least it makes everything taste better," Cole told her, but then he paused to think about it. "But it sure as hell isn't better *for* you."

And before Quinn could ask what he meant, Matt pulled his car out onto the road, half a donut on the pavement as it narrowly missed Cole's side mirror.

Matt gunned the engine and screamed out the window, "Party!" And then he peeled off into the night and they had no choice but to follow into the gloom.

TEN

Quinn pushed open the passenger's side door and stepped out into the field. The soil under her feet was spongy and uneven; fallen cornstalks crisscrossed beneath her Chuck Taylors.

Cole had turned off the highway and driven straight into the standing cornfield, stalks pushed down under his bumper like he was playing a video game or building a crop circle. High beams on, they entered a small clearing after a few dozen yards, near several other cars and trucks. Cole explained that they were hiding the cars from the road in case a highway patrol officer cruised past and was in the mood to break up a high school party.

Ronnie and Matt had already parked, and Matt, for some reason, was climbing out of his car through the driver's side window. Cole's muscle car had been cramped, but Matt's cherry-red two-seater was almost ludicrously small and impractical. It felt more like a rich kid's car than Cole's, which actually *was* a rich kid's car.

Standing in the trampled corn, Matt reached back through the window, behind the front seat, and pulled out two Frendo costumes on hangers and in clear plastic laundry bags. He tossed one to Ronnie.

"Why?" Quinn asked Janet, nodding over to where the couple was tearing into the plastic. Janet shrugged, as if she had no idea why any of her dumbass friends did the dumbass things they did.

Matt pulled the jumpsuit on over his corduroy pants and loosely tied Timberlands. He cinched the sleeves together, then tied them around his waist in a crude belt. The baggy Frendo pants looked ridiculous. To finish the ensemble, he put the elastic strap of the mask around his ears, Frendo's plastic face turned into a hat.

Across from him, Ronnie found a way to make polyester clown coveralls pornographic. She was wearing the outfit off her shoulders, leaving the front of the jumpsuit unbuttoned down to her navel. Without dropping the costume to her waist, she'd managed to wiggle her way out of her shirt. It was a lot of skin to be showing off all night. On a cool night.

Stop it, you're not her mother. Not that you had a great role model for that anyway . . .

"All right. Let's get going. Someone help me with the beer," Matt said, popping open his trunk.

Quinn grabbed a twelve-pack of lukewarm Bud Light. Matt reached over, looking ready to help, then pulled a single can from the case.

Cole joined them, forced a smile. He hefted a half keg onto the bumper. "Don't worry. You won't have to hang with these dopes all night."

Cole got a better grip, hoisted the keg to his waist, and led the way.

Once they were out of the clearing of flattened plants and parked cars, the cornfield was pitch-dark around them. Quinn could see faces, hands floating in the reflected starlight, but they all seemed to exist in a stretch of nothingness. The only hints of form around them were moonbeams and starlight reflecting off leaves, their topsides glossy, the bottoms matte.

"How do you know where to go?" she asked.

"You just know," Cole started. "The road is back there, and the barn and the party is up ahead there somewhere," he added, gesturing with his chin as he strained.

It was unclear if Matt would take a turn carrying the keg, even if asked.

There were no landmarks. No signs. They were going to find the party on instinct. Quinn didn't like the idea of relying on anyone to find her way home, but there was no going back. She was here.

"Most of these kids, they've got relatives who're farmers. Some help out on these farms themselves. They've all done this a few times." He smiled mischievously. "Or they'll get lost in the corn—"

"—and die!" Matt yelled, jumping onto Cole's back like a crazy person. Cole fell forward, bottom of the keg stamping cornstalks flat under him. "I'll protect you, new girl. If you need someone a little less low-T."

Cole shook him off, stood, and shot Matt a look that Quinn couldn't quite decipher in the moonlight.

"Hurry up, losers. Party's this way."

"Idiot," Cole muttered, but his tone seemed to be lightening.

"And he's proud of it," Ronnie said, smiling. She caught up with Matt and wrapped an arm around him, their twin Frendo costumes making them the most visible kids in the corn.

"I need a drink," Janet said. "Want help carrying that?"

Quinn told her no and the three of them walked on, Matt and Ronnie eventually disappearing into the corn in front of them.

They marched deeper into the oceans of corn, their way

illuminated by the stars and passing the occasional lost kid holding out an iPhone, flashlight on. Eventually, the atonal buzz in Quinn's ears resolved itself into music. Ahead, speakers were blasting a familiar, if still muffled, Kid Cudi song. Above the tops of the corn, she could see a warm orange firelight, the flicker of the flames punctuated with strobe flashes that were either timed to the music or near enough to the beat that it didn't matter.

They were getting close.

Whoops and screams popped off around them. More partygoers arriving. Cornstalks rustled, bent, and broke.

Quinn caught glimpses of hands and feet as teenagers skittered past. Some of their arms pinwheeled, swimming through the leaves; some of them carried six-packs, plastic looped around wrists; some had tiki torches resting over their shoulders.

And then, when it didn't seem like the firelight could get any brighter or the pulse of the hip-hop could get any louder: they broke through.

Quinn, Cole, and Janet stood shoulder to shoulder at the edge of a clearing. The expanse of dirt and grass was about the diameter of a high school's running track, maybe a little bigger. On the far side of the clearing was a barn, its doors pushed open, front and back. Quinn could see straight through to the night-darkened rows of corn out the other end.

Next to the barn was a silo, its sparse red paint cracking with age. The cylinder was maybe five feet taller than the two-story barn. Quinn had no idea what the point of a silo was, didn't even know if they were solid or hollow, but she could tell from where she stood that the structure was disused. The silo had a visible lean and the barn's roof was sagging in the middle. Without some serious rehabbing, neither building looked like it'd still be standing by the time KSH's current freshmen were seniors.

"It . . . is . . . perfect!" Janet squealed into Cole's face, then raced ahead, continuing on into the party. Quinn and Cole stayed at the fringes, taking in details, the case of beer no longer feeling heavy in her arms.

"I mean, doesn't seem like she helped set anything up, but . . . I think she's proud of herself?" Cole asked.

Quinn smiled.

Set at a remove from the barn, still close enough that rogue embers probably should have been a concern, were two firepits. One was set in a large corrugated metal brazier, while the other was simply a hole dug a few feet down into the dirt. Above one, tilted at an angle so the flames could lick his feet but not catch, was a life-size effigy of Frendo.

Someone had stolen some of the red, white, and blue bunting from Main Street and hung it around the edge of the DJ booth set inside the barn doors. The effect was that this party was a pulsing, living inverse of Founder's Day.

Next to the firepits, but far enough away so the plastic wouldn't melt, were a fleet of baby pools. Kegs jutted up from these pools like buoys, while loose cans of beer, spiked lemonades, and hard iced teas floated idly beneath the surface. Quinn had never cared much for beer. She'd learned long ago that her party drink of choice was the screwdriver. Mixed right, it was like drinking orange juice, and it was easy to mix in a way that kept her buzzed without getting out of control. And so Quinn and Cole dropped the beer at one of the pools, and then she headed inside the barn alone in search of a "real drink."

Instead, she found the dance floor, the party's pulsing, writhing heart. There must have been thirty or forty kids, drinks raised, bouncing to the rhythm (or close enough), singing along with songs spinning from the DJ's dueling iPad setups.

The DJ, a hooded figure too skinny and small to be much more than a sophomore, bopped and shook over a table. Strobes flashed from either side of his kit, heavy-duty amplifiers forming the base of the platform that stood him taller than the partygoers.

Cole came up behind her and yelled over the music, "So . . . what do you think?"

"I don't think I'm in Philadelphia anymore," Quinn yelled back, smiling. She meant it to be funny, a *Wizard of Oz* reference in reverse, but she could tell by Cole's expression that he took it as an insult. "This is much better," she added quickly. "It's lit."

"We try," Cole yelled, smiling. He had a faint liquor mustache that Quinn wanted so badly to wipe off for him.

"How do you guys pull this off? Isn't this someone's backyard?"

They moved away from the speakers, but still needed to shout.

"Not really. The house is, like, a mile away from here. But Janet really did do the legwork. She planned the party during the farming expo. Tillerson has packed up his family in the RV. They vacation, checking out the tractors and fertilizer nozzles, while we party."

He stood tall, smiling. "If we do a good enough job picking up after ourselves, nobody will ever know we were here. A victimless crime." His hair fell over his eyes in a way that made him look sad. Beautiful, but sad. And Quinn knew in her heart that if her mother were alive, she would warn her. Cole Hill was broken. He was trouble in every conceivable way a boy could be trouble. And Quinn already wanted to save him from himself. And she could hear her mother's voice say: "Exactly. Look how well that worked out for your dad."

Quinn broke away from his stare as the DJ transitioned from one of those eighties synth hits with the melt-in-your-heart chorus to something catchy-but-still-ratchet by Cardi B.

"I love this song," she shouted into Cole's face. A white lie but a necessary one. "Let's dance!"

"Oh, I'll dance," he said, looking uneasy, already looking busy thinking of boy excuses. Quinn furrowed her brow. "*I will.* But I think I need a drink first. Can I get you one? What do you like?"

"Screwdriver," Quinn said. "I'll come with you." She followed Cole as he stomped across the barn to a table in the corner that housed what appeared to be an endless supply of plastic liquor bottles and mixers. Quinn may have trusted Cole, but trust wasn't the same as stupidity. Glenn Maybrook hadn't given his daughter very many "facts of life" talks. But when he did, the talks were often in the form of things he'd witnessed firsthand in the emergency room. One such talk that had stayed with her ended with the words: "And that's why you always mix your own drinks."

Across the barn, Quinn could see beer pong tables. A big guy belched and bellowed, throwing his arms up in triumph as Matt Trent—still with his clown jumpsuit cinched around his waist—pounded him on the back and then stumbled off. At the other side of the table Ronnie, still with her plunging Frendo neckline, grimaced. She sniffed her cup and fished a ping-pong ball out with a manicured finger before drinking.

Janet had found a ledge to sit on. She had a drink in her hand and her legs crossed. She looked like the Queen of Hearts, already bored with her kingdom, searching the crowd and deciding which of her subjects would be next to lose their head.

Quinn watched Janet's expression change and followed her gaze to the back doors.

Ruston Vance was the last kid in Kettle Springs that Quinn had expected to see at this party. Everything about him, including his yellow-and-green John Deere hat and red plaid shirt, seemed out of place.

Rust spotted her spotting him, then began his way toward her. She poured some plastic-bottle vodka and some paper-carton OJ into a cup, not paying enough attention to the proportions of either.

Beside her, Cole was shuffling with some bottles, scrutinizing labels.

She didn't know why seeing Rust here made her stomach drop. Why she didn't want him to come over and talk. She barely knew him—and if anything, she belonged here less than he did.

Cole ducked down, apparently searching for a bottle opener he'd dropped.

Rust approached. He stopped in front of Quinn and shifted his hat on his head in lieu of a hello. He tried to smile but must have felt as awkward as he looked. "Quinn. Didn't expect to see you here."

"Maybe because you didn't invite me?" Quinn shot back,

not meaning to be rude and yet, there it was. But really, if he'd known about the party and was planning on attending, why hadn't he?

"I don't usually, uh, come to this kind of stuff."

Cole returned, looking surprised to see that his spot beside Quinn had been taken. He slapped Rust on the back, an aggressive hello, his demeanor shifting. What was Cole really feeling, or was he always performing, the role shifting depending on who he was with?

"Rusty," he began, "how the hell are you?" Cole made to stick out his hand, but Rust kept both of his own around a bottle of Coors, warming it like a baby bird, and they didn't shake. Instead Cole popped open his own beer, a local brand Quinn didn't recognize. "You been to the Point yet this season? Thompson says he caught a three-pound rock bass."

"Bullshit," Rust said, pulling a long drink off the bottle. "Record is two pounds and ten ounces. Something like that."

"Exactly what I said," Cole added, clinking drinks with Rust. "But you know him. Always compensating with fish for what he doesn't have . . ." Cole nodded down. The boy in plaid laughed politely, and Quinn stood there smiling, sipping her drink, thinking to herself that boys everywhere are dumb.

"You two know each other?" Cole asked, swiveling over toward her and drinking deep.

“Rust is my neighbor,” Quinn explained. “He’s walked me to school.”

Cole’s eyebrows went high, and then he nodded to show he was surprised.

“Just being friendly,” Rust said. “Hard to be new in a place like Kettle Springs. Without a friend,” he added, and the look he fixed on Cole told her that it was more than just a pleasant observation.

“Me and this guy,” Cole said, pausing to take a big sip, then motioning to Rust. “We used to be thick as thieves. Little hellions, running around.” Cole twirled his free fingers to mime running around like little hellions.

“Long time ago,” Rust said, his voice deeper suddenly.

“Oh yeah, what happened?” Quinn asked, because they seemed to want her to.

“We grew up,” Cole said before Rust could answer. “Rusty got too cool for me.”

“Nailed it,” Rust said flatly. “I got *so* cool.” And then, realizing that Quinn was getting fed up with all the passive aggression, he explained, “We drifted. Cole started playing football, and I didn’t quite have the skills.”

“I’m sorry. That sucks,” Quinn said.

“Yeah,” Rust said, taking a deep breath and then a long drink. “Stinks.”

“What position did you play?” Quinn asked.

Rust smiled and answered, "Quarterback."

"Oh." Quinn began to ask, "You still play, Cole?" before sensing that the boys weren't really listening to her anymore. She took a long sip of her drink to cover.

Woof. She'd mixed it too strong.

"You still got the Ford?" Cole asked, changing topics gracelessly.

"You know I do," Rust answered. "Seats're mostly duct tape, but she still runs—most of the time."

Cole's face brightened. "If we don't get too shitfaced tonight," Cole said, "maybe we drive up to Devil's Den before sunrise and see if we can't bag a duck or two. An unlucky rabbit."

Rust laughed, made uneasy by the suggestion. "I . . . I don't think so."

"It'll be fun. I know you've got guns in the rack. If she's up for it, we can show city girl here the ropes. I bet she's never even fired a round." Cole's expression got fake-serious. "Unless she was in a gang. Were you in a *gang*, Quinn?"

But she couldn't reply—she was too hung up on the thought:

Ruston Vance had brought guns to a high school party.

Quinn cocked a brow, started to say something, but Cole held up a silencing hand. He was still performing a bit.

"Holding the gun like this"—he made pistol fingers and

then turned the invisible gun on its side—"doesn't count." One of Cole's arms had snaked around Rust's shoulders, was making her neighbor visibly uncomfortable.

"I think I'll pass, but thanks," Quinn said when she realized Cole was being at least half-sincere about going hunting tonight.

"C'mon, it'll be fun," Cole whined. He was definitely not used to being told no.

"Leave it be, Colton," Rust said, ducking to extricate himself from the hold.

Colton. That sounded . . . like they really *had* been friends.

"Guns just aren't my thing," Quinn explained. "I don't think I'd like shooting things."

"But you do eat meat?" Rust asked.

"Sure, but that's different. I'm not putting on an apron, getting out the sledgehammer, every time I want a burger," Quinn replied, crossing her arms.

"Well," Rust began, "I only use my guns to hunt and only hunt what I eat."

"Here we go, sounding like the NRA duders in town—" Cole said, throwing his hands up.

"No," Rust shot back. He was clearly tired of Cole's puckishness. Quinn was getting there herself, and she looked at the mostly empty beer in his hand. "I'm not some gun nut," Rust continued. "I don't have any bump stocks or semi-automatic weapons. I'm not sitting in my basement with a bowie knife, carving rounds into cop killers. I eat what I hunt. I think if you're going to eat meat, you should know where it comes from and what you're taking from the world."

Quinn blinked. This was a far cry from the courteous, awkward boy who'd walked her to school. Was it because Ruston Vance was more comfortable around Cole or less?

"I just don't believe in killing, okay?" Quinn said, feeling her cheeks flush. She hadn't come out to debate anyone, wasn't prepared to. "I don't think it's humane."

"Okay," Rust told her.

"Okay?" Quinn said, staring him down hard.

"Yeah, okay." And like that: understanding. Different strokes, different worlds, reconciled. It was easier IRL than in comment threads; you had to look the person in the face, still *wanting* to like them.

"Great, so we're all besties again," Cole cut in. "Quinn and I were about to go dance, but if you're still around later, we should talk, drink. Catch up?"

"Was good seeing you both," Rust said. "I'll probably be heading out early. If I don't see you: stay safe."

And like that, the neighbor boy in flannel turned and disappeared farther into the barn.

Stay safe.

The sounds of the party resumed, and Matt came

bounding over, hooting with his arms raised. "I am the king of 'root!" he declared. "Three matches and undefeated! Not even buzzed." He belched like that couldn't possibly be true and pointed to Cole. "What about you, QB? Or you, new girl?" A steely look from Cole and he corrected himself: "Quinn—I mean Quinn, you two think you can beat me?"

But Quinn wasn't giving the question her full attention. She was thinking about what Rust had said: *stay safe*. The way he'd said it. Was that a warning? About the party or about Cole or just something people in Kettle Springs said instead of goodbye?

"You-hoo! New fish," Ronnie said, poking Quinn in the shoulder, "we're talking to you?"

"Sorry, I'm not very good at pong," Quinn said, snapping back to it. Ronnie didn't seem to like her answer.

"Beirut, but . . . fine," Ronnie said, giving a long blink, then playing with her jumpsuit's pom-poms. All the motions said "drunk," but Ronnie's eyes looked clear to Quinn, like the girl was only pretending to be tipsy. Ronnie nuzzled into Matt's squat frame, keeping a hard stare on Cole, who couldn't be giving her less of his attention. If this was flirting, the girl was bad at it.

"I mean, maybe later, but Quinn said she wanted to dance," Cole said, flashing that smile that'd probably defused a thousand arguments. "So . . . let's dance." And he grabbed her hand and guided her toward the dance floor.

As Quinn was pulled along, she spotted Janet marching out the back of the barn, throwing a look over her shoulder. Matt found a freshman to beat at flip cup. Ronnie stood at the edge of the throng, phone out, filming it all, the eye of the camera always seeming to settle back on Quinn and Cole.

ELEVEN

Glenn Maybrook stood at the sink and considered his cell phone. His hands were soapy to the point of ineffectiveness. And he'd lathered them up like this on purpose. With these hands, he could barely work a plate from the stack beside him without it crashing to the floor. But clean dishes weren't the point. Being at the sink was an excuse to kill time, get his mind off things. If he were scrubbing, he'd forget that his daughter was going to be out all night partying. A party he'd encouraged her to attend.

But then what was he supposed to do? Drag her away from her home, out to live in the middle of nowhere, and then tell her "No. You can't go make new friends!"?

Quinn was fine. He knew she was fine. She was a smart kid. She was going to bounce back . . .

He cursed himself and pushed his glasses back up his nose, then cursed himself again as a soap bubble glided across his vision.

They hadn't yet used these dishes for a meal in their new house, and the plates and glassware weren't dirty from the move. Despite their plan to eat better and to cook more, all of their meals so far had been either at the Eatery or leftovers *from* the Eatery. Turns out that grocery shopping was exhausting and the takeout choices in Kettle Springs were . . . limited.

Tomorrow they would go to the supermarket! Even if it meant a road trip. As soon as he was done with the dishes, Glenn resolved to make a list. He'd text Quinn to make sure he didn't forget anything. He'd make sure she knew it was not a rush. He'd write that first—"NOT URGENT!"—so she'd know she didn't need to stop having fun and immediately text back.

He set a dish in the drying rack and rinsed his hands.

"Well. That's done," he said to the empty kitchen. He looked down at his phone, hit the home button to check the time. A single soap sud winked at him. Mocked him.

Placing both hands on the countertop, he looked out the window above the sink. There was the sound of—what? Crickets? Cicadas? Glenn Maybrook could hear them so well through the window that he idly worried about the house's insulation.

He made a mental note to try to get the name of a good handyman. Glenn Maybrook was many things—but handy was not one of them. Having someone reliable who could fix the small things seemed essential now that they didn't have a super anymore. Glenn looked out the window, adjusted his glasses. Carefully this time, using the dry part of his wrist.

The cornstalks were infantry outside the window, lined at the edge of their yard, forever on guard.

Looking out, Glenn made a mental note to get porch lights installed. The kind with motion sensors. He should put that on the grocery list. He caught his own reflection in the kitchen window, then glanced up at the light. Anyone out there could see him or Quinn, pillboxed in the window. He'd also get some drapes.

What time is it? He'd checked a second ago but clearly hadn't internalized the info. He used a still-damp pinkie to wake his phone again and saw that it was only 8:57. A droplet of dishwater ran down his elbow and onto his new Reeboks. Earlier Quinn had teased him that his shoes were too new-looking and way too white. Her ride, Cole, seemed to appreciate them. He'd said, "I think they're cool," and offered Glenn a firm handshake. Glenn decided to take it as a compliment, not some kind of teen boy power play.

Standing alone now in the kitchen, Glenn frowned. Glenn liked the boy, even if he didn't like that he drove a muscle car that predated airbags and antilock brakes by thirty years or that his breath smelled too minty not to be covering *something* up.

No, no, Glenn shook away the thought. He would not worry. He couldn't worry. He had to let Quinn have a life. That was the whole point of coming here. This was a nice, small town. People here took care of each other. Bad things didn't happen in Kettle Springs. *Nothing* happened in Kettle Springs. Which reminded Glenn that the cable company hadn't come yet, which meant no TV, no Wi-Fi. The reception in the house was so bad he could barely stream music. He'd have to figure out where he packed the books. He couldn't remember the last time he read for pleasure—*Tonight I'll start reading for pleasure again.*

But then he heard it. It was a sound like a soft crack or crinkle. Like footsteps but more careful, no rhythm.

He strained, leaned an ear toward the window, and thought he could almost—almost—hear someone talking, hidden out there in the corn. He couldn't make out words, but it definitely sounded like someone was out there, whispering.

Then, the noises stopped.

Glenn was not really sure why, but he took a step back from the window. Without looking over, he reached a hand out, searching the still-unfamiliar wall, then flicked off the kitchen light switch so he was no longer on display. With no other lights on in the house, it took his eyes a moment to adjust.

Zzzzt!

Glenn jumped at the sound and the accompanying flash of light.

Just his phone.

He looked down into the glow:

9:00.

Why had he set himself an alarm to stop cleaning dishes and move on to the next task? *Because it's structure, Glenn. Because you're nuts.* He laughed, uneasy, and picked up the phone to silence the alarm.

WHAM!

Something crashed into the outside of the house.

Glenn flinched and the phone dropped from his hand, bounced off the counter, and landed on the floor with its screen facedown.

Glenn's body tingled with the aftermath of the scare.

This night was taking years off his life. Who was throwing rocks at his house? Kids, of course. Some dopey kid trying to prank the new neighbor. A kid who wasn't smart enough to do an actual prank, so settled for throwing rocks.

Glenn was in no mood. He hadn't driven halfway across the country to be tortured by a whole new and exotic set of late-night sounds.

Stumbling through the darkness of the house, Glenn pawed his way to the front closet, where he found exactly what he wanted: his golf club. No, he wasn't the "golfing kind" of doctor. He didn't have a whole bag, just this one, for going to the driving range.

The club didn't have the heft of a baseball bat, but it would do. He wasn't going to do anything crazy, wasn't going to hurt anyone—he just needed to look like he could and would.

Glenn felt his way back along the hallway to the back door. This area would be their mudroom once they were done unpacking.

But before Glenn could unlatch the screen, there was a second impact.

WHAM!

Standing still, he listened as the object tumbled down their roof. A split second later there was a sound like the crack of wood. Siding or a roofing shingle that would now need to be replaced.

"Hey!" Glenn yelled, spilling onto the top step of the back porch. "Stop that!"

There was no answer, so he made his way down the stairs and stood in the middle of the yard.

Stepping wide around the broken birdbath, Glenn held his golf club at the ready.

"The police are already on their way," Glenn lied. "I'd get out of here quick-quick if I were you."

No response. No sounds. No footfalls and giggling as kids fled into the night.

Even the crickets seemed to have gone silent.

He stood in the damp grass, staring hard into the dark, trying to catch sight of something, anything. His arms began to go to gooseflesh, and Glenn sighed and lowered his club, resting it on his shoulder.

The rock throwing seemed to be done.

He started back toward the house, but then he heard a familiar sound. The click of a lighter. It continued, the click-click of a wheel spinning but not sparking. He turned in time to see a blue-purple flame bloom out in the cornfield.

A large torch, flame fizzing and cracking, stood, a few yards into the field, flame reaching a foot or two above the tops of the stalks.

There was no movement around the torch. No pranksters in sight, simply fire licking at leaves and husks, ready to set the whole field ablaze.

"Jesus, kids—you're going to burn the whole neighborhood down!" Glenn yelled. He remembered the little boy he'd helped in the aftermath of the parade, how sweet all the kids on that float had seemed, how happy he was that nobody'd been seriously injured. "Put that out and get out of there. You're not in trouble, just get out of there."

He stepped toward the cornfield. Patting his pocket, he remembered that he'd left his phone on the kitchen floor, possibly shattered. He needed to call the fire department—

As he watched, the fire spread, then split.

Now the center flame had become two torches.

"Hey. Stop!"

What was the phrasing Quinn had used to describe her new friends?

"Prone to mischief" was what she'd said. But this was too much. More than simple mischief, too calculated, too targeted.

The torches burned and then split again, flame dripping into the dirt with a sizzle. He took another step back, closer to his house, happy that the home didn't *directly* border the field.

He could smell accelerant. Gas. Was the plan to light the whole field up? Was this a show just for him? He watched the four torches, flames dancing in the night.

What the fuck is going on? Glenn thought, more bewildered than terrified. If the goal was to burn up the cornfield, then this had evolved too quickly from a stupid prank to serious criminal mischief.

A wind that hadn't been there moments ago picked up, blowing smoke and heat into his face. His eyes began to tear and for the first time since he stepped outside, he allowed himself to know that this wasn't a prank.

That he wasn't safe.

Under the whoosh of the flames and wind, there was the sound of running footfalls on grass at his back. Someone had either crept up on him, flanked him from the field, or had simply *materialized* behind him.

Glenn began to spin, golf club raised, his knuckles white around the grip—

But he wasn't fast enough to stop the sharp blow to the back of his head. He was dazed, and then a tremendous pressure clamped down around his neck.

He couldn't breathe; his focus was fading. He felt the golf club slide out of his grip and onto the lawn.

"Where's yer daughter, Doc?" asked an unfamiliar voice.

But Glenn couldn't get a word out. Whoever had him in a headlock, they'd hit him too hard, were squeezing too tight.

Before he could answer, his world went from amber flames to dead black.

Glenn Maybrook awoke to the stench of rot.

The odor was only marginally better than the pain.

Glenn could barely remember what a hangover felt like, but he knew that the throbbing at the back of his skull was worse. He tried to remember if the "worst headache of your life" was more indicative of a subarachnoid or a subdural hemorrhage and couldn't.

How would he continue to practice medicine if he couldn't remember a simple diagnosis?

A spasm of pain brought him to the here and now. The ache glided along the skin of his face, reached his nose, and ebbed backward. It felt like someone was skipping stones across the gray matter of his brain.

What is that smell?

Glenn used a finger to windshield-wiper the front of his glasses, then tried flopping onto his back and found that he'd been buried up to the waist in—

In what? And why did it reek?

Flailing, without being able to sit up, Glenn made a gooey, gross snow angel. He'd been knocked unconscious and left sinking into a pile of—topsoil? No. Manure? It was somehow worse than that.

It was . . . corn?

It was corn that had been separated from the cob and left to rot. Some of it was green, some of it brown, and some of it weirdly untouched by decomposition, still a bright, cheery yellow. If the stench was any indication, the pile had been putrefying for a long time. Some of the corn was still in sacks, but pests had long ago gnawed holes into the burlap. And at the thought of pests, Glenn realized what *else* he was sitting in. There were mouse and rat feces everywhere, mixed in with the rotting corn. Wispy tubers of fungus and mold grew among the turds, some of the growths tickling his chin. Whoever had knocked him out had then carried him, half buried him, and left him here to rot, too.

But why? Glenn looked up, took in as much as he could.

The room he was in wasn't a room at all, but an enclosure in a larger space, similar in size to a bathroom stall. To his side, the floor beyond the corn pile was dirt-streaked concrete, speckled with footprints that looked like they were made by large boots.

Glenn was facing the back wall, made of solid wood paneling reinforced with chicken wire. The roof was far above him, taller than the walls of his enclosure, and in the darkness, he could glimpse concrete and steel beams. Glenn craned his neck, looking behind him to see that on the other end of the small cubicle was a chain-link door that appeared to be padlocked shut. Beyond the chain-link was a bare bulb, the only light. Under the bulb was a folding chair and a set of stairs that led up. He confirmed that he was in a basement of some kind.

He tried to stand, pushing down with his arms only to feel the suck of the corn and shit against his clothes like quicksand.

The futility of the movement chilled him to a stop.

Glenn looked down at his knees, the kneecaps poking through the corn. He stretched to grab his knees. He pinched at his pant legs, and his fears racked into sudden focus . . .

He couldn't feel his legs.

No. No, that couldn't be.

They've paralyzed me!

But. That wasn't right. He didn't *feel* disconnected from the lower half of his body. He felt like he could still move, if barely. He wiggled his toes, felt the fabric inside his sneakers.

He tried again and found that he *could* flex his knees a bit, under the corn.

Like a neon sign, the answer broke through Glenn Maybrook's fogged mind: those are not *your* knees!

With a surge of strength, Glenn dug himself out of the slop. He used his hands to free his legs enough that he was able to hoist himself on top of the muck.

And then he scrambled over to whoever else had been dumped in the cage with him.

He began to dig.

Come on, Glenn. You're a doctor. You felt those cold knees. You know that whoever's under there, they're more than "hurt."

He tossed handfuls of slop behind him, rats scurrying away from the clatter as he hauled lumps of wet, putrid corn at the side of his chicken-wire-and-plywood cage.

It was a few moments until he'd uncovered his cellmate up to the waist, then a few more until he'd dug out his neck.

One final brush was all it took to reveal the corpse's eyes.

A gasp caught in Glenn's throat, becoming a nauseous retch.

Dr. Weller.

The town's former doctor.

He'd looked a lot better in the pictures he'd left hung in his office.

Dr. Weller was buried in here with Glenn.

And Dr. Weller was very, very dead.

"Help!" Glenn found his voice, his scream all at once. The exertion caused his head to flare with renewed pain. "Help me! Get me out of here!" His words echoed around in the larger chamber above his cage.

He stood and as if trying to answer, Dr. Weller's mouth began to move. The dead man's jaw worked up and down, the lips stiff, a bad ventriloquist.

Oh God. Weller was alive. This had all been a cruel, elaborate prank.

Glenn got closer to inspect. And watched a mouse crawl out from between Dr. Weller's teeth, apparently done nibbling the dead man's tongue. Whiskers streaked with pink froth, the mouse dove off the bump of the corpse's chin and disappeared into the rotting corn.

Glenn began to scream again: "Heeellll—"

"Please don't do that," someone said, tone even but amplified by the darkness. The voice was deep. Digitally disguised. "Please just sit tight, Doctor. You're still alive. Count your blessings."

Glenn did not like the sound of that.

"Who the hell are you? And where am I?" he yelled, but his head throbbed and the place stank and after everything, he thought he was going to pass out.

"Do what's asked of you, and maybe—just maybe—you won't be among those who die tonight."

TWELVE

The heat in the middle of the dance floor was pleasant at first, but after three songs, it became oppressive. Even with both barn doors open wide, the body heat of so many kids added up.

"You're a good dancer," Cole shouted, bringing her back to the moment.

"Thanks!" she replied, even though she was thinking that this wasn't really dancing. It was really more just grinding and fist pumping. The party's soundtrack had been unexpected. Underground hits that wouldn't have been out of place after-hours in Center City mixed with souped-up honky-tonk, that Kenny Chestnut shit that would have been booed out of any house party in Philly proper. Quinn was no music snob, but at one point, the kids of KSH had started line dancing. Seriously, shuffling out into three rows—twist, turn, tap your boots. Which was weird, but if she was being honest also, yeah, kinda fun. And much harder than it looked.

Quinn scrutinized the sweaty mass of kids surrounding her and Cole. She'd misjudged them back at the school: the young people of Kettle Springs weren't boring or lily white or your oh-so-basic red state clichés.

Girls danced with girls, guys with guys, and nobody looked scandalized. A couple of black guys chilled at the pong tables, getting along just fine with cheesy-looking white boys. Everyone could hang. More than anything else had in the last strange, confusing few days, the dance floor—and maybe the drink—put Quinn at ease.

Which wasn't to say there weren't . . . moments. The kids of KSH were completely obsessed with Cole.

Everyone was eyeing her date. Quinn and Cole were at the center of it all. Guppies in a fishbowl. It was a position not entirely unfamiliar to Quinn, who'd spent most of the last year trying hard to disappear.

Her therapist said she was trying to hide, that withdrawing wasn't a valid coping mechanism. But Dr. Mennin wasn't the one who had to go to school, put up with the whispers. The more people googled the specifics, the more they found out about what had happened to Samantha Maybrook. That Mom was a dope fiend, hooked on opioids, who'd graduated to heroin. How, basically, her mom's brain had stopped telling her lungs to breathe. The thought of which made Quinn want to disappear, and when Dr. Mennin called her on it, she called bullshit. But she knew, in her heart, the woman had a point.

She'd started seeing Dr. Mennin just before the overdose—the last overdose, when Mom had promised to get clean. If Quinn wanted to float away before then, afterward she felt flattened. Her dad was the thing that kept her in the world. He pulled her out of bed. He made sure to be home when she got home from school. He took her to the movies, made her eat, lay on the floor next to her bed until she fell asleep. But eventually it did start to get better. It *did.* And then Dad finally fell apart. Grief doesn't depend on dates—that's what Dr. Mennin told her again and again.

And now . . . Now she was dancing with Cole, watching all the people watching them, and thinking about calling her therapist. If that wasn't a sign that she still needed professional help, Quinn couldn't imagine what else could be.

Suddenly the air around her was humid and cloying, and no amount of closing her eyes to reset was ever going to bring her back to normal.

As a Steve Aoki song reached its final breakbeats, Quinn found her body screaming for a time-out.

"I need a drink," Quinn whispered in Cole's ear. "Not a drink-drink. Some water."

"Cool, cool," Cole said. Thankfully, he didn't follow her as she moved through and around the dancing bodies toward the makeshift bar outside the barn, in the clearing. No, he didn't follow—instead Quinn caught a glimpse of Ronnie and Matt approaching Cole as she made her way to the two plywood-covered sawhorses that the kids were calling the "bar."

There didn't seem to be any water, so Quinn poured herself another screwdriver, this time correctly: heavy on the OJ, light on the plastic-bottle vodka. She lightened it even further with a few ice cubes that she plucked from one of the keg-filled kiddie pools, gross as the pools might've been.

Quinn pressed her drink to the side of her neck to cool herself off as she stood to the side to watch the party. There was a drunk boy, perched on the edge of the in-ground fire, looking like his friends had convinced him to jump it. Quinn looked away, not wanting to watch if this dope was about to hurt himself.

Quinn also noted that the silo had a small sliding door on its side. She watched a girl exit, a thick plume of smoke or vape following her.

The droplets of sweat running down Quinn's back slowed, then began to cool as she sipped her drink.

Without Cole by her side, Quinn was anonymous again. It felt freeing.

She wandered around to the rear of the barn, tugging her blouse from her lower back as she went. Over here the party thinned. There were a few giggling shadows, people making out in the shade of the far side of the barn. Out in the corn, she heard someone puking, the sound reminding her to look where she was walking, just in time to sidestep a suspicious-looking puddle. And then, near the edge of the high school party oasis, she saw a latecomer wandering out of the corn.

Ginger walked out of the shadows. The skater girl's hair color was distinctive, even if she'd ditched her sweatshirt for a tank top and had put some kind of product in her hair.

Quinn squinted at her.

Was that seriously a faux-hawk? Quite the fashion statement.

Back at their lockers, the girl had given Quinn a loner vibe, but then again, so had Rust, and he'd shown up at the party at Tillerson's. Maybe this was truly a unifying event. No outcasts here; the high school had come together to howl at the moon for one night at least. Quinn smiled at the thought.

"Hey," Quinn said as Ginger approached.

There was no response.

Ginger was alone and . . . staggering.

Ginger hugged her bare arms, raised her eyes, and seemed to notice Quinn for the first time.

Her lips worked, trying to speak, but Quinn couldn't make out what she was saying.

Ginger hopped forward on one foot, then paused to turn and look behind her, then stumbled to the ground.

"Ya all right there?" Quinn almost said "youse," but that would have been a put-on, an affectation—Quinn wasn't from that part of Philly.

Quinn laughed, uneasy when Ginger didn't stand back up.

Quinn stepped forward to give her a hand, but was suddenly aware that the two of them were alone out here.

In the back of her mind, selfishly, Quinn was thinking how helping Ginger could become an excuse to leave the party early, to go home to her dad. She'd had enough for one night. Helping a drunk girl home was as good an excuse as any for getting out of this field.

But as Quinn walked closer, it was clear that something was wrong.

Ginger's hair hadn't been gelled up on purpose, hadn't been styled that way. It was clotted and clumped together.

There was *blood* streaming down the girl's face.

It was coming from a huge gash above her eye. Ginger's nose ring had been torn from her nose, the blood clotted on her upper lip like too much makeup.

Every bad thing that could happen to a teenage girl at a party was suddenly, *vividly* playing in Quinn's mind.

Ginger pushed herself up to her knees as Quinn rushed to her side. Only now could she see the panic in Ginger's eyes.

And there, sticking from her lower back, was an arrow, bright neon feathers marking the end.

Of all the possible scenarios that had been churning through Quinn's imagination, none of them had factored in this kind of . . . of hunting accident? Purposeful violence? What was happening?

Quinn reached for the end of the arrow to pull it out, and Ginger screamed, "No!"

"Okay, okay—" Quinn said quickly, hands up in a panicked apology.

"Whoa," someone said beside Quinn. It was Janet. The girl was carrying two Solo cups, had been in the process of pushing one toward Quinn when she spoke, but the drink never made it.

Janet dropped both cups and screamed, cool beer hitting the dirt and dead grass, splattering up, the splash fizzing against Quinn's cheek.

Quinn was too stunned to move. Wasn't sure what to do. Although Ginger's chest was rising and falling, she felt like dead weight in Quinn's arms. The girl was slick and cold.

Quinn looked up to Janet, needing help, but Janet had her hands to her face, was screaming at the top of her lungs.

It felt like all this was happening in slow motion. The

foam of beer sliding down her chin not yet settled, Ginger's blood sticky, beginning to web her fingers together.

Janet's scream had attracted a few onlookers, but nobody was moving to help them, not yet.

Inside the barn, less than ten yards away, Quinn could hear the music continuing, the dance floor no doubt still raging.

Quinn couldn't bring herself to speak, to even call for help. Her jaw ached from clenching. Janet finally rushed over and put her fingers on Ginger's neck like she was checking for a pulse. "I can't—" she began, and then she reached into her pocket. Janet's phone bobbled in the air for a moment and she dropped it into the beer puddle.

As Janet scrambled for the phone, Quinn heard movement behind them.

Quinn watched, her lockjaw going slack, as a clown emerged from the corn.

Frendo's shoulders were uneven, set that way. His chest heaved like he'd been running.

There was a flash of screen light as Janet finally got hold of her phone, hands muddy, and brought it up.

"We need to go," Quinn said, and began to pull at Ginger's shoulders. The girl wasn't helping. She was unconscious, somehow even colder than she'd been seconds ago.

"No, we shouldn't move her, we . . ." Janet, confused, followed Quinn's gaze, saw what she was seeing, and stopped arguing.

Ten feet away from them, Frendo stopped his approach and hefted something up to his waistline.

A crossbow.

Quinn watched, too stunned to move, as Frendo aimed the weapon low and fired at them.

There was a *thwump* sound like a broken guitar string.

The arrow moved with such speed that with one blink, a flinch, it passed between Quinn and Janet and embedded itself in the dirt, missing Ginger's head by inches.

The shaft of the arrow vibrated, Quinn close enough to hear the tuning-fork hum.

The motion had been so quick, the idea of violence so foreign, that Quinn had just assumed the clown had missed. But then the girl in Quinn's arms slumped forward, Ginger giving a final shudder as air left her body.

Frendo had hit his target.

The arrow had glided clean through Ginger's head. Enough force in the bowstring to enter the base of the girl's skull, then punch out the left eye socket and bury itself down in the dirt.

Quinn stared down at the hole in Ginger's head, the blood running between her fingertips, eye and brain bits splattered in the grass under them.

Quinn wouldn't have moved if Janet's voice hadn't resolved into a single word, repeated:

"Run!"

She understood by the second, maybe the third time.

Janet had Quinn by her armpits, ripping her to her feet.

Quinn had no choice but to be dragged out from under Ginger's corpse.

Her Chuck Taylors barely up to the task, she stumbled, crab-crawled backward, as she watched Frendo begin to move again.

The clown let the front end of his crossbow drop into the dirt, then used his foot to hold the weapon steady, drawing back the cable until it clicked.

He was preparing to fire again.

"Fucking go!" Janet yelled into Quinn's ear.

This time, Quinn really ran.

Behind them, Frendo took aim and fired.

THIRTEEN

Cole Hill watched from the edge of the barn as the killer in the clown mask took aim at Janet and fired.

No. Please no.

But the crossbow bolt went wide, missing Janet but still finding purchase in *someone*. Was that Pat Horner? In the chaos, Cole couldn't tell. Next to him, standing at the door to the barn, someone had screamed to "run," while another had yelled "active shooter" and the whole place, after a lifetime of in-school drills, went nuts.

Pat, or whoever had been hit, limped along, the bolt deep in the meat of his thigh, before finally collapsing in the space in front of the bar. The music was still thumping, full blast, but Cole could hear Pat's pained screaming anyway. It was like nothing Cole had ever heard before—a half-swallowed shriek that hurt just to hear.

Cole looked beyond the boy and saw that the clown was reloading. Whoever was behind the mask wasn't flustered. He worked with methodical efficiency, foot in the bow's stirrup, what must have been powerful arms hand-drawing the string back.

Was it 100—maybe 150 pounds? How much draw weight did a hunter need when his quarry was teenagers?

"Let's go," Matt said, grabbing Cole by the arm. Matt was still wearing his own Frendo costume, the choice instantaneously in bad taste. Cole's friend had untied the sleeves and had slipped his arms through at some point in the last few minutes, maybe for style, maybe to stay warm. But before Matt could direct Cole anywhere, Matt was knocked flat on his ass by a terrified Trevor Connolly. Trevor was running full speed, faster than he ever had on the football field. Trevor barely slowed after leveling Matt, was almost at the corn, was almost safe, when a bolt hit him in the back, felling him midstride, a dust cloud following after his limp body.

Before Cole could run to help Trevor, Ronnie was there by his side. The flash of her own costume made Cole have to work against the urge to fight her. He'd never been scared of clowns, but here, now Cole wanted to push Ronnie away as she tried to grab him.

"Come on," Ronnie yelled. "Let's go. Let's go." She spun

Cole around and grasped at Matt by the fabric of his costume to pull him up.

"We need to help them," Cole said.

Ronnie slapped him. Her palm hard on the side of his face.

"Listen to me," she said, voice serious. "Stop fucking around. We need to survive this."

He didn't have time to argue, didn't think to, because there was a familiar voice coming up behind them.

Cole turned, cheek stinging, and saw Janet. Quinn was right behind. All of them headed toward the barn doors.

Janet yelled out, again: "He's trying to kill me!"

The clown was finished reloading—how long was that? Five, ten seconds?—and fired again.

A few feet in front of Janet, a guy—Jake Peps, not an athlete but a friendly enough guy who'd share his homework if you were in a bind—twitched and fell face-first into the raised firepit. The flames flared, then knocked into a cloud of smoke and cinders as Jake screamed and writhed in the burning embers.

Cole instinctually started toward Jake, ready to bat out the flames with his hands if he had to. It was a small town. A small school. He'd known Jake since kindergarten. His first sleepover was at Jake's house. Jake's mother made them French toast sticks in the morning. Like real, homemade French toast sticks, with eggs, not from the freezer. But

Cole didn't get more than a few steps. Ronnie was still holding him by the shirtsleeve. She yanked Cole back and got up in his face. "He's gone. Let it go. Matt!" Ronnie yelled. Matt clamped a strong hand around Cole's arm, the couple moving him as a team.

Janet. Quinn. Where were they? He'd lost track.

They fought against the flow of traffic. Most of the partygoers were either headed for the corn or were trying to get inside the barn as a team of kids worked to get the big, wheeled doors closed.

Instead, Cole was being three-legged-raced toward the silo.

"Come on! Hurry!" Erin Werther yelled to them, about to slide the small door shut as they approached the disused corn silo. She held the door open as they rushed over the threshold, which was her mistake, as it turned out. A bolt found its way between the door and the jamb and slapped her in the side of the head, shattering Erin's glasses, killing her before she hit the floor.

Erin's body landed at Matt's feet, who, seeing her like that, snapped, turned his head, and coughed, sounding ready to puke.

The door was still open, about a foot gap, as they all stood, horrified.

"What the fuck!" Ronnie yelled as Cole ran to the door and slid it shut, bracing the frame with his shoulder.

"Lock it! Lock it," Ronnie yelled, her voice echoing around them.

"I can't," Cole screamed at her, pointing with his eyes to the empty latch, hands still holding the door shut, feeling vulnerable. "There's no lock!"

One of the stoner kids had set up a Coleman lantern in there, and the lamp threw harsh shadows on the door as Ronnie and Matt moved in front of the light source.

"Maybe it fell. Look for it," Matt offered, his voice weak, his face so pale he looked ready to pass out.

"Dipshit," Ronnie said, pushing Matt from her shoulder and beginning to search the ground. With a frustrated expression, Ronnie crossed to Erin's body, put one foot to the side of Erin's head, grabbed hold of the fletching, and pulled the crossbow bolt out of her skull.

"Back up," she said to Cole, voice dispassionate, then wedged the bolt into the latch, forming an improvised bar. They made those things out of carbon, strong but flexible, so that they could withstand tremendous pressure and not shatter. But still: crossbow bolts could bend—it could easily slip out if their attacker *really* wanted to open the door.

That didn't matter. Everything was happening too fast. Was too insane. Using the bolt as a wedge solved a problem, but outside, there was another twang of a bowstring. The sound was far enough away that queasy relief filled Cole's belly.

The killer was moving toward the barn. He was leaving the silo alone.

Cole listened as someone screeched and someone else whimpered. But there were fewer footfalls now—people had either made it to the cornfield or were taking their chances in a hiding spot.

"We can't just stay here and do nothing," Cole said as he fumbled to pull out his phone. Inside the silo was cool and airless and way too quiet, but it could have been worse. The silo would not have been shelter at all, if the Tillerson family were using the building. It would have been filled to capacity with dry corn, if Baypen were still open and buying the crop. One small silver lining to the shitshow that was this last year.

Cole dialed in his code and swore. "No bars. No bars. Nothing!" he screamed. "Fuck this town. What do we do now?"

"What can we do? We wait," Ronnie said in a whisper, shushing him, a finger to her lips. "Someone had to have made it out. They'll get to the road. The cops will be here soon."

"But Janet . . . and Quinn . . . and everyone else. That fucking guy is still out there."

"Maybe," Matt said, taking his own phone and shining it into Cole's eyes, "but right now, they're not our problem. All we have to do now is not die."

FOURTEEN

"He's trying to kill me!" Janet screamed. "Why me?"

Quinn watched as Janet changed directions, a boost of speed to her already herky-jerky sprint. Janet burst through the stampede around her, shoving a boy so small he had to be a freshman and sending him sprawling.

Thwump!

An arrow whizzed between them, missing them both by inches. With her push, Janet had saved the boy's life, if completely by accident.

It was not lost on Quinn that Janet might have been onto something: maybe Frendo *was* aiming for her. That was the second shot aimed the girl's way.

Quinn's chest heaved, not from distance run but from panic.

Quinn pressed her back up against the barn wall. She crouched, pulling an old tire down over herself, trying to make her body as small as possible. She stayed toward the shadows and let Frendo jog past her.

"Janet!" Quinn whisper-yelled, afraid to attract too much attention. She tried again, opening and closing her fist as she did, attempting to signal Janet with a manic sort of Morse code.

With the bulk of the partygoers either headed inside the barn or off into the fields, the clown had stopped chasing them. With one hand, the attacker tipped the bar onto its side, off its sawhorse base, and made himself a hunter's blind out of the plywood. He then stood, long torso above the upturned table, and nocked another arrow.

Janet had made another extreme course correction, a curve that ended in a sudden U-turn. The move ultimately gave the clown a better shot, no more classmates for Janet to use as cover as she doubled back.

Quinn watched as Frendo stuck a gloved finger in one eyehole of his mask and pulled sideways, adjusting his sight, then his grip. He steadied the bow, following Janet with the end of the weapon, leading her.

Quinn didn't think.

If she would have let rational thought enter her mind, she wouldn't have pushed the tire off herself and dove toward

Janet. If Quinn thought about it, she would not have put herself in that kind of jeopardy for a girl she barely knew.

But she did, tackling Janet, spearing her, shoulder to waist, to the dirt. The air whooshed out of Quinn's lungs as the arrow passed over their heads, embedding itself in the tire behind them with an audible thrum, shaft vibrating.

"Why is he trying to kill me!?" Janet yelled into Quinn's face.

"He's trying to kill everyone!" Quinn yelled back.

And as she said it, a boy who'd been banging on the front of the barn, begging for entry, fell into view, an arrow through his neck.

How was that possible? Quinn hadn't even heard the click-clack of a reload. Time in this situation was doing strange things. Motion stuttered forward and stopped. In her frenzy and adrenaline, Quinn was losing full seconds, maybe even minutes. From around the corner of the barn, the wounded boy watched them, his eyes pleading, blood filling his mouth, and he reached out, vainly, for their help.

Quinn watched the boy's eyes twitch and roll, then finally still.

"We need to get to the cars," Quinn told Janet, scooting them both back into the shadows.

"Oh God," Janet cried.

"Janet!" Quinn yelled. "I don't know what direction that

is." She jabbed a finger into Janet's chest. "But we need to get to the corn. That'll give us some cover. And you need to lead us out."

"The cars," Janet said. Behind Janet's eyes, Quinn watched as the girl's confidence fought to regain control. "Okay. Okay. I can do that." But Janet didn't move. In front of them, the clearing had emptied out. At their backs, inside the barn, Quinn could hear hushed cries, the kids in there wondering what was next.

She could hear them so well.

When had the music cut off? Quinn couldn't remember.

"You need to lead the way," Quinn said, getting to her feet and then pulling Janet up with her. Staying as close as possible to each other and the cover of the barn, the two of them sidestepped to the edge of the building. They couldn't see where Frendo had perched. "It all looks the same to me."

"There. Straight there," Janet said, pointing to a spot in the corn. "We run there on three. One. Two."

But before they got two steps out of the shadows:

Fwwwtump.

This time Frendo didn't miss.

The bastard had been waiting for them to leave cover. Even while focusing on other victims, he'd never lost track of where Janet and Quinn had hidden.

Janet spun to the ground. She'd been hit high in the shoulder.

She screamed, stumbled, but didn't stop running. Janet reached up to grab the end of the arrow to pull it out.

Quinn stopped her.

"Don't. You could bleed to death."

Her father had explained this to her once. In movies and TV, they say a bullet passing through is the best thing—and it *could* be if you could get an ambulance quickly enough. But sometimes, especially if you were shot in North Philly, where the cops and paramedics cared *slightly* less, a lodged bullet could be the thing that saved your life, kept you from bleeding to death.

There was almost no wobble to the arrow's neon feathers, which meant the arrowhead was likely embedded in Janet's shoulder blade or collarbone, not soft tissue. Careful not to bump the impalement, Quinn put her arm around Janet, adding a steadying hand to her back as they sprinted to the corn together.

Ten more limping steps. That was all they needed.

Please.

With each step, Janet yelled out, not the shrill scream of an injured girl but the deep, bellowing growl of a large animal in a lot of pain.

Tough as Janet was—and she was tough—Quinn knew

she would eventually lapse into shock. They needed to be far enough away, safe in the corn before that happened.

There was a click, some distance across the clearing behind them.

And then:

Thwwuump!

Nothing. Frendo missed. By a wide enough margin, Quinn didn't even hear the whistle and thrum of a near miss. They were home free.

Quinn and Janet bounded across the finish line of the corn as one, the world instantly darker, decibels quieter, the leaves around them absorbing the screams from back in the clearing.

Quinn had no idea where she was going, if they were headed toward or away from the cars, but she figured that getting away from the barn, from Frendo, was the safest move regardless.

A few yards into the tall corn, Janet started tugging at Quinn's arm, asking to stop. But Quinn kept them moving. Janet's war howls weakened and then finally stopped altogether. The girl was heavier in Quinn's arms. Janet would lose consciousness soon. And not only consciousness, if they couldn't stop the bleeding . . .

Quinn didn't want to think about it.

She wasn't going to let anyone else die. Not when there was something she could do to help. It wasn't going to happen on her watch. Not again.

"Where are the cars, Janet? Are we going the right way?"

Janet was keeping pace beside her, leaning into her, but she didn't answer. She only groaned, like someone trying to sleep in, snooze their alarm, resist a parent's annoying wakeup call.

Leaves licked at Quinn's face, underwatered corncobs bouncing off the side of her head. The edges of the leaves felt like they were leaving tiny paper cuts. Quinn's face was wet, her hair likely curling against the stress and humidity, the ghost of her mother crawling back into her features, taking over her body.

It was quiet. Where had all the other partygoers gone? Had anyone else made it out? The escapees, the ones who'd be interviewed, crying, on the six-o'clock news?

It was so dark out here. She looked up to see why. There was cloud cover now. Was it about to rain? Would that help or hurt their escape?

Would a cool rain wake her from this nightmare? Would it wash away the sweat, blood, beer, and pain?

If she did wake, would it be in Philadelphia or in Kettle Springs?

"Quinn!"

Hearing her own name jolted her back to the here and now.

"Rust?" Quinn said into the darkness. A cloud passed as Rust emerged from the corn in front of them.

She wanted so badly to throw herself into her neighbor's arms, but she was the only thing keeping Janet on her feet.

Janet, still being Janet, couldn't help but snark: "That's good, the Mounties have arrived."

"Oh, shit," Ruston Vance said, despair in his voice as he noticed Janet's wound. Was this the first time she'd heard him swear?

"Help me with her."

Quinn let Rust take over holding Janet. She straightened herself and rolled her shoulders to get the kinks out. "We were trying to get to the cars."

"I was just there. It's not good. All the tires are slashed. Batteries pulled. This guy did that first."

"Seriously?" Quinn started to pace, then lowered her voice, unsure if they were being hunted out here in the corn: "What is going on, Rust?"

"I don't know," Rust said to her, "but he didn't think of everything."

The boy swung a duffel bag off his shoulder and let it clatter on the ground. Whatever was inside, it was heavy.

They all crouched, Rust careful to prop Janet onto her hands and knees so she didn't fall back onto the arrow and injure herself further.

He placed the bag on the dirt, took out a small flashlight, and clicked it on, cupping his hand to shield the beam.

"Unzip it." He nodded down, both hands busy.

Quinn did, working to open the bag but somehow knowing what she'd see before she saw it.

Guns.

The bag was full of guns and boxes of bullets.

Rust clicked off the flashlight.

"Here. We can't risk using this." He handed Quinn the light and she put it into a pocket.

"Guns?"

"I had them locked in the rack. The guy'd broken out my windows. I could see he'd tried, but he couldn't get them loose. And I keep shells and the Browning in a safe box under my seat." He pointed down, as if she'd know which one was supposed to be the "Browning."

"This is insane. I'm not shooting anyone. We should be calling the police, let them take care of it."

"Oh yeah," Rust asked, "and how much luck are you having with your cellular carrier out here?"

"Give me one," Janet said, lurching forward, hand grasping blindly in the darkness. The girl's voice was hazy, weak, and faraway. Quinn wouldn't trust Janet with a spork right now.

"Here, here," Quinn said, handing over her phone to Janet. "Keep trying nine-one-one."

Janet shook her head, lips turned out, an exaggerated frown.

"No. Not the phone. Give. Me. A. Gun." She was loud now, too loud.

"Be. Quiet," Quinn hissed.

"Now!" Janet raged, an angry-toddler slur in her voice. "I'll shoot the fuck, if you pussies . . ."

"Shhh. Shh. Janet, here," Rust said, whispering. He reached into the bag, pulled out a small handgun, and handed it over. "That's it, Janet. You guard our backs."

"Okay," Janet said, her head lolling down, pacified, now that she had the gun in her hand.

"I thought you said you only have guns to hunt. How is that a hunting gun?" Quinn whispered, pointing to the small gun in Janet's hand.

"It's for clean kills, Quinn. I don't want to let an animal suffer," Rust hissed. "First things first, we need to get that bolt out of her."

He removed a rifle from the duffel, took a single bullet from his breast pocket, fed it into the side, then placed the gun in the dirt next to him.

Janet didn't react. She was in her own world, turning the pistol over and over in her hands. Watching her play with it made Quinn unbearably tense.

Rust must have noticed her concern. He made a gesture with his hands and mouthed, *Not loaded*.

Quinn nodded her understanding. Okay. Nice work.

Rust had thought fast and come up with a way to keep Janet quiet without putting anyone in harm's way.

"We'll use my belt as a tourniquet," Rust said, removing his flannel shirt, then tugging at the seams to tear off one sleeve. His undershirt was sweat-stained and there were holes, but now wasn't the time to judge. "We'll get the bolt out, pack the wound. Tighten it for pressure. It's the best we can do."

"We need to get her to a hospital."

"Yeah, we do, but without a truck . . ." He clicked his tongue, frustrated. Like Quinn, he was only trying to do what he thought was best with what they had at hand. "Look, right now, I think, staying hidden out here is our best bet. The shooter would have to get really lucky to find us. Hopefully someone made it to the road and is already bringing the cops."

"So we wait like sitting ducks?" Quinn asked, trying and failing to mask her frustration.

"I don't like it, either. But he doesn't know we're armed. We can probably fire in the air and scare him off. And worst-case scenario, I figure we're here a couple hours. Parents are going to notice as soon as one of the younger kids is out past curfew."

Which reminded her. "Oh God, my dad. He's going to be . . ."

"I know," Rust said, "but don't think about it. Nothing we can do. Think about helping me with her."

"Okay," Quinn said.

"Hold her down and I'll pull it out, okay?" He turned to Janet, said her name, but she barely responded. "Janet," Rust said again. Even in the low light, Quinn could tell that her color had changed. "Janet, I know you can hear me. This is going to hurt."

"You sure you know what you're doing?" Quinn asked, squeezing Janet's arms to her side, her flesh clammy, her body limp, Quinn playing her shoulders like an accordion.

"We took a field first-aid course when I was a Boy Scout."

"You're a Boy Scout?"

"Well, I was probably eleven or twelve."

"Fuck," Quinn said. "Then swap with me. My dad's a doctor. I'll deal with it."

"Suit yourself," Rust said, sidling past Quinn to hold Janet by the shoulders.

Slipping further into shock, Janet didn't lose her essential Janet-ness. As Rust took hold of her, Janet tried waving him away. Telling him to leave her alone. Mumbling that he was a loser.

"Redneck Rust," Janet burbled. "Pew pew, small pee-pee," she said, playing with the gun in her lap.

"Whenever you're ready," Rust said to Quinn, the slightest wisp of dark humor in his voice.

Quinn yanked at the arrow. It didn't move at first, but she pulled harder, worried she was making the wound even wider in her struggle. Janet gave a short, loud scream, but Rust didn't bother trying to shush her.

When the bolt loosened, it came all at once, the blunted arrowhead disengaging from the bone, and the rest of the journey out of muscle and fat rendered into a quick *slurp!*

As soon as the arrow was out, blood started to flow, filling the wound. Quinn could've counted Janet's pulse against the ebbs, a slow bubbling fountain. She quickly applied Rust's ripped flannel sleeve to the hole, pressing down with all her might, then worked his belt around Janet's arm and chest, cinching it as tight as she could.

"I hope this works." Quinn sighed, sitting back, her hands caked in Janet's blood.

Somewhere during the short procedure, Janet had passed out from the pain. Quinn smiled to think that, with Janet's final words, she'd been able to roast Rust.

Rust checked her pulse. "Weak, but there," he said, easing off his haunches, onto the dirt. He exhaled before reaching over to lay his gun across his lap. He grabbed his balled flannel shirt, not to supplement the thin white undershirt, but to search the pocket for more bullets.

"Great party, by the way," Quinn said. The flush in her cheeks was like the tingle from a roller coaster, and before she'd spoken, she'd felt tears crowding her vision. She shook her head.

"You should see what they do for New Year's." But his

heart wasn't in it—he was focused, feeding at least five or six more rounds into the long rifle.

Quinn craned her neck and looked up. There was a thick black cloud encroaching on the moon, blocking out the stars. But still the sky in Kettle Springs was too big to be blocked out. It was so much bigger, so much brighter here than in Philadelphia; it was almost impossible to imagine both places were under the same heavens. But imagining home, even for just a moment, only made her remember that she was in Tillerson's field, which made her think:

Where is their house?

She was about to ask the question aloud when she smelled it:

That wasn't a *cloud* moving across the moon.

That was smoke.

FIFTEEN

"Holy shit! He set the barn on fire! They're going to die!" Cole screamed, then broke Ronnie's grip on his shoulder and dove for the latch. He grabbed hold of the bolt, which was still coated with Erin Werther's blood and hair.

"Don't, Cole," Matt said. "You're not the only person in here, you know. We have to decide as a team."

Cole stopped, turned back in place to look at his friend.

Matt Trent was standing, hands out, at the junction where the dirt floor of the old silo met the slating of the grain pit. Behind him there were hay bales and antique farm equipment. It must have been years since the Tillersons had used this building for its intended purpose: the silo was miscellaneous storage now.

Behind the door, Cole could hear frantic screams, some

muffled, some out in the open of the clearing. Maybe the crowd in the barn had gotten the doors open and was fleeing the flames.

Thwack.

The thrum of the crossbow.

Cole's hand tensed on the improvised latch, ready to pull out the bolt and open the door.

"Don't! He's right out there, Cole. And he knows we're in here," Matt continued.

Then the thrum came again. Where most people would be fatigued, pulling back at least seventy-five pounds of pressure to reload over and over, this maniac seemed to be getting faster as he fired.

The clown was shooting the kids in the barn as they tried to escape the fire! Cole had to help.

"We know you want to be a hero, but you have to be reasonable. We could get out of this alive," Ronnie said, backing up her boyfriend. She crept a step closer to Cole, Matt matching her, the two of them surrounding him. "You remember a few years ago? You said we'd all be running this town one day. Well, we can't if we're dead."

Cole let go of the door and the bolt, his fingers tacky from Erin Werther's blood.

"What's that supposed to mean?" he asked.

Matt made calming hands, trying to defuse what his

girlfriend had started: "She just means that you're not thinking clearly. And you have other people in here to think about. Even *if* you don't care about your own safety. Haven't since Victoria."

"We know the Baypen fire wasn't a mistake," Ronnie said, cutting to the point. "Tucker told us that you wanted to die in there."

"Bullshit," Cole heard himself saying, not wanting to get into this now. "We were drunk. We were all drunk. I'm not fucking suicidal."

"Then if you're not," Matt reasoned, "don't open that door. We're safe in here."

The smell of smoke was stronger now. Smoke and something else . . . Cole's mouth started to involuntarily water, which in turn caused him to gag.

"Get him, Matt. Now," Ronnie said, but Matt hesitated.

Fuck them. Cole whirled, was able to pull the bolt through the latch before Matt's hands were on him.

This wasn't Matt's job on the football field, and it was clear he wasn't used to it. Nowhere in the playbook was Matt Trent expected to put hands on another player. His job was the opposite: avoid contact, run and glide and catch. Everything about Matt's small, strong hands latching onto Cole's shoulder's felt wrong, a violation of natural law.

"Let go of me," Cole screamed, wedging his hand in

between the doorframe, pulling the door open at the same time that Matt was pulling him back. Cole still held the crossbow bolt, was waving it.

"He's crazy," Ronnie screeched. "Knock him out or something, Matt. Do it."

Cole could see the flames outside the silo. The barn crackled and spit, the smell of smoke and burned hair strong in Cole's nose and eyes.

He didn't let go of the doorframe, though, got a second hand on it and pulled, still not dropping the bolt. Matt may have been strong, but he was still small and Cole had leverage.

"Nooooo!" Cole gave a straining yell. Ronnie had added herself to the tug-of-war. Cole's arms felt like they were about to pop right out of their sockets.

And then, suddenly, Frendo's face was covering the foot-wide sliver of doorway.

The tapered end of a crossbow bolt pressed into the hollow between Cole's left eye and his nose, a dot of blood welling there.

"Fuck you!" Cole screamed, angry, scared, but above all: ready.

Cole gave one final burst of strength, pulling against Ronnie and Matt, getting closer to the loaded crossbow, the metal cool, then let one hand off the doorframe so he could try to stab at the clown with the bolt.

But he didn't get there. Almost, but he only nicked him.

The result of removing the one hand was like an elastic band snapping and the second hand pulled loose. With a crossbow pointed into Cole's skull—Cole waiting for the trigger to be pulled and his brain to be scrambled—Matt and Ronnie's combined strength slingshot all three of them back into the silo.

Matt screamed, Ronnie screamed, and all three scrambled to their feet, trying to close the door as on the other side, Frendo dropped the end of the crossbow down, yowling at the wide scratch in his exposed chin and neck.

Cole had done better than he thought.

Matt was the first to the handle, pulling to shut the door, but the space now wedged open six, seven inches.

Frendo had placed his foot in the tread, wedging the door open. The shoe wasn't a polished red clown shoe, bulbous and exaggerated, but a simple black combat boot.

"Open it!" Cole yelled, reeling back with his fist.

"No!" Matt yelled.

"Just a little!" Ronnie responded, finally in agreement with Cole, finally saying something tonight that wasn't hateful and cruel.

Matt yanked the door back and Cole let loose, punching the clown in the face, staggering the tall man in combat boots enough that they could get the door shut and close the latch, Ronnie returning the bolt.

They all stepped back from the wall, Cole nearly tripping over Erin's body.

"Okay," Ronnie said, all of them breathing heavy. "Can we please agree to keep it closed for now?"

And before Cole could respond, somewhere in the distance, maybe even outside the clearing, there was the distinct crack of a gunshot.

SIXTEEN

The gun felt alive in Quinn's hands.

A poisonous snake, ready to turn its head back and bite her on the wrist.

"I can't do this. I don't want to take this," Quinn begged.

"Yes, you *can* do this," Rust said. "You need to." He pointed to the barn fire, then looked down to his empty duffel bag.

At least he hadn't traversed the corn with a bag full of three *loaded* guns. Which did seem responsible. In a way. While Rust took the time to load the rifle and the shotgun, he taught Quinn the phrase "trigger discipline" and explained the different nobs, levers, and safeties.

It was hard to pay attention as the smell of smoke grew, but she tried.

"This is a shotgun and it has a fairly wide spread. You *will* hit whatever you fire at—and everything standing nearby. So keep your finger here"—he moved her hand in his, calluses scratching in the cold—"and *do not* touch the trigger unless you intend to fire."

Quinn nodded. The weapon's stock was beginning to warm against her skin. It felt like the weapon was breathing.

"Safety's on and it's already cocked. No movie stuff, you won't need to work the pump, just flick this off," he said, pointing, "and squeeze."

The smoke was getting worse and the horizon line had begun to glow. At least they wouldn't get lost on their way back to the party.

"Keep dialing, Janet," Quinn said.

The injured girl had the pistol in one hand, phone in the other, and her chin was beginning to nod. Quinn worried she was going to slip back into unconsciousness. Janet was wearing Rust's flannel now, her tourniquet and packing forming a hump on her shoulder. If she passed out again, they might never be able to wake her.

"There's no service, Quinn." Her voice mocking, frustrated. "Are you sure you paid the bill?"

"Janet. Shush. Don't make a sound," Rust said. "We'll come back and get you. Just hang tight, okay."

"I mean. If I don't shoot you two first," Janet said with a demented smile. "Just k—" She coughed twice; it sounded wet. "Just kidding. But if I see Frendo, I *will* shoot Frendo. Fucking clown deserves to die."

Rust looked over to Quinn, a pained *Should I tell her?* expression on his face. This was clearly a moral quandary for him, leaving an unarmed person thinking they were armed.

Quinn shook her head. If it gave Janet a bit more comfort, thinking she had a loaded gun and could defend herself, then maybe that revenge fantasy could help keep the girl awake and alive. The answer certainly couldn't be leaving her with a loaded handgun.

"I can't," Rust said, his conscience winning out over Quinn's input.

He loaded Janet's gun for her, then patted her hand: "Don't make me regret this. Okay? Stay awake, stay alive."

"I'm sorry," Janet said, her voice soft and vulnerable, more sure of her words than she'd sounded since entering the corn.

"For what?" Rust asked.

"That I was always so mean to you . . ." She paused. "You stupid hick."

"It's fine." Rust smiled, then stood. "I'm sorry, too, you spoiled asshole." Janet smiled and licked her lips and nodded for them to go.

"Let's do this," Quinn said.

Rust led the way and she stayed close.

The trip back to the barn didn't take long. And here

Quinn was, thinking she'd brought the injured Janet deep into the safety of the corn, when in reality they'd only traveled maybe a few hundred yards from the barn, walking a straight line.

The two crouched at the edge of the cornfield.

Quinn looked over Rust's shoulders at the fire that'd engulfed the barn, orange shadows dancing across his face and rifle stock. She worried that the off-white of his exposed undershirt made him too visible.

Out in the clearing, there was no sign of the clown—the shooter, as Rust had more accurately called him. But the maniac could have been anywhere. From here, they could only see the barn's closed rear doors, the structure blocking most of the clearing and silo from view.

Not that it was easy to look away from the barn itself.

Flames were licking the sides of the building, catching and climbing to the corrugated tin roof. Knots of wood popped, sparks flying, accelerating the flames wherever the embers touched. Sections of the barn's roof and sides would begin to collapse soon.

The smell of smoke wafting down off the barn reeked of chemicals and charred meat, made worse by the sounds coming from inside.

Cracks, screams, and the banging of fists against the closed back doors. The howl of the fire was a constant *whirring* under it all.

In the field opposite them, Quinn thought she could hear the snap of a bowstring. But it could have been an auditory hallucination, something her subconscious had been expecting to hear, dreading.

"He locked them in," Rust said, pointing with the end of his rifle to the door.

She squinted against the flames and spied the metallic sheen of a chain, padlocked in the center, joining the handles of the two barn doors on the outside. Well, that explained why their classmates couldn't escape.

"Now. We have to go now," Quinn said, raising her own gun, not feeling confident, but focusing instead on what Rust had taught her about how to use her gun. She needed to be sure to plant herself and brace the stock before firing, he'd explained. "Be careful or the recoil will break a rib."

They ran for the doors, heads on swivels, checking that a homicidal clown wasn't standing in the shadows, ready to pick them off when they tried to help.

"Switch with me," Rust said as they reached the barn doors. Even outside the building, the fire was almost unbearably hot. Quinn's lips were immediately dry, felt ready to crack. Her eyes were watering from the heat.

Quinn and Rust swapped weapons.

Someone on the other side of the door must have seen them through a crack.

"Hey. There's someone out there," they said.

"HEEEEELLPP," a voice, the gender indistinct, yelled. The word turned into a jagged, burning screech.

The doors swung outward on their hinges, then stopped short. The chain and padlock held firm, pulled taut, as the survivors inside pressed against them, panicking, looking to be saved. The entire building groaned as the doors shifted. As fists banged, ash floated down onto Quinn's skin.

"Step back!" Rust yelled at them, but now the kids inside were all screaming, becoming a raving, jabbering hive mind. They didn't ease up on the door—instead their words mingled and canceled each other out.

"WE'REDYINGHELPUSBURNINGDEADHE'S-STILLSHOOTING"

"Please," Rust screamed. "I have to shoot the lock! Step back!" Rust tried again, but there seemed to be no getting through to the KSH students inside. They'd been driven insane in their fear and pain. Rust shook his head, looked over to Quinn. "You step back, at least," he said, frustrated.

She did, not wanting to leave him alone. But not too far—she didn't want to become a target for the clown by moving too far away from the cover of the building.

Rust knelt, putting the shotgun as close as he could to horizontal, resting the butt in the dirt, the top of the padlock wedged against the barrel.

"Everyone inside get back!" he tried one more time, then fired.

The blast sheared off a chunk of the barn doors, a rain of splinters floating down. But it was the upper part—hopefully he'd avoided killing anyone.

Rust stood, reached for the padlock, then pulled his hand back. In his eagerness to remove the chain, he'd burned himself.

He hadn't needed to touch the chain, though. The doors strained, the top loop of the lock twisting. The chain loosened, then fell away. Smoke and teenagers fell out of the widening gap between the barn doors. Spines and necks were stepped on, tears running down soot-streaked faces. The doors pushed outward on their hinges and were pulled apart at the same time.

Quinn and Rust needed to take a few quick steps to the side, to avoid being crushed by the stampede. Twenty or thirty KSH students spilled out, found their feet, and then hopped, stumbled, or were carried into the cornfield.

None of them seemed to see Quinn and Rust. The two of them were, at most, another obstacle to avoid on the way to the safety of the corn.

A boy with black marks running down from his nostrils and patches of singed hair caught sight of them, then did a double take at their weaponry. He stopped his retreat. He was wearing a singed T-shirt that read "Cool Story, Bro" and a tattered and burned Hawaiian shirt over that. Earlier in the night, the boy was what Quinn would have described as "trying too hard." He probably would have been thrilled if a girl had deigned to talk to him, but now he was crying dirty tears, thankful to be alive.

The boy in the Hawaiian shirt crossed to where Quinn and Rust were watching the procession of survivors and grabbed Rust by the shoulder.

"He left the front door open," the boy managed through his sobs. "He's killin' em as they try to run for—"

But the boy's words were cut short by a crossbow round to the ear, head kicked back, neck turned to rubber.

Rust closed his eyes against the spatter of blood, the dots of it looking black in the firelight, dripping down his pale stubble.

Quinn whirled. Frendo had rounded the corner of the barn and was standing, feet planted, crossbow still raised, maybe twenty feet away.

The clown tilted his head, painted smile demonic as the flames played across his plastic mask.

Quinn didn't think. Didn't calculate the odds she'd hit him. Didn't reflect on her strong anti-gun views. The petitions she'd signed. The marches and candlelight vigils she'd attended with Tessa and Jace. She didn't even remember the frustration she'd once felt at a street fair midway, claiming the game was rigged when her BB gun couldn't shoot the center out of a red paper star.

She merely braced the rifle, took one last look at Frendo the Clown, placed her finger on the trigger.

And squeeeeeezed.

Rust had been right, she would have broken a rib if she'd held the gun any lower. As it were, she might have done permanent damage to her hearing and was going to have a helluva bruise.

Only after the blast did the clown tilt his mask to acknowledge Quinn directly.

Oh no. She hadn't hit him.

Quinn's hands scrambled to switch positions. The clown hadn't cried out, hadn't been tossed backward by the shot—she *must* have missed. Her left hand searched for the lever she needed to pull back and forward to advance the next . . .

She'd started this adventure, this rescue mission, with the shotgun. This *wasn't supposed to be her gun* and she hadn't been paying much attention as Rust explained how to work the rifle.

But then she saw it.

To the right side of the clown's second pom-pom button, there was a rose blooming against Frendo's chest. The mark spread, then began to dribble, then pump. Like a clown's water-gun flower.

She pulled the lever to her. The spent shell spiraled away, grazed the back of her hand. It was not hot enough to burn, but still warm, even next to the flames whooshing out from the barn.

She pushed forward, loading the weapon, and fired again.

The second shot dropped Frendo back.

"She did it," someone—not Rust—said behind her, a straggler leaving the barn or a survivor who'd been too dazed to run for the cover of the cornfield.

Rust was at Quinn's side, time again seeming to skip forward a few seconds. He moved slowly, working a thumb around in circles on the back of her neck as he directed the end of the rifle down to the ground with his other hand.

He'd dropped his shotgun to the dirt between them.

"It's okay. You did good. You did good," he said, soothing. "You did what you had to."

Quinn couldn't speak. Couldn't do anything but let him point the rifle's barrel to the dirt. Her grip was tight against the wood. If Rust had tried to pry the rifle from her hands, she wouldn't have let it go.

"Hey, he's dead. The new girl shot him!" someone yelled, calling some of the partygoers back to the burning barn.

Shot who?

Who did she kill?

"Who is it?" Quinn said, working the words out her dry lips. It was unclear if Rust heard. Beside them, a length of tin roofing collapsed into the barn with a clatter. Wood popped and flames whooshed.

Quinn walked forward, knowing that if the barn buckled and collapsed in the wrong direction, she'd be burned up in the resulting fireball, maybe even crushed under flaming lumber.

But she had to know.

With very little ceremony, Quinn knelt to Frendo, noting the dark half-inch hole her second shot had punched in the bridge of his nose, and pried off the mask.

Who would want to do this? Who would—

Oh. Apparently, a science teacher would.

Mr. Vern's dead eyes stared up at her, his small mustache frothed with blood and spit.

SEVENTEEN

"I can smell 'em burnin'," someone said, the voice vaguely behind and above where Janet Murray lay.

Janet blinked against the darkness, dust coating her eyelashes. Had she blacked out again? She was flat on her belly. Her mouth tasted like soil and copper. She'd fallen asleep, facedown in the cornfield.

God. Her shoulder was completely numb now. Her brain felt fuzzy, dreamy.

That couldn't be good.

She peered over at the small black gun in her hand.

It was loaded now, wasn't it?

Redneck Rust had called it a Browning. She'd known at one point, in another life, but was that a make or a model? She furrowed her brows, scrutinized the object.

It wasn't clear how long Quinn and Rust had been gone. Could have been minutes, could have been hours that they'd left her here. Alone.

"How many primary targets confirmed?"

The voice was still talking. The cornfield absorbed sound; her grogginess and the dull ringing in her ears made her hearing echo. She couldn't tell how close this voice was or even how many people were speaking.

"None confirmed. But Hill is safe." A voice, tinny and hollow, returned. There were at least two of them, but . . .

Confirmed? Targets?

They talked like cops! The cops were here!

Janet swallowed hard, trying to get enough spit down her throat that she'd be heard when she called for help.

"Not *one*?" a voice asked. "Not even the Murray girl? I was betting she'd be first to go. Vern hates her."

Wait, what? *Janet* was the only Murray girl in town.

These weren't cops. Who and what was she listening to? Why were they talking about her?

Somewhere, there was an electronic chirp. Janet looked at the phone in her other hand, suddenly worried it would give away her location. The phone was Quinn's. It was on silent. She pressed the screen down into the dirt, desperately, frantically aware that, whoever was speaking, a few feet behind and above her in the field:

They. Weren't. Cops.

"Is the new girl a primary target? Or a bonus objective, because—"

The chirp again, then static: that wasn't a phone. It was a radio.

"The barn failed! I repeat. Barn failed. Somebody opened up the back. They're running out. They're moving west! Quick! Clean up! Now! Clean up!"

"Oh shit," the voice said, groaning with exertion, sounding like he was lifting something cumbersome.

Then there were footfalls. Moving toward Janet's hiding spot. These weren't cops, her mind repeated again, not helping.

More shuffling steps. Buckles, equipment, and zippers clanging. Getting closer. Janet was sure they were going to trip right over her.

Janet held her breath, made herself smaller, felt like she was going to sob. She dropped the phone, freeing a hand to plaster over her mouth and nose. Holding any sound in.

The muscles in her shoulders and arms twitched as she flexed. She felt life returning to her body, which made the pain in her back flare. She couldn't focus. She knew she wouldn't be able to keep this position longer, her gun arm outstretched, the rest of her hugged tight in the fetal position.

Her fingers felt white, bloodless. She fought the instinct to squeeze her eyes shut as the footfalls approached.

Heavy combat boots crushed cornstalks mere inches

from where Janet was hiding. She turned her eyes up to see that the boots were connected to polka-dot pant legs.

The boots jogged by. Their owner not stopping, not seeing Janet.

Shoot him.

Shoot him!

But she couldn't, and he disappeared out of sight before she could will herself to act.

A few breaths later, there were other sounds.

Kids, screaming, crying, relieved, telling each other that the nightmare was over. That they'd be home soon. Home soon. I know you're burned, but just hold on. You'll live.

Janet was the only one who knew they *weren't* headed toward safety.

Knew that she was the only one who could save them, could warn them.

Janet tried to move to her feet. An ache shot from the base of her wound, moving outward and splintering like an electric shock. From the tips of her toes to the marrow of her shoulder blade, probably chipped, soon to be infected by Redneck Rust's dirty shirtsleeve.

She lay back down, almost falling on the gun, throwing her elbow out to catch her at the last second.

Why should she leave her hiding spot?

Yer not from around here.

That's the first thing Janet could remember a classmate

saying to her, nearly fifteen years ago. She'd ruined that boy and his OshKosh clothing. Tom Mathers. Yeah. It'd been Tom Mathers. She'd made him cry on the playground. Years later, in middle school, she'd spread a rumor that *he* was the reason they were being screened for lice. Because Janet Murray might not have been from around here, but she knew where she was going and she never forgot what they said to her along the way.

Janet Murray hadn't gotten where she was in Kettle Springs by caring about other people.

Maybe that was why she liked Quinn so much so quickly. Janet saw herself in the girl. She used to live in a city, too. Once upon a time. So Tom Mathers had been right: she wasn't from here.

Janet had been born in Cincinnati. She lived in a nice little house, had a nice little life, until Dad up and left. Her mom worked two jobs and dated desperately until she met Alec Murray while he was visiting Ohio on business. They fell in love, married in a matter of months, and then she and Janet packed and moved with him to his stupid, giant house in Kettle Springs the month before Janet started first grade.

And Janet knew from the first day, the first minute, she landed in Kettle Springs that she wasn't going to survive her terminally basic stepdad and this terminally basic town by being *nice*.

But the truth was that she didn't wind up hating her

classmates as much as she wanted to. Frankly, she didn't hate anyone. Outside of a few instances of schoolyard weirdness, especially in those first years, the kids of Kettle Springs were kind of cool. They were woke. To a point. Well, woke-er than their parents. And by the time she got to high school, if not well before that, Janet considered herself one of them. For better or worse, Kettle Springs was her home, was her town, was now where she was from, fucker.

And so, it was not acceptable that her people, her friends, her classmates, were running straight into a trap while she could do something about it. This was her party. They were her guests. She couldn't allow it. And she had the will and the firepower to stop it.

Janet pushed herself to her feet and left her hiding place, shoulder throbbing.

Her legs felt like they were about to buckle out from under her, jellied knees breaking inward, but after two steps she was walking, then two more and soon she was running.

"Back!" Janet screamed, tried to scream, but the word came out as a wheeze.

She could do this. That clodhopper in the combat boots: she could outrun him. She could kill him.

She could save everyone.

"Get back!" she yelled, finally finding her voice. "Run! There's more than one clown!"

EIGHTEEN

In January 2014, Samantha Maybrook slipped on the icy front step of her family's trinity home, in the Fairmount district of Philadelphia, and chipped her tailbone.

It was a small chip. About a fingernail's width.

It took three days of the bruise worsening—Samantha was willing to miss work, but unable to sit and enjoy her time home—for her to agree to get an X-ray.

Yes. She'd broken her coccyx. Which wasn't great, but the injury wasn't life-threatening. The doctor was happy to report that the chip wouldn't require surgery. They'd medicate and keep an eye on mobility and bruising. If the fracture didn't heal in a few months, then, and only then, would a referral to a specialist be on the table.

The doc was in-network with their insurance, but

Samantha Maybrook could have gone to Penn or Jefferson. The coverage she got being on her husband's insurance was great. No. She'd gone to this doctor even before she and Glenn had been married, she argued, and she liked him.

The doctor prescribed her two pills: a stool softener, because the pain of straining on the toilet could be the worst part of an injury like this, and an opioid for the discomfort. The opioid, ironically, would cause constipation, so at least in the first days, she'd better double up on the stool softener and drink plenty of water.

That first night, when she'd been worried about the effects of the painkiller and only taken a third of a pill, a dusty sliver so small she'd needed to take it with a spoon, Glenn had joked about Quinn's junkie mom and Quinn had laughed.

Neither of them were laughing on the way to pick Samantha up from rehab in February 2017.

Or stuck in funerary traffic, snaking down from the service at Laurel Hill Cemetery.

That death had meant something. Had fundamentally changed who Quinn Maybrook was.

But *this* death . . .

Quinn didn't know what she expected to feel, having taken a human life—even a life that had ended while doing a horribly evil thing.

She looked into Mr. Vern's face. The Frendo mask had

slipped off easily. The exit wound from her second shot had popped the back of Mr. Vern's head like a water balloon. His crossbow was at her feet, and Quinn noticed that Mr. Vern's weapon had a bright pink camo pattern. Why would anyone make a pink camouflage crossbow? So strange. The whole thing was just so strange.

"There's a lot of burns," Rust said, interrupting her reverie. The neighbor boy put a hand on her shoulder and guided her back from the body and the soon-to-collapse barn.

The survivors from the barn were arranged behind them in a half circle.

The group coughed and trembled despite the heat. There were maybe fifteen in all. Most had run off into the cornfield without looking back.

"What are we going to do? Some of them look like they can't even walk," Quinn said, scanning the scene.

"We should head out to the road," Rust said, nodding in the general direction of where the street had to be. "We still need to get an ambulance out here."

It sounded like a good plan and Quinn couldn't argue. Frankly, she was too exhausted. She didn't even know if she could handle the half-a-mile walk back to the main road.

Rust was gathering up their stuff when Quinn heard the scream.

"Run!"

"Janet?" Quinn asked, turning to face the sound.

"Run!" Janet yelled again, before she could be seen. "Run!!"

Two or three bodies broke through the edge of the cornfield ahead of Janet's warning.

"There's more clowns! They're coming! Run. Run! Run!!!"

Finally, Janet limped to the edge of the clearing, looked to the group of survivors, then spotted Rust and Quinn, and bounded toward them.

Janet was holding the handgun out in front of her, waving it around. Quinn flinched. They'd come so far, only to be shot by their friend, hallucinating from her trauma and armed because Rust felt guilty leaving her with an unloaded gun.

"It's revenge! You've got to listen," Janet raved, her voice pleading. Even from this distance, Quinn could see Rust's borrowed flannel shirt had been blotted solid with blood and dirt. Janet must've noticed how she was holding the gun then and pointed it up at the sky.

"This isn't one person," Janet continued. "This is revenge. They're killing *us* because—"

Brrrmm. Brrrrmm.

The loud rev of a motor drowned out Janet's words.

The sound caused Quinn's muscles to lock up, stop midstride.

Quinn's vision got sharper by degrees and the smell of

smoke returned, possibly because the wind changed, possibly because the adrenaline drip was back.

Quinn was no longer tired, because she'd gone back to being terrified.

At a full gallop, Frendo the Clown followed Janet out of the cornfield. He was no longer carrying a crossbow.

Instead, the clown carried a large, whirring circular saw. It was a two-handed piece of equipment—a weapon—its blade measuring at least a foot and a half in diameter. The end under the clown's elbow spewed thick gray smoke out into the night.

The clown was faster than Janet, and it wasn't long before he'd closed the distance. She seemed to sense he was there, though, and turned to face him before she was overtaken.

She couldn't get the gun up, though. He swung once as Janet attempted to dive away. From this vantage, it looked like he barely connected. He grazed Janet's chest, a fine mist of blood fanning out into the air. Rust's leather belt snapped loose from around Janet's shoulder and her compress unraveled as she ran backward.

"No!" Quinn yelled, raising the rifle. If she couldn't run to Janet, she could at least shoot the bastard.

Janet wobbled forward as Frendo stepped back. There was an unsatisfying click as Quinn attempted to fire at the clown. She hadn't advanced the bolt. It didn't matter—she didn't have a clear shot, anyway.

"Get down," Rust screamed to Janet. She was five feet away now, the clown maybe six.

The follow-through of the clown's first swing had thrown the attacker off-balance, but instead of falling, he let the momentum of the heavy, whirling blade drag him around.

The clown, broader in the chest and shoulders than Mr. Vern, made a complete 360 in a ballerina's pirouette.

Coming back around into a second swing, the circular saw cut Janet's head from her body. She fell backward in a halting, dislocated heap, the pop of the handgun sounding only once, as Janet's head hit the dirt.

Quinn wished she'd looked away, hadn't seen Janet's body trip over her own face.

With Janet out of the way, Rust took two more steps toward the clown and pulled the trigger.

Sparks flew from the end of the shotgun, blasting this Frendo backward into the dirt.

There was no need for a second shot. The left side of Frendo's torso had been blown apart, the man nearly torn in half.

The motor of the circular saw idled, then died, the clown's hands letting off the throttle.

And like that, the clearing was back to quiet.

Behind them, more of the barn collapsed in a soft rustle of ash and cinders.

"Why are they doing this!" someone yelled, but nobody offered an answer.

Rust tapped Quinn on the elbow, pointing.

Janet had been right. There was more than one clown. A lot more than one.

To the south, the direction of the road, two clowns stepped out of the cover of the cornfield. One carried a long, hooked blade, the other a chainsaw, gently idling, waiting to be revved.

From the far side of the barn, another clown sucked his teeth, the sound getting them to turn, his body language gloating that he had flanked them. He had a crossbow—no pink accents—at the ready. Had this been the one who'd shot Ginger, the murderer who'd started this whole thing? It seemed right. He was huge, where Mr. Vern had been quite reedy in class.

To the east, dragging behind him a mewling, babbling freshman, came a Frendo with two hands on a wooden staff. No, not a staff: a pitchfork, his victim impaled at his feet, stuck in the tines. To the side of him stood another clown, smaller, slimmer, hefting an ax.

They were surrounded on at least three sides, the clowns seemingly unconcerned that their victims had guns, that the kids had already blown away two of their members.

The men in the masks walked in sync, cinching closed

the noose. The clowns stalked forward on heavy boots, looking ready to cut and chop and shoot them down.

"RUN!" Rust yelled, lowering his gun to his waist and firing at the nearest clown, the big one who'd crept from around the front of the barn with the crossbow. The shot went wide, only peppering the clown's side and shoulder. The man spun and howled, but not before getting a shot of his own off, the arrow sailing into the small crowd of survivors.

Quinn didn't need to be told again. She followed Rust, advancing a new round into the rifle as she went.

They needed to run north, toward the only place there weren't visible attackers. Or was that what the clowns wanted? Were they being herded?

Paranoia nagged at Quinn as she ran. This was insane. This wasn't a lone-wolf shooter; it was a nightmare army made of Kettle Springs' goofy mascot, multiplied. She remembered one of Janet's last words, her warning: this was revenge.

Juking past him, Quinn and Rust gave the injured clown with the crossbow as wide a berth as possible, Rust shuffling with his pant pockets, presumably grabbing for more bullets—no, shells, they were called shells, he'd been serious about that distinction when they were talking in the field.

They were passing between the ruined barn, smoking

bodies littering the parted front doors, and the silo, when Quinn heard a voice cry out.

"Rust, Quinn! Over here!"

Cole Hill was standing in the doorway to the silo, was waving to them, then suddenly disappeared, looking like he'd been yanked back inside.

Quinn turned, and two of the clowns—the pitchfork and the ax—were in pursuit, while the other three had begun to descend upon the group of barn survivors. The stunned and defenseless kids were trying to scatter unsuccessfully.

Without stopping, or really aiming, Quinn turned the rifle on the two clowns and fired. No hits and neither pursuer seemed fazed. It was a waste of ammunition.

Quinn and Rust fell onto the silo door, now suddenly closed. Rust yanked at the handle and . . .

Nothing.

The door held firm.

"Let us in!" Quinn screamed, taking hold of the door handle and trying for herself. Rust let go and fumbled to feed two shells into the shotgun. Dropping one into the gravel and dust as his hands shook, he bent for it.

The clowns were bearing down on them. One with his pitchfork held aloft like a javelin, the other choking up on his ax.

Quinn could hear a scuffle on the other side of the door.

"They'll kill us, too!" a voice screeched.

"Fuck yourself. Open that door."

Rust pumped the shotgun, his back against hers, leaning for support. Quinn sobbed, banging an ineffectual fist on the door.

"Open this door or I'm blowing it down," Rust screamed, then punctuated the threat with a blast from the shotgun, aimed behind and above them.

There were footfalls and laughter behind them. The cackling was strained and evil, the sound of someone enjoying killing.

"Please," Quinn gasped, one last time.

Quinn closed her eyes in anticipation of the end. Hoping death would be quick.

And then she fell forward, Rust's weight on top of her, crushing her.

NINETEEN

Cole had opened the door to let Quinn and Rust in. He'd had to punch Matt Trent in the face to do it—so the situation was a win-win. Cole had fantasized about laying Matt out for, well, years now—probably ever since he started talking about how much better things used to be way back when and dropping the word "cuck" into his insults. Even if Cole's knuckles throbbed and had already started to swell a bit, it was worth it. It shut Matt up and Ronnie, too. She stopped screaming to help him close the door again.

But as they slid the silo door shut, a steel-toed boot and a white-gloved hand wedged into the doorway. The clown on the other side grunted in opposition as they tried to roll the door the last few inches closed.

Cole couldn't move, couldn't let go, or the clown would get in. Fortunately, Rust noticed.

"Get back," Rust said, nodding to Cole. Rust was still on his back, shotgun barrel angled up. Quinn clawed at dirt and corn, crawling out from under him.

Cole smiled. It felt good to smile, just like it felt good to still be on the same wavelength as Rust. Even after all this time. Even in this situation.

Cole backed away from the clown's grasping hand and the doorway. Knowing what was coming, he turned and covered Ronnie's face and neck with his arms, protecting her from any shrapnel or stray pellets.

The blast echoed around the empty wood cylinder above them.

Cole turned back to get a glimpse of a ruined stump retreating, oversize glove gone, destroyed by the buckshot, a single naked digit remaining, dangling by a thread against a wrist.

They closed the door, locked it with the bolt.

Outside, the clown cried for help. It was a woman's voice, high-pitched, babbling, crying about her hand being gone.

Cole looked over to Rust and nodded, satisfied—good job. Somehow, he knew from the start of it that the gunshots he'd heard weren't the cops. He knew it was Ruston who'd come to the rescue.

Quinn gasped then, turning his attention. She'd crawled eye-to-eye with Erin's body. "What the—" she said, but Cole knew there was no explaining. Not now. Instead, he just offered a hand to help her up.

"What the hell?" Rust yelled, standing. "Why didn't you open the door for us? We could have died!"

"I tried," Cole said. He looked over at Matt. He was sitting on a milk crate, rubbing his jaw, face red in the lamp-light. "*Someone* didn't want me to."

"You think that was a good choice of costume, Trent?" Rust began crossing to Matt. "Why the hell do you still have it on?" He had his shotgun turned around, holding the beveled stock out, making it look more like a baseball bat. Cole had enjoyed punching Matt, but Rust would cave his skull in, if he followed through.

Ronnie must have seen where this was headed. She hopped onto Rust's back, but Rust was strong and pissed and he just carried her with him like he was hefting a load of grain.

"He didn't mean it," Ronnie said. "Don't hurt him."

Rust raised his arms, shrugging her off: "He's an asshole."

"Fuck you," Matt said, as ever not making the situation better.

Rust was about to lunge at Matt again when Cole cut him off with a bear hug. "I'm just happy you're alive," Cole said into his ear. "We've got bigger worries now." He turned to Quinn, reaching an arm out for her shoulder but not close enough to make contact. "You okay, Maybrook?"

"I'm not dead," she said, smiling nervously.

They all went quiet, still; Cole could hear everyone's breathing. Outside, the handless clown's screaming had quieted and turned to a sad, helpless blubbering.

"Look, I'm sorry," Matt said, his hands pleading. "I *am* an asshole. We were just scared."

Rust stared him down hard. "Fine. Whatever," he said. Cole knew that the moment was over but not forgotten.

And then outside there was an angry roar. The door shuddered against its lock. There was a loud crack. Splinters flew at them, an ax-head buried in the door, a five-inch chunk of wood knocked inward.

"They're going to get in!" Quinn yelled. She still had her gun and was pointing it toward the door, out the new hole the ax had just chopped, menacing whoever was out there. "Back away or I'll shoot!"

Cole knew that Rust had spent a lifetime hunting. For the early part of that life, Cole had been there, but this girl: she was brand-new to it. And seemed to be doing fine.

She poked the barrel of the rifle out the ax hole, fired.

Like that, no more whacks with the ax came.

"Hey." Rust put a finger to his lips, waved them over. "We have to get out of here," he said, his voice hushed and conspiratorial. "We're vulnerable. They don't need to get in. They can just burn us out like they did with the barn."

"Well, what do you suggest, Sarge?" Matt asked. Ronnie patted his shoulder, trying to quiet her boyfriend. But Cole knew she had very little control over Matt. Nobody decided what Matt Trent said or did, most times not even Matt Trent.

"How many more shots do you have?" Ronnie asked.

"I left my bag back in the corn," Rust said, then worked the action. "So not as many as we'd like." The gun was a Winchester 1300 that Cole remembered from their childhood. Its wood accents looked like something from the Old West, at least compared to the sleek black tactical shotguns Cole had seen on YouTube. Rust slid the action a second time, revealing that the chamber and magazine of the shotgun were empty.

"That's not good," Cole said.

"No. Not great. But good news is, Quinn's got . . ." Rust paused, counted on his fingers. "Four or five rounds left. I can't remember."

"Then she should hand it over," Ronnie said, her voice going loud for a second. She looked to Quinn, who was still watching the door. "Gimme the gun, new girl," Ronnie continued, then pointed a thumb to herself. "Miss Kettle Springs Riflery 2019."

Quinn looked back, gave Ronnie Queen and her Frendo

jumpsuit a once-over, and then scoffed. She looked to Rust to back her up and he shook his head.

Quinn, a slight smile at her lips, ignored Ronnie's request and turned back to keeping the rifle trained on the door.

Ha! Cole liked this girl.

"What's in these boxes?" Rust asked in a whisper, indicating the half of the silo that looked like an extension of Tillerson's garage.

Cole shrugged.

"You didn't check?"

"Didn't seem to be anything useful and we had, like, other stuff on our minds," Cole said.

Rust shook his head again. "Help me, then. Whether they try breaking down the door or just setting us on fire, they'll be back soon. Stay on the door, Quinn."

"You're doing a great job, Maybrook," Cole said, mostly just to watch Ronnie grimace. Ronnie was hugging Matt's shoulder now, sullen that she'd been denied the weapon, both of them useless.

Cole helped Rust unstack boxes and random farm equipment.

"Got to be something useful we can take before we head out the back," Rust said, pulling open a box of *Farmer's Almanac* books that looked like they dated back to the fifties.

"Head out the back?" Cole asked.

"How long you been living around farms?" Rust asked, finally some humor in his voice. "This is a grain bin."

"I know that. So?"

Rust stamped his foot on the grating under them, the sound causing an echoing *BONG*. "It's old, but not old enough it doesn't have a loading pit. I can see from here"—he peered down into the grating—"that it's a conveyer belt and not an auger. It'll be tight, but we can crawl out the back while the clowns are watching the door."

"That's—" Cole started, a hand on Rust's shoulder as he worked to unstack another crate. "That's some good thinking, man."

How much had they both changed since they'd been on speaking terms? The skin on Rust's face seemed aged, lived-in. Cole had been filming prank videos, practicing his alcohol poisoning, and curating his social media presence, while Rust had stayed doing what he'd always done: living.

Rust's expression changed.

"Hey, weren't there kids smoking in here?" Rust asked, louder, to the room.

"Yeah, why?" Matt asked, standing away from where he and his girlfriend had been stewing.

"Probably not the best idea," Rust said, hiking up a small crate to his chest. The case was a little bigger than a shoebox and had two rope handles.

"What is that?" Cole asked.

"My guess . . ." Rust walked back to the dirt flooring of the silo, off the grating, and gently set the box down. ". . . is that it's the only fishing gear Paul Tillerson uses." He slid open the lid to reveal a box full of weathered, weeping dynamite sticks.

"Holy shit, that looks dangerous," Cole said.

"Looks to me like our way out," Rust said, staying crouched. "Who's got a lighter?"

"Ronnie?" Cole asked, putting his hand out.

Ronnie looked at him, frowned, then partially unzipped the front of her Frendo costume, reaching into the pockets under her jumpsuit and producing a cheap gas-station Bic.

Quinn still had the rifle pointed at the hole in the door, but had backed up to join their huddle. "We made it this far. Please don't kill us all," she said.

Sound advice.

"I won't," Rust said, using the tips of his fingers to gently lift one of the sticks of dynamite from the box. Its side was slick with what looked like sea salt and olive oil, but Cole knew enough to guess it was actually nitroglycerin. "Okay, Cole, find the hatch to the loading pit and get everyone down there."

"What about—"

There was a slam at the door, the ax returning, attacking a different spot from where Quinn had been aiming, old wood cracking.

Quinn pulled the barrel of the rifle over and fired, doing even more damage to the door. Cole watched Rust flinch, nearly dropping the dynamite.

"Stop her," Rust looked up and said. "One spark and—"

"You missed, girly," a voice taunted from the other side of the door.

Cole crossed to Quinn. "You've got to stop shooting," he whispered. "We don't have ammo to waste. We need you."

Cole watched her expression slacken as she turned to him. Cole's father had avoided Vietnam, but he had a brother who hadn't. Cole had never met his uncle, but Arthur Hill spoke highly of him, said it was a shame he'd gone crazy shooting. Cole never understood that expression—gone crazy shooting—until right now, looking in Quinn's eyes. A few minutes ago, if Ronnie had tried any harder to take the gun away from Quinn, it wouldn't have ended well for Ms. Queen.

"Come on," the voice outside said. "They probably ran out of ammo."

"Get back or we'll blow you all up!" Matt yelled.

They looked at him, Rust swearing under his breath.

"What? I'm trying to buy us some time," Matt whispered, and shrugged. If they made it out of this, Cole decided that he was punching his lights out again.

Outside, there were two quick pulls of a ripcord and suddenly the familiar buzz of a chainsaw.

"Now, Cole, now," Rust yelled. He was twining the short fuses of two sticks of dynamite together, lighter pinched between his teeth as he worked.

Cole didn't hesitate; he dropped to the floor and started yanking at the grating until he found a three-by-three section that pulled up with a rusty O-ring.

"Everyone get in there," he said. Ronnie didn't need any urging. She went first, stepping down carefully given that there was only about two and a half feet of clearance between the grating and the floor of the pit.

She looked back up at Cole, her hair somehow still in a neat ponytail. "Now what?"

Somewhere behind them, chainsaw bit into wood and sawdust began to flow, turning the inside of the silo into a snow globe.

"Crawl! Up the belt," Cole yelled, pushing Ronnie's head down with his shoe. "You're next, Maybrook," he said, pressing Quinn toward the hole, needing to use force as she started to plant her feet.

"What about Rust?"

That was a good question. What about Rust? The ancient dynamite didn't seem to have much of a fuse.

"I'll be fine," Rust said, looking up to Cole from where he was crouched, working frantically. "Really." Rust's eyes were locked with Cole's, pleading. Lying. "You *need* to go. Now."

Cole understood. And it killed him to understand.

"Yeah. He'll be fine, now get in there," Matt Trent said, then smiled: "Or I'll give you back that punch I owe you."

Without being able to tell Rust goodbye or good luck, Cole Hill was shoved down into the pit.

Matt followed after, the boy in the clown suit making sure Cole went.

TWENTY

Quinn had never been scared of the dark.

And for her, tight spaces didn't mean claustrophobia.

And before tonight, she'd never even thought to be afraid of clowns.

Quinn's fears tended to be more specific. Most of them more to do with whether her dad was going to be okay when she left for college, or whether she was going to let her team down during a volleyball game.

But under the silo, crammed into a situation where she needed to crawl through a shaft only as wide as her shoulders, in total darkness, she better understood some universal fears.

"I can't see anything!" Ronnie said. Her voice was muffled, even though she was only inches in front of Quinn.

"Just keep going," Cole answered. Quinn could feel one of his hands on the bottom of her shoe. He was steadily applying pressure, pushing her forward. She would've done the same thing for Ronnie, but she had to keep her grip on the rifle and use her other hand to claw herself up the incline of the conveyer belt.

"Please don't shoot me!" Ronnie said, prodded with the end of the rifle. Quinn hadn't done it on purpose, but . . .

Would it make you crawl faster?

The small, cramped passageway smelled like dry corn and earth, but there were metal treads clattering against their feet and elbows. Rust had been right, this cramped passageway *had* to be leading them to the surface.

Something with a lot of legs—a roach, a centipede—crawled over the back of Quinn's hand. The creature felt like a small feather duster, playing across her knuckles. Along with clowns, the insect rounded out the list of fears she hadn't known she had until tonight.

"Keep going," Cole urged.

Quinn could no longer hear the chainsaw. Above and behind them, the clowns were likely still carving into the silo door, but she couldn't hear much beyond her own hot, ragged breathing.

The corn silo was no longer in use, so what incentive was there to keep the conveyor belt functional? If there was no exit, if it had been boarded up or cemented over years ago, then it felt very possible they would all suffocate down here.

Quinn tried not to think about it, kept fighting for the inches of progress she was getting.

"I feel something!" Ronnie yelled, stopping short. Quinn's reaching hand touched the skin of the girl's calf, pushing up the clown jumpsuit. "It's the end, it's . . . ," Ronnie stammered. "It's dirt!"

"So dig, then," Quinn said, Cole patting her on the shoe to indicate he agreed.

Matt said something, but Quinn couldn't quite decipher it.

"Can you fucking calm down, Trent?" Cole said. "We're all cramped. Take deep breaths."

Quinn could hear Ronnie straining against something, digging, wincing with exertion.

"I've got it. No more dirt. It's grass!"

"Keep going!" Quinn said, trying to encourage her.

A second later, a dirt clod fell into Quinn's open mouth. She shut her eyes against the rain of damp soil, the blackness just as complete as the tunnel around her had been.

Then she smelled it: not sweat or corn or exhalation, but fresh air, rushing in and filling their small tunnel.

Suddenly Ronnie was no longer in front of her. Quinn surged forward, and a grime-flecked hand reached down to help her out of the tunnel.

Quinn sent the rifle up first and let Ronnie take it, before crawling out of the dead grass and dirt hole like she was being born again.

Standing, knees shaking, Quinn helped Ronnie pull out Cole, then Matt.

"Where is he?" Quinn said down into the darkness.

"We've got to go," Cole said.

Quinn knew he was right; the tunnel had deposited them less than ten feet from the base of the silo. Quinn could hear the chainsaw, even though she couldn't see any clowns.

The group retreated to the edge of the corn before Quinn stopped.

"We have to get to the road," Ronnie said.

She was holding the rifle. *Quinn's* rifle.

"No. We need to wait for Rust," Quinn told her.

"Ronnie's right," Matt said. "The road. We need to get help."

"Why the road? If we can make it to Tillerson's house, we can use their landline to call for help," Cole said.

It was the connection that Quinn had been trying to make earlier. If the Tillersons were gone for the weekend at a farm convention, they'd be no help, but they would still have a phone. Shelter of some kind.

"And you know how to get there? You know for sure what direction it is?" Ronnie asked Cole, daring him to disagree.

"If the road doesn't work, we can follow it back to the house. Let's let that be plan B—"

"Give me my gun back," Quinn said, interrupting her, tired of this shit.

"*Your* gun?" Ronnie asked, the emphasis all wrong, looking down at the weapon in her hands.

"Yeah . . . my gun. I want it," Quinn demanded, amped up, ready to fight Ronnie for it.

But then the silo exploded.

The air was almost solid in its heat and rush, the warm hand of a god gently pressing everything flat as a fireball turned night into day for the span of a few seconds.

It didn't feel like Quinn had lost consciousness, more like a long blink.

She lifted her head, looked around them, and saw that the corn had been pushed flat by the blast, every plant bent at the base of the stalk by the force of the explosion, and Quinn, Ronnie, Cole, and Matt had been bent down with it.

Quinn groaned, struggling to sit up, and when she managed, she could see that Cole was already sitting, watching where the silo had been and sniffling.

Ronnie's hair was smoking, but there didn't seem to be any actual flames threatening to burn away her hair product. Quinn crawled over to the girl and took her rifle back.

They blinked at each other for a moment, watching the

hole in the ground where the silo had been. There was no way Rust had gotten out of that alive.

"Well, he did it. He blew them up," Cole said, more to himself than anyone else. "Crazy fucker sacrificed himself to stop them."

"Not all of them," Matt said, pointing.

And there, in the middle of the clearing, another Frendo the Clown stepped through the smoke and fire toward them.

He wiped his long, curved machete on the side of one pant leg.

Peering through the smolder, the clown smiled and pointed his blade to them.

What other choice did they have: they ran.

TWENTY-ONE

Glenn Maybrook had driven across the country, taken a job in a town he'd never heard of, never even visited, upended his daughter's life, and possibly forever damaged her trust in him. Yes, he'd done *all* of that and he'd done it to preserve his own sanity.

In retrospect, he could say all he wanted to about a fresh start for both of them, but, in reality, moving had been a selfish decision.

He'd done all of this so that he wouldn't have to practice emergency medicine for one more goddamn day.

And yet.

And yet he was losing this patient.

"How do you expect me to treat her with nothing but tweezers, an old scalpel, and a shitty first-aid kit?" he asked the darkness surrounding him, then pushed his luck: "It's not even sterile!"

"You didn't have any medical supplies at your home. We had to make do. Just do your best," the voice said.

"My best? Someone shot off her fucking hand!"

His patient moaned. She was still wearing her clown mask, breathing heavy against the plastic slit. She'd screamed at him when he tried to remove it.

Another clown, a big man who'd also been wounded, buckshot in his shoulder, had been the one to bring her in and usher Glenn out of his cell to help.

"I don't care what the man on the speaker says," the big clown hissed. "If you don't save her, I will kill you."

After the threat, the clown left, climbing up the steel steps, leaving behind Glenn and the crude operating table.

Glenn was alone in here with the patient, though he was still being watched. But from where? Was there a camera, somewhere above him? Did that mean his jailer was in the next room, or was he two towns over? Could Glenn run up those industrial-looking stairs and get away?

No. No, he couldn't. Like it or not, there was a woman on the table in front of him who would die without his help.

"Can you feel this?" Glenn asked, poking the end of the tweezers into the middle of the wound.

His patient moaned, but he couldn't be sure if it was in response to anything he was doing. She'd been moaning a lot.

He looked at the smudges on the tweezers. He'd have to be careful with how much he was handling his operating equipment. He'd tried to wipe his hands the best he could with the pitiful roll of gauze he'd found in the kit, but his fingers were still caked with a putrid slurry of corn and rat shit—everything about him was far from sterile. Even if Glenn could stabilize her, she'd need most of the antibiotics in the Midwest to stave off infection.

"This?" he asked again, poking, and the woman gave a high-pitched shriek through her clown mask. She was breathing her own air in there, and it was going to take more and more effort to draw breath as she dipped further into shock.

Someone had placed a plastic zip-tie around her wrist, cinching off the blood flow. It was crude but efficient. Might have saved her life. Had at the very least prolonged it.

Over his career, Glenn Maybrook had seen plenty of gunshots, but very few as messy as this. First of all, shotguns weren't exactly popular in Philly. Second, the blast had been from such a close range that the meat of this woman's stump had been . . . cooked? He frankly didn't know that was possible from a muzzle flash.

Before removing the zip-tie, Glenn would need to cut away the charred skin with his scalpel, remove any pellets he could reach, then throw on as many sutures as she would allow him to with the small loop of cotton thread and no anesthetic. There had been a Motel 6 sewing kit tucked in the white plastic first-aid box, which would have been laughable if it wasn't the only thing right now standing between his patient's life and death.

"Can you tell me your name?"

"Frrrrr—"

The woman tried, struggling through what must have been blinding pain.

"Frendo," she said finally, then maybe the strangest part of a strange night: she laughed.

"Okay, Frendo, I'm new in town, so I'm going to take off your mask. You need to be able to breathe properly."

Being back in an operating room—of sorts—made Glenn braver than he should've been.

"Doctor. I wouldn't," the voice above him said. The voice on the speaker was no longer using the Darth Vader distortion. It didn't matter, as the voice wasn't familiar anyway.

"I'm going to do what I need to do to keep this person alive."

"Suit yourself."

His patient fought him, but he got the plastic mask off and . . .

And . . . *holy shit*. He'd been joking about the new-in-town thing, but he *recognized* the woman on the table.

It was their waitress from the Eatery. Her distinctive beehive hairdo had been tamped down inside of a skullcap, probably to keep her looking as uniform as she could with the big clown.

"I don't know what you did to get like this," Glenn started, holding her steady so she'd look him in the eye. "But ma'am, you are severely injured and I'm trying to help you."

He squeezed her good hand, tried to put as much bedside manner into his voice as he could muster, under the circumstances.

"Now, can you please remind me of your name?"

"Muh . . ." She swallowed. "My—my name is Trudy."

"Okay. Trudy. I'm Dr. Maybrook. You waited on my daughter and me—"

"I know. I remember," she said as she forced up a smile, "and I hope your little slut dies slow out in that field!"

She tried spitting at him but couldn't connect.

Glenn dropped the woman's hand, stood back from the table, his head throbbing like he'd been sucker-punched.

Quinn! They'd asked for Quinn when they'd taken him. Somehow she was involved; somehow his daughter had become a target.

Trudy was laughing again, cackling really, half out of her mind from pain and warped by evil.

"Think about what you do next very carefully, Dr. Maybrook," the voice above him said. "Your daughter isn't dead . . . yet."

He nodded, a big exaggerated movement that could be picked up on a camera to show that he understood.

Glenn Maybrook put aside the Hippocratic Oath for a moment and poked the end of the tweezers deep into the exposed, chipped bone of Trudy's radius.

He did *some* harm.

Trudy gave half a strangled scream before promptly blacking out from the pain.

There. Now he could stabilize his patient.

Once that was done, he needed to find a way out of this. A way to get back to Quinn.

TWENTY-TWO

It pained Quinn to admit it, but Ronnie and Matt had been right.

Credit where credit was due: heading to the road turned out to be the right move.

She knew as soon as they stepped out of the corn and saw headlights growing on the horizon.

They were going to be saved.

Cole grabbed Quinn's hand. "Be ready."

She nodded.

Quinn waved with the rest of them, but kept glancing to the ditch, then the cornfield beyond. It was hard to move through the rows without leaving a trail. From the slight elevation of the road she looked out at the stalks.

Quinn had wasted two shots, firing blindly back at the clown with the machete, as they'd run to the road.

There was no indication that they'd been followed. It seemed like the clown had given up, but Quinn watched over her shoulder anyway. She felt certain their attacker would be diving through onto the road at any moment.

But the clown must have either gotten lost or given up.

A truck slowed. Quinn was ready to run to it, jump in the bed, if need be.

Quinn could hear country music as the truck approached, louder as the windows rolled down a quarter of the way.

"Please help us!" Cole yelled.

With the glare of the headlights, Quinn couldn't see the driver's face. And as the truck began to creep, she gripped harder at Cole's hand, dug her nails in. He squeezed back and she realized that they were both expecting the same thing:

They were thinking this was too easy, that there'd be a man in a clown mask driving the truck.

"Whatyer ya doin' out here?" the driver yelled, a drawl thicker than any Quinn had heard during her time in Kettle Springs. The driver kept on the brakes but didn't stop, moving them out of the way with the rumble of his grille. The group split as the truck nosed forward.

Matt and Ronnie stayed with the passenger side, Cole and Quinn on the driver's side, ready to talk with the driver.

She made sure to point the gun at the asphalt, not wanting to scare him.

"Whatever it is, I don't want any part in it," the man said.

"They're trying to kill us. You have to help us!" Quinn said, shaking away Cole's hand and reaching out for the driver's side mirror, ready to pull the truck to a stop if she had to.

The cab of the truck smelled like skunk and burned metal. Any other day, the driver would have been a complete ghoul, someone to cross the street to avoid. But he wasn't wearing a Frendo mask, wasn't flecked with blood, so to Quinn he looked like a superhero.

"Who's trying to kill you?" the driver said through the window, addressing Cole, not Quinn, then nodding over to the two teenagers dressed like clowns, at his passenger's side window. "And why are they dressed crazy? It ain't Halloween."

He kept the truck moving, but slow. Quinn could tell he didn't like this situation any more than they did.

"Sir, we need help," Quinn said. The truck rolled, tires crunching gravel and old blacktop. But slower now, slower. She kept her hand on the cool metal joining the mirror to the door. "There are masked psychos out here. They killed our friends. They may still be killing our friends. We got away, and we need to get the police."

All she needed was for the driver to take a second, listen

to her words, register the terror in their faces, that they weren't joking.

He stopped, thank God.

But then there was a thud on the far side of the cab.

Matt had kicked the passenger's side door, then slammed a slick, open hand on the window, the glass around his fingers fogging.

"Would you let us in, you methhead, podunk fuck!" Matt yelled. "This is an emergency!"

The driver turned to Quinn, eyes sad, resigned: "Not playin' your games, kids."

There was a rev of ignition, the truck peeling out. The mirror was yanked out of Quinn's grip. Cole threw an arm around her waist and pulled her back, her feet nearly crushed under the truck's rear tires.

They watched his taillights go, the fields and road becoming much darker in their absence.

Nobody said anything until hope of a ride was truly lost as the truck disappeared behind a bend.

"What the fuck, Matt?" Cole yelled. "Why'd you do that?"

"Me? How was I supposed to know that coward was going to take off—"

"Shut up," Quinn said to him. "Just shut up."

Matt didn't argue. He just shrugged and went back to holding on to Ronnie like she was the only thing keeping him standing.

Quinn paced up the road a few strides, then back, keeping her eyes on the horizon, searching for movement in the corn. There was nothing—just rows and rows of crops split by an empty stretch of highway.

"Look, Quinn," Ronnie started. "Matt made a mistake, but that doesn't make you King Shit."

"You know what?" Quinn sputtered, the gun feeling powerful in her grip, assuring her at the very least that she was Princess Shit . . .

Cole put a hand on her shoulder to calm her before she could say something to make the situation worse. "Done is done," he said. "Let's just focus on getting out of here alive."

"Okay. Which direction is the Tillerson house?" Quinn asked. "We'll walk that way. If another car comes, we'll try again."

Matt and Ronnie didn't argue.

"North. We'll see the turnoff. That way," Cole answered, and pointed.

They began walking. The silence uncomfortable. Quinn couldn't shake the images of Rust. His bloody undershirt, his stubble, his goofy smile, the fuse. And Janet, her skin perfectly buffed, lips glossed, her bursting through the corn to warn them that there was more than one clown.

But Quinn didn't have to be alone with her memories for long.

They didn't get far.

"Look!" The first exclamation sent the skin on her neck prickling.

"Oh, hell yes!" Matt cheered.

The road at their backs was bathed in red-and-blue lights.

The cops had arrived.

Or, at least, a single cruiser.

It was enough. The sheriff was here.

"Took him long enough," Ronnie said. Never satisfied, even as the boys cheered and waved.

The sheriff pulled to a stop a few feet in front of them and opened his door. He didn't shut off his lights.

He was just as big as Quinn had remembered from the parade and the diner, taking time to put his hat on his head, even as Quinn and Cole started babbling at him.

"Thank God you're here."

"Call for backup!"

The sheriff didn't answer, simply crossed to them, his cruiser sideways, not completely blocking the road but pulled into both lanes.

"Where's the party?" he asked. "I need you to break it up *now*, Cole."

"Dunne," Cole said, stepping forward. "I know I'm not your favorite person, but there's people out there dressed as Frendo. It's . . . nuts. They're killing everyone. You need to do something."

"Sheriff," Dunne said flatly.

"What?!"

"I'm not 'Dunne' to you. I am not your buddy. So before you start in, you will call me 'Sheriff Dunne' and treat me with respect."

The expression on Cole's face quickly transitioned to disbelief. Quinn watched Cole pull his sharp features under control, contort them into something that approached a combination of sincerity, respect, and patience.

"Sheriff. I apologize. You need to get on your radio and call for backup. There's at least one left. Maybe more."

"One what?"

"One *clown*, Sheriff. They've got crossbows. Axes, too. They're—"

"And you've got guns." He looked to Quinn, acknowledging her for the first time, noting that she was still holding a shotgun. "And these two dumbasses are dressed like Frendo." He indicated Ronnie and Matt. "How much have you had to drink, boy? Am I on camera right now? Where's the fake blood from? Or did you kill a pig—"

"Sheriff, please, you have to listen," Cole said.

"My switchboard's Christmas lights right now. Maggie's off for the night, so I had to pick up myself. Someone tells me Tillerson's B-field's on fire. I hang up. Then someone else gets on the line, tells me that it's a mushroom cloud, that the Iranians have really done it this time. Have dropped the big one," the sheriff said, waving Cole out of his face with one hand. "There is a panic brewing, and I drive all the way out to investigate and *yours* is the first face I see, Hill."

Quinn saw Cole swallow hard. Take a deep breath. He had a thousand things to say, but like Quinn, he was too dumbstruck to even know where to start.

"Sheriff Dunne. You have to understand that I know how this looks, but—"

"Enough out of you," the sheriff said with finality. Dunne looped a thumb into his gun belt and adjusted himself. Something about him looked uncomfortable. He was sweating despite the cold air and seemed to be looking back over his shoulder. Quinn couldn't figure out for what. "Uh, Queen, Trent. Or, you." He pointed to Quinn with a thick finger.

"Maybrook," Quinn said, offering her last name.

"Why are good kids like you involved with a loser like this? Cole, get in the car. I'm going to run you for causing a public nuisance."

"This is insane. People are dead!" Cole protested. "And they're still out there; the clowns are still out there killing people!"

With that, the sheriff snapped. He grabbed Cole by the neck with one hand, and bent Cole's wrist behind his back with the other. "Yeah, people are dead. Your mama, your sister. People seem to die when you're around, Hill. And I've had about enough."

"Let go of me—" Cole started, then tried his best to turn back as Sheriff Dunne ripped open the rear door and shoved him in.

Quinn started toward them, but a cool hand appeared on her shoulder, gently tugging her back. "Don't," Ronnie whispered. "You'll make it worse."

"Just tell him the truth, Quinn!" Cole shouted as Dunne slammed the door.

TWENTY-THREE

Cole Hill had always kept his hair a little longer than the squares had.

Growing up, it wasn't that he disliked the town's population of farmhands and altar boys. Or that he thought he was better than them because his family had money.

No. A buzz cut simply wasn't his style. Even from a young age, Cole knew he was different. Janet called it star power, but, in hindsight, she might have been using the term sarcastically.

Cole lay facedown in the back of the car, hair flopped into his eyes, staying where Dunne had thrown him longer than he needed to, wedged between the cushion and the front seats. He felt defeated, but weirdly safe. Cocooned in here, he felt the knot in his chest unclench for the first time in hours.

And it wasn't like the kids of Kettle Springs had stayed squares. Seemed like during middle school, around when everyone got a phone, they grew into themselves.

Lately, when he hadn't much felt like getting out of bed, never mind getting a haircut, Cole's hair had gotten even longer, but it hadn't been a deliberate fashion choice.

His eyes stung with salt; the hair covering his vision was oily from where Dunne had grabbed him and forced his head down.

The sheriff's hand had been sticky, the size, heat, and consistency of a glazed ham, fresh from the oven.

Dunne was an asshole. And maybe he had an unhealthy obsession with Cole Hill's behavior since Victoria's death.

But Dunne wasn't stupid. Wasn't negligent. Cole took solace in that.

The big bastard would listen to Quinn and then he would take action. He'd have the state troopers and the FBI out in that cornfield before first light, guns drawn, evidence bags unfurled.

But really sweaty hands, big guy . . .

For some reason Cole was fixating on that detail as he picked his face up from the rubberized back seat of the cruiser. With all the time he'd spent in the holding cell and small interrogation room in the Municipal Building, Cole had never once been in the back of Dunne's squad car. The seat wasn't leather, wasn't pleather, but smelled funny, must have been some special material that could be hosed down if someone bled or puked onto it.

Cole pawed at the seat, climbing up so he could watch out the window as Quinn explained what was going on to Dunne.

He watched Quinn, her expression pleading. These windows must have been treated, somehow, were double thick or bulletproof, or something, because Cole couldn't make out the words.

He could see that Quinn was trying her best to remain calm, but he watched fat teardrops gather at her chin, some dripping off, some gliding down her neck, as she related what'd happened to them tonight.

Ronnie and Matt flanked her, each nodding silent assent.

Dunne listened but didn't nod himself. He didn't look incredulous or skeptical, but he wasn't digging out his handkerchief, either. He stood back at a remove, Ronnie's and Matt's eyes ping-ponging between the new girl and the sheriff, Ronnie's hand on Quinn's shoulder.

Cole could see the dark spots, growing darker on Dunne's chest and shoulder as the man listened, occasionally offering a quick one- or two-word prompt that must have been "yes" or "go on" as Quinn seemed to get more visibly frustrated.

Dark spots.

That wasn't sweat. That was blood. And it was coming

from the *inside* of Dunne's uniform. Like he'd recently changed his clothes, was bleeding into this new shirt.

Halfway through making this connection, Cole's hands had dipped down to the car door's handle, but there was no handle. This wasn't a normal car door.

It was the back of a cop car. There were no power windows, no pull knobs to unlock the door. And there was an iron mesh partition dividing the front and back seats. This car was built to keep people—criminals—in.

FUCK. How could Cole be so stupid?

He slammed both hands on the window and was able to pull Quinn's attention.

She looked to him, confusion blooming. Ronnie's hand already dipping, grabbing at the rifle.

"One! Of! Them!" Cole screamed, timing his words with slaps at the glass, needing to be heard and understood quickly.

Sheriff Dunne simply smiled, dipping his left hand down to his service weapon, the leather buckle already unsnapped. Cole hadn't even noticed him do that.

Quinn tried to duck away and pull up with her weapon at the same time. She was fast but not fast enough. Dunne flashed out with his right arm, grabbing her in a headlock as Ronnie pulled the rifle away.

Not looking at the girl, but keeping eye contact with

Cole as he screamed and beat at the glass, Sheriff Dunne removed his gun from his belt and brought the butt down on the side of Quinn's temple, dazing her.

He let her out of the hold, giving himself some distance to wind up and aim, then hit her again with another quick knock. The impact of the gun's butt sent her to the asphalt, sprawled on her back.

Quinn was unconscious, possibly dead.

Ronnie and Matt looked down to Quinn at their feet, then back up to Dunne, who was rubbing at his shoulder, wincing, cursing something about the wound there.

Ronnie made eye contact with Cole and *smiled*.

Sheriff Dunne pointed to Ronnie and Matt, then said something, delivering an order and hiking his thumb back to the cornfield.

Matt knelt, gathering up Quinn in a fireman's carry, and disappeared down into the ditch, headed for the corn.

Ronnie adjusted her grip on the rifle, propping it in one hand, then looked back to Cole, and mouthed *Pow!* while shooting a quick gun-finger in his direction.

"Fuck you!" Cole screamed, which seemed like the only logical response to the betrayal.

Ronnie gently shook her head like *We both know you won't* and followed Matt down into the cornfield.

Dunne adjusted his hat and pointed his chin into his

collarbone as far as it would go, looking down at the roses of blood that were spotting the front of his shirt. He frowned.

The sheriff returned to the cruiser, ignoring Cole until he could no longer take his screaming.

"Shut your mouth, Hill, or I'll call off the rest of the plans, drag you onto the side of the road, and put a bullet in your head myself."

TWENTY-FOUR

"When that tweaker drove up, God," Matt said, his mouth next to Quinn's ear, "I thought we were done for. Thought he was going to ruin everything."

Quinn's hearing felt . . . wet, like she'd just been in a wave pool and still had water rattling around in her skull.

"Couldn't believe it," Ronnie said, a couple of feet away. "What are the odds? Nobody drives that road. That was quick thinking, though, baby. You saved us."

"I . . . ," Matt said, suddenly bashful. Quinn could almost feel his blush, despite the world wavering, threatening to crash back into complete darkness. "Thank you."

It sounded like he didn't get a lot of compliments. Least of all from Ronnie.

"How should we do it?" Matt asked.

"I say we change her first. To make things easier."

"Oh def," Matt replied.

What were they talking about? Change her into what? Matt's grip slackened and he readjusted Quinn's body, hand on her ass, digging in for purchase and boosting her up, balancing her top half over his shoulder. It would have been simpler for him if he were taller or she were shorter.

"Hey, I see that hand," Ronnie said. "Don't be a creep."

Pffft. Matt blew a raspberry, the sound so sudden and loud Quinn had to stop herself from flinching. So long as Ronnie and Matt thought she was unconscious, she was inclined to keep it that way.

"Look. If you want to go all women's lib, you can carry her," Matt said. "Gimme the gun. We can switch. She's heavier than she looks."

"You're a child." Ronnie tsk'd, then changed the subject back. "We can probably just find a rock and bash her skull in. No ballistics there. Makes it look like we got lucky, took one of the clowns down with *improvised* weapons."

"Yeah. That'd earn us some hero points, too."

"Don't know how many hero points we'll be getting . . ." Ronnie trailed off. "We didn't really save anyone."

"Well, I mean, we saved each other. Isn't that important?"

"Important," Ronnie said, a slight giggle, the fucking psychopath. "Important *and* romantic."

Quinn kept her eyes closed, but she could hear that they were stepping out of the cornfield, into the clearing. The strong smell of burning confirmed it for her.

"Whoa," Matt said.

"Yeah. Not exactly according to plan. Silo's fucking *gone*. Who could have seen that coming? Dunne's going to be pissed, but, the way I see it, this does nothing but help us. We're—careful!"

Matt tripped, then caught himself. Quinn fought the instinct to grab onto him.

"Ugh, gross," Ronnie said. And Quinn couldn't help it, her curiosity was too strong. She cracked open an eye, trying to keep her lashes knit in case Ronnie was looking at her.

There, in the dirt, Janet's dead face stared up at Quinn.

Matt either hadn't seen the body or had tried to step over it and slipped in the girl's blood. He kicked her head, rolling it over so that it followed them, was still wobbling slightly, gauzy dead pupils locked with Quinn as she looked down from over his shoulder.

"That's fucked up," Matt said, his voice losing something, no longer playful, undeniably disturbed.

"I know, babe, but that could have been us. If we didn't choose the right side of history. They'll make it worth it, though."

Quinn closed her eyes again, not wanting to see any more horrors as they crossed the clearing.

"What do you think happened to her dad?" Matt asked.

"Whose dad?"

"Hers. Janet's."

"Stepdad," Ronnie corrected.

"Like *that* makes it okay," Matt said. "Last time I saw him, this one was shooting at him."

"Oh please. She wasn't shooting at anything." Ronnie paused. "He's probably back at Baypen, waiting for the delivery. He saw we had everything under control. No thanks to this bitch." Quinn felt the butt of the rifle pressed into her thigh.

If she'd done anything to make Ronnie Queen's night a little more difficult, she was proud.

Quinn tried to focus, parse what had just been said. Janet's stepfather was one of the clowns? Was he the one with the machete who'd survived the silo blast? The thought gave Quinn a shooting pain over her left temple, a vein there throbbing, feeling like it would burst at any moment, killing her. Or maybe the one with the chainsaw? He could have been any of them, frankly. What did it matter—they were all fucking nuts.

Matt came to a stop.

"If we lay her here," Matt explained, "it'll be like we surprised her while she was chopping up the bodies."

"You're fucking sick," Ronnie replied. "I love it."

With that, Matt Trent hoisted Quinn over his shoulder.

She would have had all the wind knocked out of her on impact, if her fall hadn't been cushioned by something soft.

The back of Quinn's neck was wet. Her left leg was on grass, but her right was up on something, knee propped on something squishy. She tried to hold still.

"So," Matt said. "You giving her your suit or . . . what?"

"They're the same size. Why don't you take yours off?"

Quinn could smell cooked meat. She kept her eyes shut, tried not to tremble, tried to hold the terror and the sobs in.

They were standing over her, arguing about who would strip off their Frendo costume so they could put it on Quinn, framing her, and Quinn was lying on . . .

She could feel wetness, cold and tacky in the night air, under her hands.

Bodies!

Matt had tossed her onto a pile of bodies! All in different states of dismemberment, some hacked to death by Janet Murray's stepfather.

"Look, she's moving."

Quinn fought the strong urge to open her eyes, see what was around her. The image couldn't have been worse than what she was imagining.

"Shoot her."

"No. No more gunshots. Quick. Find a rock."

It was now or never. Matt and Ronnie thought Quinn was coming to, didn't know she was already *here*.

Quinn threw herself toward where Ronnie's voice had been. She didn't open her eyes until she was fully upright, stomach muscles crunching and burning with the sudden activity.

The night was still dark. She caught the outline of Ronnie, standing in front of her, holding *the* rifle.

Her rifle.

Quinn roared one hand to the wood of the stock, one hand to where Ronnie had her fingers already wrapped around the grip and trigger.

"Oh shit!" Matt yelled.

Quinn grappled with Ronnie, their faces getting close, while Matt tried to get out of the way of the barrel of the rifle.

Quinn smiled, feeling the blood of her dismembered classmates dribbling down her back. Trying to work her sore mouth to speak.

"What?" Ronnie yelled.

Matt had one hand on Quinn's shoulder and the other wrapped around the barrel of the gun—a cartoon move, like he'd be able to catch the bullet after it'd been fired.

"I said," Quinn started between clenched teeth: "Trigger discipline."

She mashed Ronnie's finger down.

The bullet tore through Matt's hand, sending the boy spinning away. He landed facedown on the pile of bodies where Quinn had been, seconds ago.

For a moment, Quinn thought—hoped—he was dead, but then he began to grip at his ear, screaming. Or . . . what was left of his ear, the flaps of it dangling down his exposed skull. Fresh blood shot from the side of Matt's face, visibly darkening as it hit the air, and splashed onto the dead grass and bodies, oxidizing in the open eyes of the corpses.

"Ayyyeeeeeee!" Matt screamed, the sounds he was making barely human.

Seeing Matt, Ronnie began to scream, too. Her eyes were frantic. "Matt, holy shit! Are you okay?" she asked.

Matt didn't answer in words, and Ronnie still wouldn't give up the rifle.

Ronnie slipped in a black, coagulated puddle, and seizing the chance, Quinn lifted up an elbow and brought it down on Ronnie's chin.

Ronnie's head cocked back, her neck like a spring, but still the girl's eyes were ferocious and lucid, her grip on the gun still tight.

Fuck it. Quinn needed to get out of here while she had the chance.

Quinn gambled that Ronnie didn't have many rounds left and that she'd been lying about being a great shot.

With both Ronnie and Matt sprawled below her, reaching for each other on the pile of bodies, Quinn broke into a run. She staggered, trying her best to remember which way they'd come from and which direction was north.

Behind her, Ronnie screamed. It was a guttural sound of betrayal, the screech of someone who'd been cheated, didn't think that life was fair. Someone who seemed ignorant to the fact that she'd condemned all of her friends. Damned them, sold them out, killed them.

Quinn pumped her arms.

Fifteen feet until she was in the clear.

Even with a head start, some distance, she could hear the oiled click-clack as Ronnie advanced the rifle's bolt.

"Don't shoot!" Matt yelled to Ronnie. There was an uneasy second where Quinn thought Ronnie would ignore him.

Quinn crashed into the field, but not before hearing Matt say:

"We'll catch her. There's nowhere for her to go."

TWENTY-FIVE

After a silence of what was probably minutes, but felt like hours, Cole Hill asked, "Why?"

At first Sheriff Dunne didn't acknowledge the question, but then he reached up, adjusted his rearview mirror so they could look at each other through the mesh partition, and spoke.

"For the laughs? Isn't that what you've said in your videos?"

Cole crossed his arms, wouldn't give Dunne the satisfaction of a response.

"'Why?' I've been asking you the same thing for years, Cole. I know your father has, too. But you never seem able to give either of us a good reason."

"Don't talk to me like you're—" Cole started, but Dunne held two fingers up to stop him.

"If you want me to tell it, let me tell it. If not, we'll be there soon. You can try to piece it all together yourself . . . in your final moments."

Cole nodded. Hearing he was going to die didn't have much of an impact. Didn't shake him like Dunne probably thought it would. Cole had already assumed that this was how it ended.

"Now you probably have some choice words for me and my . . . brothers and sisters out there. You'd call us murderers. Psychopaths." Dunne enunciated every part of the last word. *Sy-co-paths.* "What happened tonight will haunt me for the rest of my life. See, people from *my* generation, we have what they call empathy."

Cole scoffed. People of *his* generation. History wasn't Cole's best subject, but he could remember a thing or two that Dunne's generation had handled poorly.

Dunne continued:

"Why do it? Well, first there's the ideological element."

"Well, you've got to stand for something, right?" Cole asked.

"Shut it. *I* came up with this part. This is my gospel. I'd been thinking about it long before Victoria, but after what happened, after what you and your friends did to her . . ." Dunne paused, waiting for a denial, but Cole wasn't going to give him the satisfaction. If any two people in town knew how much Cole regretted that night at the reservoir and what happened to his sister . . . well, it was Cole and his father, but Sheriff George Dunne was a close third. He'd been the one to investigate the accident.

"What I realized was that you and all your little friends who'd been out there that night, even the ones not directly responsible, are bad. Whether you was born bad, or made bad by your phones, by the internet, by the music, by *social media*, I dunno." Dunne said the last phrase with complete disgust. "But I'm not blaming those things, because what does the cause matter? It's the result that matters.

"Way I like to explain it . . . you and your friends are a blighted crop." He motioned out the window, into the darkness of the cornfields to either side of them. "That's why we didn't have a choice. If a farmer has fungus or beetles or any other scourge, it spreads if you don't take steps to eliminate it. Cut and cull. Root out the problem. Burn the whole harvest if you have to, lose the crop to save the land. Then let the field lie fallow for a couple seasons."

"So you're going to wipe out an entire generation of the town, because, what—you think we don't respect you enough? As if your generation gives a fuck about us. Everything was better way back when, but when we try to tell you how things are now, you don't want to hear it. Make Kettle Springs great again . . . You're not *only* a psychopath, you're dumb as shit," Cole said.

"Well, now you're just being rude and proving my point,"

Dunne said, surprising Cole by turning, the asphalt under them switching to the grit and bumps of dirt road. "Which gets us to part two, the *practical* part of the problem. The why and hows of the solution."

Cole wasn't sure where they were driving, but he knew they weren't headed back to town.

"Now on the practical side of things, you ask, 'How could you get someone to buy into what needs to be done?' and I'll admit, that was harder. But you and your friends helped.

"The stunt at Founder's Day—that was what did you all in. Got people thinking we needed to act fast. For months we'd been bringing everyone together—everyone who we thought would listen and had a part to play. We called it the Kettle Springs Improvement Society. Didn't tell them everything at once and didn't tell *every*one *every*thing, but why do that? You'd scare them off. Even as we did it, it scared off Dr. Weller. He was one of our most vocal supporters, early on, but he threatened to turn rat. Which was a hiccup, but we fixed it. We fixed it together."

"So you don't only murder children, is what you're saying."

Dunne turned back to face him, the car wobbling.

"Stop actin' like you're children. You fight and fuck and drink. You are not children. You grew up too fast." He paused. "Maybe that's the cause."

Dunne turned back to face the road, got himself and the wheel under control.

"But convincing the town that we needed to cull was not as hard as you'd think. I mean, we didn't say it right away like that. You can't say it all yourself. It has to seem like their idea. So you nudge. You tell people they're right, tell 'em what they want to hear, you listen—really listen, not pretend listen—but then the whole time you're doing that listening, you're pushing the boundaries forward. Reshaping morality. Drawing a new line in the sand while nobody else is watching, then wiping away the old one. And the whole time you know . . . You know where it's all leading."

"Killing a bunch of high school kids at a party," Cole said, simplifying.

"Don't say it like that! Don't make it sound like we planned it that way. The party was just . . . convenient. We knew where and when and that all your . . . social circle would be there. It was the perfect opportunity to save our town." Dunne was proud of himself.

He smiled back at Cole, teeth glinting in the rearview mirror.

"You'll never get away with it," Cole said. "All those deaths; all those people involved. Many of them even dumber than you are."

"But that's the brilliance of it, son. You seen the news lately? No one's going to doubt what a troubled, heartbroken teen could do. When armed."

"Wait, wait," Cole shouted. "You're going to try to pin this on me?"

"You'll be saving the town, Cole. We'll make it look like a suicide. You and that new girl and the Vance boy. That's why we used crossbows and chainsaws to cut down on the ballistic evidence. But I think once I get back out there and start making an official report, I'll find you three presented us with more evidence, not less."

"Quinn was our accomplice? Are you fucking nuts? It doesn't make sense."

"It never does. These senseless crimes."

"We barely know her. Nobody's going to believe that. You assholes are going to jail. I mean, the ones we didn't kill . . . ," Cole said, leaning forward.

And then without warning, Dunne stomped on the brakes. Cole's face collided with the mesh partition.

"*You* didn't kill anyone, Cole. Not tonight. So, please, don't be a tough guy. Got it?"

"Fuck off," Cole whispered, wiping the blood from his newly split lip.

Dunne resumed driving but more slowly, the road narrowing now.

"But why *not* the new girl? Three people doing the killing is more believable than just one. Isn't it?" Dunne asked. It was like he was legitimately asking for Cole's input, his help shoring up his rickety alibi. "The love triangle. Trudy thought of that piece of it. The Maybrook girl, she's only been here for, what, four days? That's long enough. Romeo and Juliet only knew each other for what? Three? This is practically the same thing."

Cole wasn't going to point out that was fiction. And that Romeo and Juliet hadn't beheaded anyone with a circular saw.

The sheriff continued musing, almost to himself. "I suggested we have her kill her dad, too. Because these thrill killers usually do that anyway. It was the stress of moving, leaving her friends behind."

"You know the thing that gets me?" Cole said. "How you pretend to care. Even in your insane way, you pretend to care. You're all so worried about what's wrong with the kids, when you're the ones selling us guns, telling us times were better when men were men, pretending that global warming is a hoax, and turning hate into a team sport. I mean, yeah, you have taken it all a step further, sure, but it's not like anyone over the age of fifty has ever *really* given a shit about us. You guys may be homicidal lunatics, but, hey, at least you're being honest about how you wish we were dead."

They were quiet, listening to tires on gravel.

"That was beautiful, Cole. Thank you. I should add that to your suicide note," Dunne said, leaning over, opening the glove box. Dunne held up an envelope marked "Dad." The handwriting was so close to Cole's own, Cole had to blink, try to remember if he actually had written the word. "It comes with a full confession. Not the particulars of the spree killings, but enough. Should be pretty ironclad. One of us in the Improvement Society is a lawyer—he looked it over, made sure that your father wouldn't be legally culpable for any of your actions, might even get another insurance payout. Drop in the bucket, for a man of his means, but every little bit will help."

Money, of course. The false hope that the one rich guy in town could pull everyone out of their shitty lives. If he would only reinvest in the town. Cole had heard it all before.

"My dad may be an asshole, but I doubt he'll buy what you're selling."

"People can surprise you," Dunne said, oddly cheery.

Cole looked out the window, the silhouette of the shuttered refinery blocking out the stars.

It figured that this would be where it ended.

"If it makes you feel any better, think of yourself as a phoenix. Your death becomes a rebirth. Baypen reopened. Kettle Springs saved."

"Frendo wins," Cole said softly.

"Frendo wins. And a little drop of Baypen makes everything better." Sheriff Dunne nodded, lapsing into silence, his master plan explained. He reached out and depressed a button, a garage door opener strapped to his dashboard radio.

Somewhere in front of them there was a whirr of metal

and machinery. Gears worked against rust and heat-warped parts, the shutter of the loading dock miraculously still operational, after the fire.

Cole looked up to see the charred face of Frendo the Clown, a giant mural painted over a double-wide bay door, the steel rising up, becoming the clown's open mouth.

Dunne pulled the cruiser onto the factory floor and shut the engine, cutting the lights.

There were a few fluorescent lights somewhere to the right, forming a circle of light that ended around the stairs leading up to the foreman's office, but the rest of the factory floor was dark.

There was a knock on the driver's side window that caused Cole to flinch.

Frendo the Clown had appeared out of the gloom and motioned for Dunne to roll down his window.

Frendo lifted his mask and it took Cole a moment to place the bald man. Tall, but still toady, with bland features, and still somehow married to Miss Kettle Springs. It was Janet's stepdad. God. How could he? Did Janet's mom know? Where was she tonight? Without her husband and daughter, that was certain.

"Oh, you got him," Mr. Murray said. "That's good. At least something tonight can go right."

"Nothing has gone wrong," Dunne said, sounding angry. "They all knew the risks."

"Sure. Sure they did."

"Did he say if he was coming down or not?" Dunne asked. "If he wants to see it? To say goodbye to the boy, at least." Dunne smiled, glanced back to Cole.

"Yes. He said wait for him. He needs a minute."

"Okay, then," Dunne said, looking over toward the lights. The new fluorescent bulbs had to have been recently installed. There was no way they'd survived the fire. The lights were throwing hard shadows across pipes, mixing tanks, and suspended walkways. There was very little debris on the factory floor; the firefighters had cleaned most of it away with their hoses. The refinery was structurally unsound, the building condemned, but there was plenty of infrastructure that hadn't burned.

Mr. Murray apparently couldn't take the silence, so he spoke again. "He could be praying, don't you think?"

"I don't presume to guess," Dunne said, a chastisement. "If he said wait, we'll wait."

Cole felt nauseous.

He could now see the noose dangling from one of the burned-out catwalks. The walkway that led up to the foreman's office.

Suddenly Cole knew *who* they were waiting for and his heart broke.

People can surprise you.

TWENTY-SIX

Quinn's calves ached, but she knew that as long as she kept running perpendicular to the rows, she would stay in the right direction.

Would you believe Trent's the best tight end the team's had in a decade?

Cole's words from the parade came back to her as she ran.

There were no footfalls behind her, but she knew that Ronnie and Matt were in pursuit. They had to be. They wouldn't let her go. Couldn't.

She hoped the rifle shot had done enough damage to slow them down. That the bleeding hadn't stopped. Matt would be inducted into some kind of hall of fame, if he could still be the best tight end with a hole in his hand and one of his ears blown off.

Quinn felt her strength return, like when she was in training, at camp. She'd run until she felt ready to collapse, and then something would click and she'd find a second full gas tank she didn't know she had. Quinn huffed along, trying to maintain her pace, ten rows, then twenty. It was possible she was still miles away from the Tillerson farmhouse. Possible she'd somehow drifted off course and missed it. But that would be okay, too: she'd keep running until the sun came up, until she ran into someone who could help, even if that someone was in Ontario.

After a few more minutes, another half mile maybe, Quinn reached a simple dirt road. This had to be it, the driveway. She looked both ways, then continued in the direction of the farmhouse.

At the end of the drive, she spotted a pickup truck, the tires looking a little flat and the hood dusty, but otherwise intact.

The truck was red, brick-colored, and had a cream stripe across the side. Quinn tried pulling on the driver's side door as she passed. It opened, but she'd need the keys. She wasn't lucky enough to find them waiting in the ignition, or under the window shades, or in the glove box where she took a moment to check. She'd have to go inside to look for them.

Quinn walked up the front steps and in through their screened-in porch. To the side of the front door was a broken swing, one chain dragging on the ground. A pile of weathered Fisher-Price toys lay stacked in one corner of the porch. Quinn couldn't decide if the smiling, oversize, mildewed plastic caterpillars and dogs were more of a *sad* detail or a *creepy* one.

She approached the front door, held her breath, reached a hand out, then stopped. The knob was streaked with dirt and soot, big dusty fingerprints on the white of the doorframe. There was no telling if the prints were fresh or not.

She'd made it this far. She couldn't start acting stupid now. It didn't seem possible that Ronnie and Matt could have beaten her to the house—she would have seen them and she knew she was fast . . .

But she wasn't about to walk into a trap.

Quinn left the porch and walked around the back of the house, peering in windows, stopping and listening twice, seeing if she could hear anything if she stayed still, ear flat to the siding.

Nothing. The house seemed empty.

And the back door didn't have any smudges.

She said a half-second prayer and turned the knob: the back door was unlocked.

Back in Philly, leaving town on vacation with a door unlocked was like asking to be robbed, but out here, the closest neighbors were miles away. If she'd grown up here, she wouldn't have bothered, either.

She pulled open the door, a metallic creak she couldn't stop.

She listened. Nothing.

The door opened onto a coatroom that saw regular use. The small room smelled like sweat and feet. Beside the rubber doormat, there were stacks of work boots, heavy-duty gloves, and a thick layer of dirt and grass clods, presumably scraped from the sole of the boots with the flathead screwdriver that'd been tucked into the molding.

Quinn shivered. Inside the house was as cool as outside. The Tillersons must have turned off the heat when they left town. Reaching up, Quinn grabbed a jacket. Slipping it on over her bloody clothes, she immediately felt safer and warmer. She wondered if this was Mr. or Mrs. Tillerson's coat. It smelled faintly of burned leaves and perfume. Or maybe that was fertilizer.

Quinn moved from the mudroom into the kitchen, with black-and-white linoleum tiles and pastel cabinets. The fixtures could have been green, could have been blue, it was hard to tell in the darkness. She looked to the countertops, her blood chilling at a utensil drawer left open. But, no, Ronnie had the gun. Even if Ronnie and Matt had somehow been able to beat her here, why would they bother ransacking the place for knives?

Quinn's eyes scanned the dish rack: mismatched cutlery,

mugs, plastic plates with cartoon characters, and a large, chipped cleaver. If they'd been in here looking for weapons, they would have taken *that*.

Quinn pulled the cleaver out from between a mug and a plate, trying her best not to clatter. The blade was top-heavy, but like wearing the jacket, having it made her feel more comfortable.

She turned from the sink and saw the phone on the wall, spiral cord dangling from the handset.

If only she could think of the right person to call.

A 911 call would reroute to local police. Wouldn't it? She could call her dad. She had to call her dad.

But when Quinn held the headset to her ear: busy signal.

Quinn wasn't surprised. This was the way it was. Whether the line was dead from a deliberately cut phone line or an unpaid bill, it didn't matter.

She'd find the keys to the truck and be out before . . .

She sniffed the collar of the jacket, then the kitchen air. There was a scent wafting in through the doorway, coming from down the hall.

She moved to investigate.

The smell . . . It was burned meat and chemicals. A turkey that an absentminded grandmother put in the oven still wrapped in plastic.

Following her nose, Quinn reached a double-wide entryway and stopped. She remembered the smudges on the door handle and held the cleaver up, ready to defend herself.

She peeked in.

Shit.

She stifled a gasp. Frendo was sitting on the Tillersons' living room couch.

She pulled her head back, flattening herself against the wall. When would it end? When would it *fucking* end?

When she *made* it end, she thought.

Quinn swung around the corner, cleaver high, ready to do what had to be done.

"Hah!" she yelled, a karate movie entrance.

But Frendo didn't move.

He didn't even flinch.

He was . . . dead? She watched the clown for a moment, then stepped out onto the carpet, the material thinner in this room than in the hallway. She had her cleaver held high, but didn't need the weapon.

She came around the front of the couch and realized that he must've been one of the clowns caught in the silo explosion. He'd somehow made it to the farmhouse, despite the burns over most of his body, then had sat down to die.

His eyes were milky and lidless.

Frendo's mask had been melted to his face by the heat. Blisters had sprouted on the clown's exposed flesh, pale white fissures glowing in the moonlight from where the skin met the edge of the plastic.

Quinn took a few steps and poked him with the flat end of the cleaver. He didn't move, didn't blink.

This clown didn't matter.

He was dead.

Good. She sighed and remembered that she needed to find those keys. Ronnie and Matt had to be on their way here, and who knew what kind of backup they'd bring.

Quinn looked around the room, playing a game of "I Spy"—crocheted doilies, a video game controller, a pair of slippers . . .

There. On the coffee table. Between a stack of magazines and a small bowl of individually wrapped caramels: the metal glint of keys.

Quinn crouched, began to creep toward the key ring, her hands out.

Beside her, outside the front door, the porch groaned. A small sound, but enough to startle her.

Quinn looked over to keep an eye on the clown:

He was still dead.

She looked to the door, still for a moment. She heard no footsteps, no other squeaks or groans.

There was nothing out there. It was just the kind of sound old houses made.

She dipped her hand down, snatching up the key ring, then crossed to the front door, holding her cleaver out in front of her.

Was this the right way to do it? Would she be better served by exiting the house the way she came in? Head to the truck the long way, around the back of the house?

No. She was alone out here. No more jumping at shadows.

She pulled open the door and peered out onto the Tillersons' depressing porch.

Four feet away, the screen door had been soundlessly propped open.

Ronnie stood in the threshold, frozen there, like she knew Quinn had heard her try the first time and had not wanted to chance another step onto the porch.

"Hello," Ronnie said, then charged at Quinn, shoulder slung low, rifle butt out like a battering ram.

"Youuuuuu die," Ronnie screamed, a battle cry as she took two running steps and closed the distance into the living room.

Hand still on the knob, Quinn tried to swing the front door into the girl's face, but the door only bounced off the side of Ronnie's body as the girl gave a grunt, barreling through into the living room. Her golden ponytail bobbed as she tried to use the end of the rifle like a club, lashing out and narrowly missing the end of Quinn's nose.

Quinn backed up, knees taken out by the arm of the couch, spilling backward into the roasted clown's lap, charred flesh flakes raining down on her.

Ronnie stopped at the arm of the couch and brought the gun around and pointed the barrel at Quinn.

"Don't move," Ronnie said.

But moving was the only choice, hedging her bets because Ronnie hadn't chosen to shoot at her yet.

Quinn crab-walked off the back of the couch, the edge of the cleaver cutting the dead clown as she went. The smell of cooked blood filled the room, nauseating.

"Fuck, that's gross," Ronnie muttered, gagging.

Quinn heard the rifle clatter as Ronnie struggled to aim.

Over the far cushion of the couch, Quinn kept moving down the hall. She found her feet, then juked toward the direction she'd come, the kitchen and the back door, but then remembered that there were possibly two of them.

Matt might've taken up position at the back of the house.

She needed to go deeper into the house, kick out a window in one of the bedrooms if she had to and—

BAM! Plaster and drywall exploded inches from Quinn's face. Ronnie had fired at her.

"Stop," Ronnie yelled from the living room, but Quinn didn't stop. She was going to get away or die trying. Quinn dove farther down the hallway and pushed into the first door she came to before Ronnie could fire again.

She shut the door behind her, but there was no lock.

Who didn't have a lock on the fucking bathroom door!?

The window! Quinn jumped into the tub, pulling the

shower curtain closed behind her, as if the vinyl could deflect a bullet.

"Shit," Quinn said, tugging at the base of the small window, age or a lock holding it shut. She banged on the glass with her palm, textured and opaque for privacy, desperate to get it to move.

Behind her, the door creaked open.

Quinn whirled.

Ronnie stood on the other side of the shower curtain, a shadow, a grim reaper in cheap nail polish ready to take Quinn away.

"Did you know more Americans die in the bathroom than any other room in the house?" Ronnie said, a sick, tremoring laughter in her voice.

No. Not like this; not killed by *her*.

Frantic, Quinn jumped out of the tub at Ronnie, not peeling back the curtain but instead jumping *through* it.

Plastic rings snapped above them, some giving way, some tearing at the vinyl, the shower curtain collapsing on top of them like a parachute.

Ronnie bounced back into the bathroom door, slamming it shut, barely space for the two of them to stand in the space next to the sink. Quinn's hip collided with porcelain as Ronnie bucked forward, her head thudding against the corner of a towel rack.

Under the curtain, Quinn managed to get Ronnie's

gun pointed away from her, but couldn't see exactly what Ronnie was doing, if she were ready to attack from another angle.

But Quinn could discern where Ronnie's head was.

Quinn brought the cleaver down, making a sharp, soft sound she wasn't expecting.

Swit.

There was no bone crunching, not even a scream, as the cleaver dug into shower curtain, separating the section of Ronnie's skull with the ponytail from the part with her exquisite bangs. Ronnie instantly slackened against Quinn's body, the small whimpering groan she gave too much, too pitiful in the close quarters of the bathroom.

Quinn let go of the cleaver, leaving it there, handle pointed out, as if keeping Ronnie's brains intact on either side of the blade somehow made Quinn a kinder person, less savage.

Even as Ronnie's body wilted, Quinn stepped on the barrel of the rifle, just to be sure. Then she peeled back the vinyl to reveal Ronnie's face.

"Ronnie," Quinn said, trying to meet the girl's blank, dreamy stare in the low light. "Ronnie? Where did they take Cole?"

Ronnie wasn't dead. But it didn't look like she'd be able to answer.

"Ronnie?" Quinn said. "Please."

Please, before you go, you terrible piece of shit, do something for me, make amends for the pain you helped cause.

Before Ronnie Queen died, she didn't speak.

But she did sing.

"Ehhhhh," Ronnie began, a childish smile at her lips, one of her eyes starting to drift inward. "Lit-tel drop of Behhhhhhh . . ."

She didn't get the rest out. But Quinn knew what she was trying to say. She could remember the view from her bedroom window.

"Makes everything better," Quinn finished, gathering up the rifle.

Quinn stumbled on preschool toys on her way out the porch's screen door.

She'd made it halfway to the truck when headlights flared at the end of the driveway.

It was probably too much to ask for it to be a helpful mid-western family in an RV, returning from vacation.

It only took a second for her to realize that Matt was still alive and that he was tearing down the driveway toward her.

Quinn remembered back to the Frendo scarecrow, how Ronnie and Matt had left it in the middle of the road. They'd planned this whole thing out, all in an effort to stay close to Cole throughout the night. Matt had even tried to coax them to park farther away; it was Janet who had shot that down. In the spotlight glow of the oncoming car, Quinn realized it'd been Ronnie and Matt's job to keep Cole safe. But safe for what?

Quinn ran for the open cab of the truck, diving inside just as Matt zoomed past, nearly taking the door off.

Quinn watched as Matt applied the brakes. He was moving too fast; he avoided colliding with the house, but the ass end of his two-seater crashed into one corner of the screen porch.

"No!" she heard Matt yell as she tossed the rifle onto the seat next to her and began to fumble with the keys.

Matt's back tires spun out in the dust, engine revving, but the porch roof was pinching him in place. Finally, the car got traction and was able to pull free, the sound of more wood cracking.

But instead of driving after her, taking another dive-bombing run at the truck, Matt got out of his car. Maybe to come after her on foot, maybe to inspect the damage to his ride. Quinn kept searching for the right key on the ring.

"Oh no," Matt said. Quinn looked up again; there was blood coating the side of his head, down to his ruined hand.

If Matt thought the damage to his car was bad, wait until he saw what Quinn had done to his girlfriend.

Quinn inserted the right key and the engine turned over on her first try.

Miraculous.

Matt crossed in front of his car, limping toward her now. He was seemingly unarmed, opening and closing his fists, not even wincing as he worked the damaged one.

He stumbled, grabbing onto the front of his car, staining one of the headlights red with his blood.

"Newwww girl!" he yelled, slurred and pained.

Quinn reached for the gearshift and had a sudden, terrible realization.

This truck. It was an antique. A real slice of Americana.

It had a manual transmission.

She looked down between her legs and began to despair.

Three. There were three pedals.

"Why are there three?!" Quinn screamed into the empty cab.

"Do not test me," Matt said, yelling at her, still a number of yards away, weaving drunkenly as he marched to her. He stumbled and fell, too far from his own car to use it to prop himself up.

He didn't seem like a threat. And she had the rifle. But she did not want to waste the bullets on him.

Quinn knew enough to know that one of the three pedals was the clutch. Now, did you need that pedal depressed in order to start rolling? She had a fifty/fifty shot.

She hit both the gas and the clutch, moved the gearshift to 1, and . . . nothing.

Wait. Not nothing. There was sound, revving. With

her feet still on both pedals, she felt around in front of her, flashing the headlights accidentally. She squinted against the sudden illumination, then watched as one of the meters on the lit dash began to count RPMs.

The needle was halfway up. That seemed like enough, right?

Matt was screaming again, but a different sound now, frustrated, rage-filled. He made it to his feet, but was down again before he could make much more progress toward her and the truck.

Quinn lifted her foot from the clutch slowly, but maybe not slowly enough. The truck jerked forward. She had to lock her elbows to stop the bridge of her nose from colliding with the steering wheel. Tensing from the force of the sudden acceleration, she pressed her weight farther onto the gas and she ran . . .

. . . right into the side of Matt's car.

There was engine smoke and Quinn coughed.

Quinn blinked the world back into focus, her fingertips humming, ears ringing.

There were two blood streaks on the truck's hood and Quinn's hand fumbled to get the gearshift to R, and this time she went lighter on the gas, slower on the clutch. There was a horrible crunching sound, part fiberglass, part flesh, as she eased the truck back.

She'd ended Matt Trent's screaming in a fairly spectacular

manner, crushing his head between the bumper of the truck and the side of his own car.

Her only thought: *At least I saved a bullet.*

Who even was she anymore?

She left the truck's engine on and gathered up the rifle, unsure how to check how much ammo she had left.

One side of Matt's car was crumpled in, but the paint job helped hide the boy's blood.

Matt's sporty two-seater was an automatic. Even though the passenger's side door was hanging off, scraping the road and throwing sparks, Quinn was able to drive it just fine.

She peeled away from the Tillersons' and headed south until she could see Baypen blocking out the lights of the town.

When the building was about a hundred yards ahead of her, she cut the headlights and crept forward, parking a good distance from the factory and proceeding the rest of the way on foot.

Whoever was in there, she didn't want them to know she was coming.

TWENTY-SEVEN

Glenn Maybrook made a show of checking the corpse's pulse.

Again.

He pinched Trudy's intact wrist in one hand, mouthed counting aloud, then set her arm back down on the table. He'd been doing this for an hour now. Occasionally he'd try holding a conversation with her, lift her shortened arm and help her flex the elbow joint. The motions were an approximation of physical therapy. Soon rigor would start and the charade would need to end. But hopefully he'd be gone long before that.

She'd waved in and out of consciousness while he'd placed all the sutures he could. Even with a sewing needle and thread, the stitches held together well when he snipped off Trudy's zip-tie tourniquet. But the second time she'd blacked out, she hadn't come back. Her last minutes awake hadn't necessarily been lucid, but she'd been able to speak. She alternated laughing and crying.

Trudy called him terrible names with one breath and begged for his forgiveness the next.

The man on the speaker hadn't said anything in a long time, and Glenn was starting to suspect something was changing. That the clowns were moving to a new phase in their plan, their eye-in-the-sky leader's attention turned elsewhere.

Over the last ten minutes or so, Glenn had tested this theory. He posed questions to the voice on the speaker, had pushed the limits of insulting him, just to elicit a response. But he got nothing.

Glenn Maybrook was alone down here.

That was good.

There was the crunch of machinery somewhere above him, then the sound of a car engine and wheels, then voices.

Something was happening.

He had to make a decision.

He looked at Trudy's body, then to the mask on the floor, then finally back to his small jail cell. Dr. Weller's corpse was buried inside, a feast for rodents and rot. That would be him if he didn't try to make a break for it. There would be two dead doctors in Kettle Springs.

Using both hands, Glenn gripped Trudy by a dead shoulder, lifting her from the table, and began to peel away her jumpsuit. It was baggy on the thin woman and even if they weren't made one-size-fits-all, this one would fit Glenn Maybrook just fine.

A few minutes elapsed as he stripped the jumpsuit off the corpse and changed into the costume over his clothes.

The mask was the final touch. It smelled like sweat and death and extra-hold hairspray.

There were voices above him as he worked. There was arguing, then crying, and Glenn could recognize one of the echoing, booming voices as his captor.

It hadn't been a trick, he hadn't been ignoring him: somebody was too busy to watch Glenn on the monitors.

He stretched the elastic band over his ears, not yet wanting to pull down the mask and obscure his vision.

He picked up the scalpel.

If someone came down here, he'd have to strike quickly, before they realized what was going on.

If you're still alive out there . . . Hang on, Quinn.

"I love you," Glenn Maybrook whispered, finishing the thought out loud as he began to climb the stairs.

TWENTY-EIGHT

"Dad," Cole said. "Don't do this."

Arthur Hill walked out the door of the suspended foreman's office. The room's windows had been broken out in the fire, but the floor and the catwalk around it held firm.

Cole's father approached the railing above them and raised his voice to be heard on the refinery floor:

"Don't call me that."

The three of them—Cole, Dunne, and Mr. Murray—watched Arthur Hill descend the metal stairs from his office. It took a long time for him to reach the factory floor. Which meant Cole had a lot of time to think what he would say to get him to reconsider. To get his father to realize how *wrong* this entire night had been.

They'd left the sheriff's car somewhere in the gloom behind them and gathered under the noose and light.

There was a soft clank-clank from his father's shoes on metal stairs.

"Don't try anything," Sheriff Dunne growled, and squeezed Cole's arm as his father approached. What was he going to do? Cole had been put in handcuffs, hands behind his back.

Mr. Murray stood between them, Frendo mask perched on top of his bald head, his arms crossed. He never struck Cole as a guy in good shape, but now he wheezed impatiently, glancing up to the lit catwalk, positively giddy to hang Cole from it.

Eventually, Cole's father reached the bottom step and began to walk toward them. He stepped into the shadows with them and stopped.

"Please, Dad," Cole said. Trying again to reach him. "This is crazy."

"You haven't been my son for years," Arthur Hill said, not acknowledging Cole's pleading. "But you knew that. I lost you long before the reservoir."

"However I disappointed you, I don't deserve this!" Cole yelled, already frustrated, too angry to try to appeal to reason. "I was sad without Mom!"

Dunne dropped a hand down to Cole's back, then twisted

the chain connecting the cuffs. The metal pinched his wrists.

"Sad, so you killed your sister? That's quite the revelation," Arthur Hill said. Cole could see the blankness in his eyes. That the word "accident" wasn't in his vocabulary. To him, Cole was a murderer—plain and simple. The man in front of him was hollowed-out and dangerous. He wanted to make someone pay for Victoria's death, and Cole realized that someone was going to be him. "Is *that* why you took away the one thing in life I had left? And I assume that's also why you burned down the factory?"

The cuffs tightened another notch around Cole's skinny wrists, Dunne punctuating his father's question.

Cole thought about his mom. About the late nights and chartered jets to Columbus. The chemo.

"Sure. I've been a shitty son, but I never meant . . ." He stopped—what did it matter. "You know what? There's no convincing you. You were never much of a father. But I never thought you were a psychopath—"

Dunne shook him by the cuffs, a dog with a rat.

"Oh, so you blame him now? Or is everything that happened because you're a misunderstood snowflake? Which is it?" Dunne was tall enough he needed to bend to hiss into Cole's left ear. "You and your friends never stop blaming other people. Never think about the consequences of your actions. It's pathetic."

"George." Arthur Hill nodded his head and Sheriff Dunne relented. Cole felt blood start to return to his hands, the fingertips stinging.

"Don't think this was easy for me. My solution, when I first raised the subject with George, had been more targeted. Just you. Dead. That's all I really wanted. Maybe your skull broken, about a foot of dirt as your grave. It took a little convincing to go along with all this . . ." Arthur Hill motioned to his side. "This Frendo business."

Mr. Murray tensed. Cole had a hard time reading what had upset him. That the sainted Arthur Hill thought he'd allowed his stepdaughter to be murdered in the name of something silly?

Cole's father held up a hand to Mr. Murray.

"But I came around. Sheriff Dunne's not wrong. It's not just you; it's your generation. You're all rotten. But it's only *you* who got my little girl killed, Cole." Emotion returned to his voice, but none of it for Cole: "God. She looked so much like your mother . . ."

"You don't think that I wish every day that I could trade places with her?" Cole said, not trying for hyperbole, just stating a fact. "Think about what you're doing, Dad. You can stop this if you just—"

Before Cole could finish, his father's hands were around his throat.

"I told you not to call me that," Arthur Hill said. This close, his eyes were red, not with tears, but with mania.

Cole tried to speak, but he couldn't.

The hands tightened.

His father's thumbs against his windpipe, Cole could feel their intent to kill.

"What is it you want me to stop, Colton? It's already done."

Cole's face began to pulse, feel hot.

"*You* took everything! My livelihood. *You* took Victoria. *You* burned these people out of their hope. So I took what you care about and now I get what *I* want."

Dunne cleared his throat.

Arthur Hill's thumbs eased back, just enough to let a little air slip in between Cole's clenched teeth.

"Damn it, fine," Arthur Hill told Sheriff Dunne. "Let the town take its revenge."

He let go.

Cole dropped to his knees, coughing and sputtering.

"That's right, Arthur. Let *us* do it," Sheriff Dunne said, moving to pat Arthur Hill on his shoulder, but his target shrugging away.

"Just do it," Arthur Hill said.

Dunne hefted Cole to his feet and bent his arms back as he walked Cole forward. Arthur Hill stepped out of the way and Mr. Murray followed, wearing the smile of a kindergartner.

Arthur Hill had said his piece.

Talking was over. Death was here now.

Cole tried to slow their progress, stamping his feet, dropping to his knees only to be hoisted up, his shoulders feeling ready to dislocate. The sounds of his struggle echoed through the empty warehouse. The air felt damp the deeper in they marched. There was the sound of dripping somewhere. Was it possible that the water from the fire crews still hadn't dried?

"I never even liked your grandfather's clown," Cole's father said, voice raising, sick insane humor creeping into his otherwise flat affect: "But I have to admit, he's grown on me tonight."

Cole fell forward onto the foot of the stairs, metal biting against his chest, the side of his face, unable to put his arms out and protect himself. Dunne finally pulled him up, only to push him over three more stairs before letting him drop again.

His body couldn't take this, but he also didn't want to freely climb the makeshift gallows. There was a landing, then a turn, another half set of stairs, and then they would be out on the catwalk with the noose, the position chosen to spotlight Cole's hanging body.

Madness. Hate. Insecurity. Tradition. The American Dream.

Cole's thoughts spiraled as his toes dragged, looking for purchase on the stairs but finding nothing.

The last thing Cole was going to see before his neck snapped was his father standing twenty feet below him, looking up with a disappointed expression on his face.

"Pick up your feet and walk," Dunne said, urging Cole around the turn, up the final set of stairs. "Be a man. Stop making this harder than it has to be."

"But it doesn't have to be!" Cole screamed, knowing that there was no reasoning with any of them anymore.

Dunne lifted Cole by his belt with one massive hand and tossed him, throwing him so far up the final set of stairs that he almost tipped over the banister. While he was momentarily free, Cole considered jumping down to the factory floor: splat. He could kill himself a minute ahead of schedule just to piss off his dad, make it harder to stage his death like a suicide.

Still prone, Cole looked back down the steps, his lower lip bleeding. Bleeding *again*, if this was the same cut from the back of the cruiser, wider and deeper now.

On the landing below Cole, Dunne made an *after you* motion, urging Mr. Murray forward. The bald man started up the steps toward Cole.

Dunne was breathing heavy. The big man lifted his hat and mopped at his hairline with the back of one sleeve. The sheriff grimaced, mustache twitching, the chest of his uniform on one side now sodden with blood and sweat.

Good. Rust had done more than pepper him.

"You know the plan!" Arthur Hill yelled up from the factory floor. "I'm sorry I choked him, but don't add any more defensive bruises!"

"Get moving," Mr. Murray said, leaning over Cole.

Janet's stepdad lacked the height and gravitas of Sheriff Dunne, but in a way that was more frightening. He was a friend's dad who'd always been hard to talk to whenever Cole was over at Janet's. Now Cole could see why:

Guy was a sick fuck.

Mr. Murray pulled the Frendo mask down off the top of his head, adjusting it over his eyes. It wasn't a mask now, but an executioner's hood. Janet's stepdad lifted Cole up and carried him a few feet, the rest of the way out onto the suspended walkway. They were now higher than the small bank of fluorescent bulbs. Below them, through the metal slats of the catwalk, the noose was visible.

Cole was lifted up.

Mr. Murray held Cole steady, keeping him on his feet with an arm around his waist. Then, his movements clumsy in the mask and gloves, Mr. Murray reeled in the noose, hand over hand. His foot caught in the slack of the rope for a second before he was able to pull up a few more feet and work it free.

Once he had the loop of it above the railing, the slack of it coiled in a messy pile at their feet, Mr. Murray slipped the noose down around Cole's neck.

"Wait," Sheriff Dunne yelled, climbing the final set of stairs with obvious effort.

The catwalk groaned as the big man joined them. The entire structure shuddered against the extra weight. Scorched, corroded metal squeaked against itself. Dunne held both hands out for balance, slowed his walk to baby steps.

Cole held out a half second of hope that the structure would collapse and kill these two fuckers along with him. But the groaning calmed, and Dunne made it the rest of the way.

"Can't forget this," Dunne said, stuffing an envelope—Cole's suicide note, his father no doubt had copied his handwriting—into the waistband of Cole's jeans. "I added the extra bit from the car, too—thanks for that."

Besides the Frendo mask, Dunne was the only person smiling.

Moving slowly, almost tenderly, Dunne brought Cole forward and touched his forehead to his.

"Was it worth it?" Dunne asked in a whisper, getting a grip on the back of Cole's neck. Cole could feel his intention, the way Dunne's stubby fingers twitched.

No matter Cole's answer, Dunne was getting ready to hoist him over the handrail. It would be a much shorter fall than the one Victoria had taken. And a quicker death, since Victoria had still been alive in the ambulance, squeezing Cole's hand.

God. Maybe Cole *wanted* this.

He didn't answer Dunne's question, instead gently pulled against his hold to get a look down below them, one last glimpse of his dad.

"Stop!" a voice screamed, somewhere below, the word echoing up to them.

Dunne pulled his forehead away. Under his mask, Mr. Murray gave an impatient growl.

The three of them looked down to see Arthur Hill, stepping into the fluorescent lights under the walkway.

The shadows were harsh and sharp from up here.

One shoe. Then the other. Then hands.

Arthur Hill had his hands raised above his head, a preacher imploring his congregation. Maybe he'd finally seen reason.

No.

His hands were up in surrender.

With a rifle pointed at Arthur Hill's spine, Quinn Maybrook prodded Cole's father forward into the circle of light.

"Take that rope off his neck or I'll kill him," Quinn said.

Sheriff Dunne chuckled, hand still firm on the back of Cole's neck.

"This new girl," Dunne said, admiration in his voice. Then he turned to Cole. "I'm impressed."

Then, so fast it was hard to register the movement, Sheriff Dunne dipped his hand down to his service pistol, drew, and fired down at her.

TWENTY-NINE

She had slipped in through a broken window and wound slowly, carefully, to get to where they were holding Cole. A few amber safety lights lit her way through the maze of suspended gangways and metal scaffolds that supported the industrial mixing drums and pressurized vats of the refinery.

From the noose, it was clear what they were planning to do—she would need to act fast.

If she had to kill again to stop them . . . what was a few more clowns?

She didn't take much stock of her hostage, simply put the rifle to the older man in the white shirt and slacks and walked him into the corona of light.

"Take that rope off his neck or I'll kill him," Quinn yelled up, her voice carrying.

"This new girl," Dunne chuckled before muttering something to Cole that she couldn't quite make out.

Dunne pulled his gun and fired down at her, no regard for the man in the white shirt between them.

"Dad!" Cole yelled.

The first shot took Quinn's hostage in the shoulder, spinning him toward her, knocking the barrel of her rifle down and away.

Dad?

They both fell back, the man—Cole's dad?!—knocking her down, falling on top of her, his white shirt instantly blooming red.

Dunne's second gunshot slammed into the concrete beside Quinn's head. Dust stung her eyes as she tried to roll out from under Cole's dad.

Quinn sat forward and brought the rifle up, eyes watering, struggling to find her aim.

Dunne was the biggest target, aiming down with one arm extended, the other holding on to Cole. But . . .

She couldn't take the shot. Dunne had pulled Cole over to him and was using him as a human shield. But Cole clearly wasn't going to go down without a fight. He roared, his voice cracking as he kicked up with both feet against the railing in front of him. The move jostled Dunne as he fired at Quinn, his shot flying wild and ricocheting off the steel crossbeams above them.

Dunne steadied himself as Quinn worked herself out from under Cole's father.

Cole swung around in the sheriff's grip, wriggled himself to an about-face, and buried his head into the wound on Sheriff Dunne's shoulder.

Whatever Cole was doing—possibly biting the sheriff in his shotgun wounds—Dunne screeched in pain. The other clown—Janet's stepdad?—tried to pry the boy off Dunne, but was no help.

Dunne rushed forward toward the edge of the walkway, pulling Cole by his noose, and with a large overhanded swipe flung Cole over the railing and off the side of the platform.

Quinn watched Cole enter free fall.

No.

But Cole's neck didn't snap.

He wasn't descending fast enough for that because Janet's stepdad had caught his ankle in the slack of the rope. The bald clown had been pulled from his feet and was holding the edge of the platform for dear life. He held tight for a panicked moment before losing his grip and falling.

The heavy man in the clown costume did a complete flip in the air before stopping abruptly, both legs breaking backward as he slammed onto the factory floor.

As that Frendo howled in pain, Cole dangled by his neck, feet bicycling in the air, hands cuffed behind his back, his face turning blue as he choked.

"Look what you did!" Sheriff Dunne screamed down at Quinn, finding his aim again with the handgun but not before Quinn had squeezed the trigger on her own rifle.

Dunne put a hand to his stomach, pulled back a fistful of blood, and smiled down at Quinn. At her feet, Cole's father moaned, regaining consciousness.

Above her, Cole gave a few final bucks in the air, before going limp. His toes were pointed down, maybe two feet from the floor.

Then there was a crash somewhere behind her, a flash of light as metal tore through metal with deafening squeals.

Quinn. That was Quinn's voice!

Glenn Maybrook could hardly believe it.

He looked down at the scalpel in his hand. He was trembling. Two decades in an ER setting and nervous shakes had never been a problem.

He forced his hand still.

This was it. He could do something. He could help her. He could save her. He had to save her! Sure, he'd gone a little insane down there with two corpses. Insane enough that one of the two corpses *was* now mostly undressed, cold on her slab, but this was it, now that he was stumbling through industrial wreckage, toward the sound of voices. He could help.

Then there was the pop of a gunshot, and Glenn thought, *God, no.*

He burst from his hiding space behind the mixing drums.

He ran up the short gangplank in front of him, only to need to go back down. His legs felt weak, his vision wavering. Maybe it was the mask doing things to his peripheral vision, messing with his balance.

Your daughter needs you. Move, you shithead.

There were bellows from grown men, none of the voices Quinn's.

"Look at what you did!"

Glenn hit the ground when he heard the third shot ricochet around, nearly causing him to put the scalpel in his own chest, but he found his feet, pulled himself along in the darkness.

He turned toward the light, disoriented, catching a glimpse of Quinn, prone under a spotlight.

His girl. Strong. Alive.

Aiming a rifle.

And then there was a crash, headlights—and Glenn Maybrook needed to dive out of the way to keep from being crushed under the wheels of a speeding pickup truck.

Quinn turned to see the final pieces of shrapnel clatter from the large hole where the front end of the truck had torn down one of the factory's loading bay doors.

The red-and-cream pickup streaked onto the factory floor. At the last possible moment, the driver gave the wheel a yank to avoid crashing into the back of Dunne's parked cruiser.

The truck slowed, wending its way around where Quinn lay, then sped forward toward Cole.

Quinn couldn't watch. Cole was about to be smashed like a piñata against the truck's front fender.

But then the truck slowed and instead of hitting the dangling boy, the truck simply nudged against his hip. The truck crawled forward, lifting the weight of Cole's body, easing his weight off the rope around his neck.

Cole seemed to rouse, his knees streaking the bloody hood of the truck as he struggled to stand: coughing, alive, the hood of the truck becoming a platform, saving him.

Alive.

And Cole wasn't the only one.

Ruston Vance kicked open the truck's driver's side door, only to duck back in as Dunne leaned over the railing and fired down at him, a bullet sparking off the metal of the doorframe.

Quinn's neighbor crooked the barrel of the shotgun into the corner of the truck window and fired up, sending Dunne running to the end of the catwalk, toward the stairs down to the factory floor.

Rust stepped out of the truck and into the light. His face was puffy and burned. His white undershirt had gone black from the dirt and blood, but he was alive.

He was alive!

And he had his duffel bag slung over his back, which meant he had ammunition.

She couldn't take her eyes off Sheriff Dunne. He was still on his feet. Gutshot but alive, his boots clanging on metal as he worked his way down the first set of stairs.

Quinn stood, legs feeling bloodless and rolled flat. Cole's father was facedown by her feet, still groaning.

Quinn looked to under the lights. On the hood of the truck, Cole was gasping, unable to get his hands up, the rope still around his neck, constricting his airway. He might not have been saved, if his larynx was collapsed.

They needed to help him. Fast.

His Frendo mask still on, Janet's stepdad had stopped crying about his shattered legs and had begun crawling toward the bumper of the truck, dragging himself forward with his elbows.

Rust aimed his shotgun up at the stairs and fired at Dunne. Sparks flew from the handrails and metal steps. Sheriff Dunne winced but seemed unharmed, continued clattering down onto the landing, one more set of stairs before he was on the warehouse floor with them.

"Quinn," Rust yelled, pointing up toward Dunne. "Keep on him."

Dunne steadied himself and fired back down at Rust, missing.

Rust was finished issuing orders. He was walking around the door, ready to help Cole off the hood of the truck. The Tillersons' truck, Quinn finally recognized. She was unsurprised that Ruston Vance could drive stick.

Quinn advanced the bolt on the rifle, hoping for at least one more bullet, knowing there probably wasn't one.

On the hood, Cole wriggled against Rust's grip, dazed enough he didn't realize he was in the process of being helped.

Suddenly, Cole disappeared around the side of the truck, pulled off the hood by his legs, neck stretched out as he began dangling from the rope again.

Frendo was holding on to Cole's heels, trying to finish the job by putting all his weight into it. There was a slug trail of black blood behind him from where he'd dragged himself from his landing site.

Rust put the end of the shotgun to the man's chest and blew Janet's stepdad apart. He did this casually, how someone might swat a fly. He continued hoisting Cole up, using both hands now, dropping the shotgun and his bag at his feet.

There was too much to watch. But Quinn had to stay focused.

There was one more thing to do.

Quinn arrived at the base of the metal stairs and looked up. Dunne stumbled, missing a step. He had his gun out in front of him, but his hand wavered. He looked barely able to focus on her, the barrel shaking. The wound in his belly had flowed over his belt and was now streaking his pant legs.

The skin of his face was the same color as his mustache: gray, pale, dead.

No matter what else happened in the next minute or so, Quinn had done that. There was no living through a wound like that, this far from a hospital. She'd killed him for sure.

"Well," Dunne started to say as he took one step down toward Quinn, finally finding her with the end of his weapon. "You did g—"

Quinn fired up at him.

The sheriff's hat blew back off his head. He slumped to his knees, stairs rattling, then to his stomach, then rode down the remaining steps on his face, ending in a bloody mass at her feet.

Dead. Sheriff Dunne was dead.

In the gunsmoke and truck exhaust of the factory floor, someone coughed.

Quinn let the rifle hang limp in her fingers, but not drop, and made her way over to where Rust had successfully cut Cole down, was laying his body in front of the truck and administering CPR.

An inhale caught in Quinn's throat, turned into a lump of dread. Had Cole stopped breathing? It was all too much. That they'd gone this far, done so much, for Cole to die anyway.

Quinn felt her vision blurring, but she was too dehydrated for the tears to fall.

Rust pulled his head up from the ground and Cole's face followed.

Oh, wait . . .

That wasn't CPR. That wasn't CPR at all.

Cole Hill, red-faced, a tracer of white around his neck, returned Ruston Vance's kiss. Passionately.

"Um. Maybe let him breathe," Quinn said, collapsing beside the two of them.

It felt good to sit.

The two boys stopped kissing, at least temporarily, and looked over to her.

The pair looked natural together. For the first time all day, something made sense. They worked together—and not just because both looked like they needed about a month in the intensive care unit.

"How did you? You know . . . ," Quinn asked, too tired to articulate the whole question, her hand down on Rust's black duffel bag.

"I lit the fuse on the dynamite and ran like hell out the front," Rust said. "Didn't know how long I'd been out. Woke up, found my bag, then went to the Tillerson house. Seems like I kept missing everyone. They aren't going to like what we did to their truck . . ."

Out behind the circle of the lights, someone moved.

She'd been wrong about Dunne being the last threat.

This final clown had almost caught them unaware.

Almost.

Quinn wondered who it could be under that mask. Whether it was anyone from Kettle Springs she'd met. Most likely it wasn't. Most of the people she'd met were dead.

The clown was stumbling, judging from the blood on its jumpsuit, was probably already mortally wounded.

Wounded but not harmless. He was carrying a small knife; she could see the glint of its blade even in the darkness and haze.

Without standing, Quinn raised the rifle, getting the man—or curveless woman—in her sights. The motion feeling like muscle memory by now.

Somewhere her mother screamed at her.

But like a lot of Samantha Maybrook's motherly advice, this piece was coming too late. Quinn had already taken lives. Too many.

"No," Cole screamed, hoarse. He scurried forward, fumbling on his knees, hands still cuffed behind his back, trying to tip the rifle up with his shoulder and failing.

Quinn squeezed the trigger.

Click.

The bag—there would be more ammunition in the bag. She looked down, hand on the zipper.

"Quinn," a familiar voice said, out in the darkness.

"Dad?"

One of Glenn Maybrook's white Reeboks—not so white anymore—stumble-hopped forward and he fell.

Quinn threw the gun away, the expanse of it feeling clammy in her palm. The rifle hadn't betrayed her, though—it hadn't seduced her. It had just let her do what she wanted to do. Survive. Kill.

Cole had his head in her lap, and he nodded and whispered to himself in a rasp: "Cool shoes . . ."

Quinn stood, running to her father. She removed his Frendo mask.

The two of them were quiet, holding each other for a moment.

"Sorry I made us move here" was the first thing her dad said. "Please get me a doctor that's not me."

The most able-bodied among them, Quinn gathered the injured up, leaning them against each other.

They walked to the door. The first glimpses of morning light were cutting through the darkness like a second chance at life.

THIRTY

TWO MONTHS LATER

"Hey guys, we're LIVE here at the Main Street Eatery and—" Cole looked up. "Oh c'mon. I'm just kidding."

Their waitress was aghast, didn't seem to think Cole was funny. This woman had worked with Trudy. Maybe even *liked* her.

Rust put his hand over Cole's, lowering the phone to the table.

Cole had done this bit, or something like it, a few times now. Whenever they went out to eat, basically. It *was* a joke and it *wasn't*. It was Cole Hill, owning his infamy, trying to disarm people in town who might still harbor certain preconceptions about the boy millionaire.

"Sorry about him," Quinn said, and the waitress shrugged, regaining a little color as she took their order.

A lot had changed over the last two months.

They were wearing light winter jackets, for one thing. The draft coming from the windows next to the booth was too strong for the heat inside the old diner to contend with.

For another thing: around 20 percent of the population of Kettle Springs, Missouri, was either dead, headed to prison, or had moved away.

"How's your dad?" Cole asked Quinn. He snuggled up against Rust, the fairer boy looking uncomfortable only for a moment before easing back into his seat. Quinn got the impression that for Rust, it wasn't so much being comfortable with who he *was*, but who he was *with*. Cole still had that star quality, and Rust preferred not to be quite so visible.

"Dad's good. But if I have to nail together one more sign, I'll lose it," Quinn answered. "Nobody wants them on their lawns."

"Why more signs?" Rust asked. "Isn't he running unopposed?"

"Exactly," Quinn said, laughing.

Glenn Maybrook was still seeing patients, but he swore he'd give up his practice completely as soon as the town found a replacement. Hopefully before he was officially sworn in as mayor. But Quinn wasn't sure her dad could stop being a doctor, no matter how hard he tried.

The table lapsed into quiet. Quinn sipped her coffee. Cole started to check his phone, but then caught himself and laid it, facedown, on top of the napkin holder. Rust tried to pretend that he wasn't watching the door of the diner, making sure he had an eye on every patron. But Quinn could see that the boy was still worried, coiled, ready to strike. Of the three of them—and they were *all* in counseling, were all exhibiting symptoms of PTSD in one way or another—Rust was the one who seemed least likely to "get over it" anytime soon.

To treat Rust's burns, the doctors had shaved his head. Now that it was growing back, his hairstyle was asymmetrical, much shorter on the burned side. Redneck Rust, Eagle Scout and noted plaid enthusiast, looked like a punk.

His boyfriend, on the other hand, had gained ten or fifteen pounds and trimmed his long hair. The weight showed in Cole's face, making him look handsome, bigger, more like you'd expect of the captain of the football team. His eyes were no longer sunken, and because it was now winter, he'd started wearing zip-up sweatshirts and hunting jackets.

To Quinn, sitting across from them in the booth, it was like the two boys had switched places.

When Quinn looked in the mirror, she couldn't see many physical differences, but she bet they were there, that her father could spot them.

And yes, she did *feel* different.

Her hands would occasionally shake, and she kept lights on around the house all the time. Little things, but not insignificant. You didn't get over killer clowns quickly. Her dreams were terrible, but her dreams had been terrible since Mom. But then she'd lived through something terrible. No one expected that she wouldn't be changed by the experience.

In the immediate aftermath of the attack, Quinn had been the one who convinced her dad that they needed to stay in town. Easy as it would be to leave it all behind, she felt that they couldn't retreat. This was their home now. Blood had been spilled to make it that way, and leaving now would have meant the bastards won.

Arthur Hill and George Dunne's plan had worked. The two of them and their twelve (that the FBI knew of) conspirators had *saved* Kettle Springs.

Though not in the way they'd intended or anticipated.

The town's population might have been decimated, but in the days and weeks after, there was an influx of new life. Television news media, state and federal law enforcement, and even a handful of true crime documentarians had flooded the town. All these new people needed places to stay and places to eat, and their residency had offered a sustained months-long boost to the economy.

Quinn had declined multiple offers to speak on-camera about her experiences. But that didn't mean other kids weren't talking. One production team had secured an exclusive with Cole and Rust, to be interviewed together, and had already presold the planned three-part miniseries to Netflix.

Some of the thornier locals were bristling at the attention, but most appreciated these outsiders.

The cameras and reporters made Quinn feel safe. Extra eyes were always on the lookout, ready to catch a clown or a clown sympathizer that may have escaped the initial roundup.

Most of the clowns, especially Sheriff Dunne, hadn't been tech-savvy enough to cover their digital footprints. Even if they had survived and succeeded in killing Quinn and her friends—they would have been caught.

There was no doubt in her mind that they would have been caught.

Shortly after the arrival of the FBI, there had been a round of questionings and arrests. Arthur Hill's phone records, the sheriff's office emails, GPS of any phones that had been pinged as attending Kettle Springs Improvement Society meetings: no accomplice was able to hide. Not that there were many living accomplices. Ironic, Quinn thought, that it was the phones they hated so much that had gotten them caught.

School had come back into session at the beginning of December. Around twenty of the returning students had been in the Tillerson B-field that night. Most of them had survived being locked in the barn and had then escaped into the corn before the clown reinforcements had arrived. Another fifteen or so of the KSH student body simply hadn't gone to the party, which in Quinn's mind was a point in favor of staying in on weekends. A win for sweatpants and bad TV.

No, the "blighted crop" of Kettle Springs hadn't been culled. And even if Cole, Quinn, and Rust had died in that refinery, the clowns wouldn't have won. The kids would have persisted.

Quinn took comfort in that. The fact that history bent toward progress, no matter how hard the assholes tried pushing back.

Their food arrived and they all sat up straighter. After a few bites, Quinn put her forehead to the cold glass of the window and looked down Main Street. Businesses had been quick to remove Frendo-themed window displays. Demand for white paint and power-washers had been at an all-time high as people removed the clown from murals and signage around town.

"Theater looks about ready to open," Quinn said. The Eureka was under new management and someone had fixed the marquee so all the letters would light, not just the *E*, *K*, and *A*.

"It's coming along." Rust nodded. He'd been helping with restoration after school.

"What are they going to play opening weekend?" Quinn asked Cole.

Cole chewed, his mouth full of blueberry hotcakes,

swallowed, then spoke. “I don’t know. I’m letting Ms. Reyes choose. Probably something old and dumb.”

Cole had been a rich kid before, but now he had access to money he’d never have been able to spend if his father were alive. Now he had “Buy up Main Street” money. Quinn wanted to ask if there was any news, any developments, on the insurance front, but it all came back to one very touchy subject with Cole:

From the amount of blood at the scene, the extent of the manhunt that ensued, Arthur Hill had been declared legally dead, but there was still no body.

Drones had been used to search the cornfields. Dogs brought in. Blood had been found leading from where he’d been shot, out one of the exits of the Baypen factory, but there the trail went cold. With acres on either side and a six-hour head start before any search crews could be rerouted away from plucking kids out of Tillerson’s B-field, there were many directions Arthur Hill could have run, but more places he could have just died, alone and cold.

It was like the corn had swallowed him up.

So Quinn didn’t ask about Arthur Hill. She focused on her chipped beef, on small talk with her friends, and on the future of Kettle Springs.

EPILOGUE

Terry stole a glance behind him to watch the only passenger in the small jet.

The man was seated in the second of two rows of seats, body angled into the aisle, in full view from the cockpit.

Terry watched the man open and close his fist. He'd been repeating the same motion for hours.

The lone passenger was clenching one of those stress balls, passing it back and forth between his hands, but focusing on his left. The man grimaced against each squeeze, and Terry guessed that it was some kind of physical therapy. For an injury.

But Terry wasn't being paid to guess. Wasn't being paid cash, neat little stacks that added up to over six times his normal charter fee, to guess.

The man with the stress ball was traveling light and he wasn't going *too* far.

Under the sunglasses the man had a familiar face. A familiar face that Terry could swear had hired him before. But Terry wasn't going to allow himself to try to place the face.

Normally Terry would just yell back into the cabin, but today he used his headset to say:

"Landing soon. Please take a moment to check your seat belt."

This wasn't Terry's first flight to Cuba since normalized relations. But it was the first where he'd quickly googled "Cuba extradition with US?" before takeoff and wished he hadn't.

This guy wasn't visiting the country to search for classic cars or pick up a few boxes of Cohibas.

The man hadn't removed his sunglasses the entire flight. Instead of stowing his black garment bag flat in the compartments above his seat, he'd hooked the hanger of the bag over a headrest and laid the bag flat, seating the bag across from him like his suit was an extra passenger.

Must be one hell of a suit, Terry thought, and prepared for landing.

A few things had become clear to Arthur Hill, in the wake of his failure.

First, he realized that money wasn't everything. But that it was enough to keep you alive and out of jail. If you kept cash on hand.

Second, he realized that failure was temporary. If you were determined enough to see your plans through to the end.

Third, and this one was important: he realized that if you wanted a job done right, you had to do it yourself.

That was what he'd done wrong. He'd tried to approach revenge like a business and *delegated.*

But if he wanted something done right, he had to do it himself.

This was the mantra he repeated over and over, as the pilot dropped the landing gear and made their final descent onto the island.

The pilot had recognized him. Arthur was sure of it. Either from past flights or from the news. It didn't matter where, really.

That flash of recognition three hours ago was all the prompting Arthur Hill needed to disengage his seat belt, ignoring the pilot's announcement that they were landing, and slip into the plane's cramped bathroom.

He brought his garment bag with him.

George Dunne had been right: there was power in symbols. You could get people to rally around them. Pin their hopes on them. And *this* symbol was Arthur's legacy. His birthright.

Balanced in the small bathroom, he pulled up his jumpsuit and pulled down his mask.

Then he sat on the small aluminum toilet, waiting for touchdown and taxiing to be finished.

These Phenoms were considered "very light" jets. There would be no ground crew he had to worry about, just finding his way off the runway or out of the hangar after disembarking.

The knife was heavy in Arthur Hill's hand and he wondered if this was going to be as easy as it seemed.

He'd been responsible for dozens of deaths. But not the one he truly wanted. And that was because . . .

If you want something done right, you have to do it yourself.

ACKNOWLEDGMENTS

It takes a village to raise a book. And thankfully *Clown in a Cornfield* was raised in a kinder village than Kettle Springs.

Tremendous thanks must go to everyone at HarperCollins, Writers House, and Temple Hill Entertainment.

David Linker and Petersen Harris have been kind, funny, patient, and supportive throughout this process, and the book owes its existence to them. Even if sometimes they lapse into sports talk, leaving me baffled.

Further thanks to Camille Kellogg, Jen Strada, Jenna Stempel-Lobell, Alison Klapthor, and Jessica Berg. Editorial and design masters who stopped this from being a series of run-on sentences, printed incorrectly. And thanks to everyone at Harper's marketing and publicity teams.

Thanks to cover illustrator Matt Ryan Tobin, someone

whose incredible work I've always admired, but never dreamed would grace one of my books!

Wyck Godfrey, Marty Bowen, and Alli Dyer at Temple Hill. Alli was an MVP when it came to the book's small-town America verisimilitude.

Alec Shane at Writers House: a super cool, no-nonsense guy in a business that can be *mostly* nonsense.

I know there are a fleet of other people at these institutions who've helped shape the book, all deserving of thanks, and if I had *all* their names we'd just add a couple pages and roll credits.

On the personal side of things:

Big thanks to writers Scott Cole, Patrick Lacey, Matt Serafini, and (although he lives in Australia so doesn't get to hang as much) Aaron Dries. Many writers get to have peers, a circle, but not many people get to call that circle their best friends.

Also shout out to my non–horror writer friends (yes, I have a few) Kyle, Josh, Chuck, Andrew, and Becca.

The Athenaeum of Philadelphia, for letting me creep around for hours a day.

My Twitter (it's @Adam_Cesare!), YouTube, and other social media families: thank you for the quality content and for being very nice to me for too many years.

It's very possible that you were drawn to this book by the cover and Clive Barker's lovely quote. I've been a lifelong fan of Mr. Barker; his writings, art, and films have changed my life for the better, so to have him praise my work is a surreal experience. Thank you, sir. Deepest thanks also to Madeleine Roux, Paul Tremblay, Grady Hendrix, Nick Antosca, and Stephen Graham Jones. A writer's life is a harried and email-heavy life. That these tremendously talented creatives were there to correspond and offer kind words is humbling to say the least.

Jen, to whom this book is dedicated, who's signed herself up for a lifetime of me reading grisly descriptions of death and dismemberment as she tries to drift to sleep. She wanted me to tell you that she abhors violence, hate, and senseless cruelty. That she hopes to see them erased from the world. And I do too, but that's kind of what the book's about, isn't it?

My in-laws: Susan, Harvey, and Mike, who've welcomed me into their family not unlike that movie with John Lithgow and the Bigfoot. They knew I was strange, but they grew to love me anyway.

My parents, Carol and Richard, who not only raised me right, gave me every opportunity in life, instilled in me a love of reading, art, and wonder, but also probably were WAY too permissive with the types of movies they'd allow their kid to see. They are the best.

Thank you and love to these people and more.

And to you, the reader, for giving the book a chance and

making it this far. If you liked the book: please review. If you didn't like the book: also review, but maybe try it one more time before you do?

Thanks,

Adam